Break

The

Fence

Break The Fence

A. Mehlhorn

Bibliografische Information der Deutschen Nationalbibliothek:
Die Deutsche Nationalbibliothek verzeichnet diese Publikation
in der Deutschen Nationalbibliografie; detaillierte
bibliografische Daten sind im Internet über dnb.dnb.de
abrufbar.

Verlag: BoD · Books on Demand GmbH,
Überseering 33, 22297 Hamburg, bod@bod.de

Druck: Libri Plureos GmbH, Friedensallee 273, 22763
Hamburg

ISBN: 978-3-8192-2768-4

Cover erstellt und gezeichnet von Alex A. Mehlhorn.

To everyone not feeling brave enough.

Reader´s discretion is advised.

*"My poems were as wide as my arms were not.
They were as loud as I was silent."*

Betty, Tiffany McDaniel

1982

Prologue

I wake to the moon shining through my curtains. *Two a.m.* I guess. I release myself from the warm comfort of my sheets to go downstairs. In the kitchen, I fill a glass of tap water and throw it back in four loud gulps. Just as I turn to go back to bed, I hear a familiar sound, unusual for the time of day – since it's not even day at all. I check the clock to make sure. Two a.m. *Definitely night. Plus, I stepped up my time guessing game.* The comfortable rhythmic squeaking of wood on wood on our front porch continues and I open the front door to investigate. As expected, or more unexpected, Dad is sitting in his rocking chair on our porch, looking up at the moon, mumbling something under his breath. He doesn't seem to have noticed me yet, so I try to listen to the words he's breathing out.

"How's the big sky up there?" He asks the sky and one might think he's talking to God, but something in his voice suggests the question was directed at someone else entirely. He sounds different when talking to God.

"Why are you out here?" I ask, letting him know I'm here. But he doesn't answer. "I thought you hated the night." I push further.

"I said I hate the moon." The squeaking continues.

"How?" I'm still standing in the doorway, so Dad's back is turned towards me. And in the dim light of the moon, I see his shoulders rising and falling with a deep breath.

"It's the eye of God, watching in empathy and disappointment. I feel like the moon and the stars are judging me. Speaking in an ancient voice I no longer understand." He plays at the brim of his old cowboy hat. And for a second, I think he might be sleepwalking or he just spent too much time with me and turned into a poet overnight.

"Squirrel, want me to tell you a story?"

But before we can get to it, a bang coming from the direction of the junkyard shoots through the air, setting Jewel, Trixie and the girls into turmoil. The story slips through the noises, flying away to join the stars above, forever lost in the wild night sky.

Untold. Locked away between Dad and the moon.

Book One

The Cross

"His eyes were so brown they made me hungry."

The Bad Ones, Melissa Albert

1980

Chapter One

Friday means band-night at Hell's Saddle. The place is filled to the brim with leather-booted drunk men and their wives, while green and yellow neon lights bring more color into the red air. Mom is taking orders, mixing drinks and tapping beers while singing along to "A Horse with No Name". She must've heard this song being played a hundred times by a hundred bands by now and since I'm always here, I know it like the back of my hand too. I'm sitting at the counter watching her and occasionally scan the bar or gaze up at the band. But right now, Mom is what catches my eyes most. She looks pretty with her ruby waves in a loose bun at the top of her head like that. Dad thinks so too and always tells her, to which she still blushes like a sixteen-year-old. Though she's concentrated on satisfying the guests, I see her looking past me at the door – impatiently. I know exactly what she's thinking, because I think it too. *What happened to Eve that she's so late?*

Most guests are swaying to the music, singing along arm in arm, sharing good ol' Folkspine lore, ordering new rounds and – of course – drinking. Those that can't do any of those things are either passed out in their booth or slowly and wobbly making their way home.

Behind me, the little bell chimes, announcing someone either gets to go home to crash out or comes in to enter a state of almost crashing out. Except it's not. I turn around to see Eve finally standing in the doorway, looking messier than usual. *Has she been crying?* She runs behind the counter, throws a quick "So sorry, Love" at Mom, who's tapping beers like a mass production for our most loyal regular, and disappears behind the beaded curtain, shielding the employee area from the rest of the bar. When she reemerges, she's got her ash brown bob pinned back around her face, has gotten rid of her purse and wrapped a black apron around her hips. I notice she's wearing a turtleneck even though it´s summer.

"Trouble with Dan again?" Mom asks as Eve joins her behind the counter.

"Let's talk later. Doesn't seem like you've got time for my drama right now."

"You neither, mind you. Here, take these to Jeffrey."

Mom nods at the beers.

"'Bout time someone reacts to your job ad." Eve complains and skillfully places eight beers at once – four in each hand – in front of the regular Jeffrey. He's standing at the bar, swaying to the live music. When he hears the full glasses come down on the wooden counter in front of him, he nods and smiles at Eve, taking a little more time than necessary, grabs the beer and stumbles to his peers at their booth. As expected, he spills some of the holy golden liquid. Since this is his fifth round, I took a mental note of checking if Jeffrey leaves a trail of beer behind him.

Mom notices the puddle as Jeffrey's booth genuinely cheers at him for bringing in the next round and sarcastically for wasting some of it. She shoots me a look. *The* look.

"I've got it, Mom."

"Thanks, Sweetie." She throws me a wet cloth. I copy Jeffrey's path until I've reached the small puddle and soak it up with the cloth.

"Ah, little one! Didn't know ya were here too. Helpin' out yer mom, eh?" His moustache is covered

[19]

with beer foam. He's a real nice guy, even when he's drunk, so I happily shoot him and his seven companions a smile.

"You name it. Have fun, you guys!" *He's in guest mode tonight.* On some evenings, he takes up the role of unofficial security guard at Hell's Saddle. He's really got it in him. Once, he knocked out a guy who groped Mom and since then, he's been holding the title of *The Devil of Hell's Saddle*, which he loves.

I wipe the wood once more to make sure the cloth has soaked up all the beer and make my way back to the bar, throwing the cloth behind the counter. It lands in the sink. *Yes!*

"Good throw, Alex!" Eve has finally realized I'm here. After fights with her husband Dan, and especially on band-nights when Hell's Saddle is packed, she tends to miss out on her surroundings. *Can't blame the woman.* In addition to being one of the only two people that *officially* work at the busiest bar in town – my helping hands and Jeffrey's security mode don't count – and having the probably worst rotten man in all Folkspine as a husband, she's got the most annoying son too.

"Hiya, Eve." I gift her a smile, which comes out more empathetic than intended.

I spend the night swiping up after customers, rinsing glasses and taking out empty Whisky, Tequila and Vodka bottles. *Jesus, no one drinks like countrymen.* At around half past eleven, the band closes up their performance with "Southern Nights." The bar's still filled, though it's just the regulars at this point. Hell's Saddle's the only place around town that still offers bands a chance to perform once a week. And since Folkspine is right the middle of Colorado, we're west enough to have the bar be a proper Honky Tonk and north enough to have it be surrounded by mountains and forests carved and grown by God Himself. I'm just glad we got no desert coming up from New Mexico. The people love Hell's Saddle's western charm, so we never have to worry about not getting enough customers. The only worry around here is not having enough employees – which is why we wait and pray for a reaction to the job ad Mom put up around town – and running out of beer. As the band gets to the "Blow in the night" part, Mom tells me to go to the jukebox to switch it on once the song ends and the band's said their last thanks. Cheering and clapping follow after the song comes to an end and a couple of bows and waves later, the band has cleared off the stage. *My cue.* I choose "Thank God I'm a Country Boy" on the jukebox and John Denver fills the air. Mom throws me a Thumbs Up. *Good.*

At half past twelve, she announces last call. I check for more puddles, Eve mixes some drinks I'm glad I don't know the names of and Mom went over to Jeffrey's booth to have a chat with him. My gaze falls onto them as I sit at the counter and scan the floor. They keep glancing over at Eve, speaking in low tones. His cowboy hat rests on the table, his beard is still covered with foam and his wrinkles look deeper than before. His buddies are shouting and laughing at each other, but Jeffrey doesn't bat an eye at them. After what seems like an eternity, their conversation seems to come to an end. I know this because I see Jeffrey touching Mom's shoulder. It's what he always does when he's done having a talk. An *important* talk. *Adult talk.* I'm impressed he's still got the brains for an adult talk after all that beer.

Mom leaves his booth and makes her way back to the bar counter. She positions herself next to Eve and eyes her from the side while rinsing some glasses. Eve doesn't react to Mom's worried gaze. Both women continue with their work and I keep on lending them a hand when needed. No time for talking through Eve's family troubles on a band-night. Though I feel all itchy, wanting to know what happened.

Chapter Two

After a *lot* more songs and even more tapped beer, Mom turns to me.

"Alex Honey, why don't you go home? You've helped enough already." *She's in "worried mom" mode.*

"It's fine, Mom. I want to close up with you guys." I try to reassure her.

"You are twelve years old." *Thanks for letting me know.* "I appreciate your concern, but I can't let my child daughter work a bar all night long." *Never mind. She's in "I feel like a bad mom" mode.*

"Eve and I can manage. We're done here soon anyway." She glances over to Eve, who nods at Mom's statement. She didn't register a word Mom said. Just nodded when she heard her best friend and boss say her name. It's after the nod that she thinks over what Mom has just said.

I know Mom feels bad, even though it's always my idea to help her out, so I'll do her the favor. Just as I open my mouth to agree with her, Eve seems to have understood what Mom's been telling me and steps in.

"But you want your child daughter walking two miles at one in the morning?"

"Shit." Mom only swears when she's stressed or proper pissed off. Luckily for everyone in the bar, stress is the cause of her swearing. "I'm so sorry, Sweetie. I'll call Dad to come pick you up with the truck." We both know Dad is already asleep since he needs to get up in about four hours to start working the farm. He loves to get up with the sun in the summer. When the nights are longer, though, he always seems to be a little sadder than usual. Right now, he's fast asleep and it seems like I'm the only one who remembers, given Mom is already drying her hands on her apron and walking towards the phone.

"Mom." She grabs it from the wall and starts dialing. "Mom!" Her hand stops and she turns to face me. "Don't worry about it. I'll go to the back and lie down, okay?"

She sighs. Maybe in relief, maybe in guilt.

"Yes. Thanks Sweetie. I won't be long, I promise."

"Holler if you need two extra hands." I say getting up from my seat at the bar counter.

"I won't." She shouts after me.

I walk past the counter and part the beaded curtain. I step through it and turn right into the lounge. After having this place passed down to her from Grandpa, Mom almost took more time decorating this tiny room than the actual bar. The walls are covered with black and white pictures of Grandpa and his work partner building the place and finally working at the bar. Mom stuck the photographs in chronological order on the walls. She initially wanted to have them framed and hung up in the public space of the bar, but decided against it, because of Hell's Saddle's history. Now, the only picture out there is the one of Grandpa standing on the freshly built stage playing air guitar. It hangs right next to the stage, looking over the dancefloor. But the picture of Grandpa at opening night is my favorite. Mom always tells me how much her father has worked for this place and how proud he was of it. You see the joy written in his face in this picture. Next to him is his work partner. Dan's father. Eve's father-in-law. He and Grandpa started the Hell's Saddle business together. Up until the day Grandpa couldn't take his partner's alcohol addiction and bar fights anymore and threw him out. *Brennans.* That's where my family's hate towards Brennan men started. Grandpa had it with Eve's father-in-law, Mom has it with Eve's husband and I have it with her son and nephew. Mom told me the whole story about the origins of Hell's Saddle. How the business started off with two friends and how one got lost surrounded by all the alcohol. But before that, they were standing in front of the bar under the Hell's Saddle sign, which is the same as now, looking safe and sound. Between the pictures, one finds a carefully selected variety of tapestries, a Colorado flag and some of the drawings I used to do when I was even younger.

I walk in to find the leather couch, which has offered me a good night's sleep a bunch of times before, occupied. *Of course.* Abel's lying there, right on my spot. Funny thing, his mom's called Eve. We are both used to the muffled music, glasses clinking and shouting people on the other side of the wall. But besides that, the fact it's the middle of the night and he's lying on the comfiest couch in all Folkspine, he's not asleep. He's just staring straight ahead at the ceiling above, arms crossed behind his head. The blue neon light right above the couch shines a weirdly calming light on him and his moles.

Sometimes my body fills with jealousy when I look at him – which remains a mystery because I know that boy probably has the hardest life in town. At least next to Eve. Still, I sometimes wish I could be him. Like, just for a day. When the girls at school asked around who they would swap places with for a day, they looked at me all crooked when I said "The Brennan boy." That's his nickname in basically all Folkspine. As if everything that he portrays is the history of his messed-up family. Sometimes, I feel myself pitying him. But just for the small moment before his and his family's actions come to mind. Then, the annoyance and hate take over. Just like now.

"Great, it's you."

"Jesus, Pony!" He shoots up and faces me like he didn't hear me come in. *Is he blushing? No, wait. That's just one cheek.*

"It's Alex. Has always been. Will always be." I demand.

"But you've got such nice hair."

The Pony-horror began years ago, when I decided to only wear my hair in a ponytail and Abel decided to give himself the right to give me a nickname. I considered wearing my hair down just so he'd stop, but I figured he'd just think of another nickname and God knows what that would've been. And since Pony doesn't involve any real insult, I decided to stay true to my signature hair.

"Save it, Brennan. We ain't friends." *It's a pain in the ass, I even have to remind him.* "And why are you here anyway? I didn't see you come in."

"When I got here, it was just your mom opening up." I *did* come in way after Mom today. I begged her to let me come help her out at the bar tonight, but she made Dad insist I finish helping him on the farm first. "If you don't know if you'll take over the bar or the farm yet, you gotta learn how to work at *both* places." She explained. So, Dad caved – *like always* – and I went out to get my boots dirty in the dung.

"She told me I could stay here for a while. We had a fight at ho-"

"Yeah, I heard. Sorry 'bout that." It's true. We aren't friends, but since Mom and Eve are – and Mom talks like a book – I know what's going on for

Eve and Abel at home. And I *do* feel sorry. Though I don't know what today's dispute was about.

He nods in appreciation and smiles at me. For a second, we stare at each other awkwardly.

"Wait, what did you want here again?" He breaks the silence, squinting at me.

"To lie down. But I see you already did that for me. So, thanks for that." I turn around to go back and help Mom. *There's always work to do and that's definitely better than having to be in the same room as Abel Brennan.*

"Oh! Sorry. I can leave."

I turn over my shoulder. He's sitting up now, struggling to push himself off the couch to get up.

"No. Don't worry 'bout it." I sigh – in guilt. He lets himself fall back, which sends a wave of exhaustion through my body as I realize how bad I need to let myself fall back too. It *is* late after all and Mom said Eve and she can manage. *Okay Mom. You win again.*

"Move though. I need to sit down." He scoots to the right end of the couch and I sit down on the left with another sigh. "Thanks."

He smells like pot, which isn't to my surprise. I recognize the odor because of him and from walking past James, his cousin, in the school's hall.

"Were you helping out again?"

"I am *not* having small talk with you." I close my eyes. In the dark of my eyelids, I still see the neon signs Mom put up all around the bar.

"Right." I hear him smiling through the word, which only makes his presence more annoying.

Chapter Three

When I wake up to Mom stroking my shoulder,
Abel and the noise on the other side of the wall are
already gone.

"What time is it?" I blink at her face.

"Late. Let's go home."

I look around to figure out where I have just woken
up. Once I've recognized the leather underneath me
and the wall decor around me, I answer Mom.

"Be right there."

"Lock the front door behind you, please." Mom lays
her keys into my lap and leaves the room. I take a
minute to get accustomed to the big white light
above. The neon blue is gone too. A good stretch
and a yawn later and I'm up and walking back out,
through the bar, towards Mom's green Flying
Fishbowl. Through the windshield, Mom makes a
gesture of turning her fist mid-air. *Right. Lock the
door.* I put the key in its hole, turn it and Mom
throws me another Thumbs Up. I walk towards her
car, open the passenger door and fall into the seat
with a big sigh.

"Worked a lot today. Huh, Honey?"

"Hm." Is all I can muster, still affected by the sleepiness crashing onto my head. I hand over the bar key to Mom and she puts it into her purse on the backseat. She then starts the car and pulls onto Main Road. As I watch the sleeping Folkspine, my mind wanders back to a couple hours ago. When Eve came in, red eyes. When Mom talked to Jeffrey, worried – his hand on her shoulder. When Abel was lying there, with a reddened cheek.

The sleep has worn off now. I'm awake, my head racing from person to person, minute to minute, trying to put together what happened over at the Brennan's before Abel got to the bar. Before Eve got to it a couple hours later. *This fight must've been different than the ones before.* By now, Mom would have normally filled me in. It's our routine. Whenever I help out at the bar and Eve and Dan had a fight, Mom tells me about it on our ride home. "He just drank too much again. Said some awful stuff to the both of them. This time he grabbed the remote and sent it flying through the tr-...living room."

But tonight, not a word. She's just driving in silence, keeping her eyes on the road. She didn't even turn on the radio like she normally does.

"Abel was in the back." I eye her from the side.

"Oh, right!" It's like I've just woken her up. Pulling her away from her thoughts.

"He came in shortly after me. I told him he could stay in the back and wait for Eve."

"And you didn't care to mention that to me?" We leave the busy part of town, driving past the hair salon Eve used to work at before her husband became the way he is. Around the time Abel was born.

"You know I can't stand the guy."

"Well, first of all, I was busy tapping hundreds of beers tonight. And second of all, why can't you two just be nice to each other?"

"Just 'cause you and Eve are friends, doesn't mean me and Abel have to be too."

"*Abel and I.*" She corrects while taking a right turn onto the trail that leads to our farm. "I didn't say you two should be friends. I just think you could start acting like decent human beings and not like war opponents. Especially you, young lady. That kid's got nothing on you."

"I just don't like him. He's a Brennan, alright?"

"And what difference does that make? Eve's a Brennan too."

"Not by birth." I do love Eve like a second Mom. As Mom-number-one pulls into our driveway and parks the car right in front of our porch, Jewel starts barking from inside the barn. The slim curve of the moon shines above our house. She turns off the motor and sighs. *Oh crap.*

"Honey." *Yep. Lecture time!* "I don't like Dan either. Heck, I hate the guy, but just cause he's a bad person, doesn't mean his son is too."

"His nephew is, though." *Not to mention his grandfather. But Mom knows this better than I.* "I just don't trust the Brennan guys." James, Abel's cousin, is a Brennan by birth. Just like Abel. He's five years older than me and a shithead. I know I shouldn't know words like that at my age, but when you spend a quarter of your life in a bar, you learn fast. *Plus, I'm tired of people treating me like a fragile butterfly wing.* I've seen James' gang pushing around kids on their way home from school, smoking cigs in alleys and lingering before the bar waiting for drunk men to give them some of the sacred poison. The gang consists of James and his friends, Glen and Alan.

[35]

And Abel. It's a small group, but enough for James to feel like he's the king of a people. He's acting like he's got the three of them on a leash, though it seems like he's only *really* got Glen and Alan under his influence. I'd like to say he's got no word whatsoever over Abel, but that'd be a lie.

"You mean James?"

"Yes, Mom. I mean James. The guy who groped the chest of a thirteen-year-old as she was walking home from school. The guy who punched one of your beloved regulars because he wouldn't give him a beer. That James."

She looks at me concerned.

"Okay, you win." *Didn't expect that.*

"Stay away from James." *Believe me. I'm trying my best.* "But give Abel a chance." *Expected that.*

"Sure, Mom." I mumble as I open the passenger door and step out into the warm summer night. She follows after me.

"Uh, Mom?" I turn to face her. "Why *was* Abel in the back, though?"

"I just told you. To wait for Eve."

"And he couldn't just stay at home *with* her?"

It's dark, but what's barely left of the moon shines enough light on Mom for me to see her tensed-up shoulders.

"No." And that's it. *Guess tonight isn't the night for me to find out what happened.*

Chapter Four

I get up late the next morning. The sun's shining directly into my room, making its way through my curtains. *Eleven.* I guess. I don't take long to understand where I am, so I slide away from underneath my covers and start heading downstairs. It doesn't smell like coffee or Mom's eggs. Despite her working late, Mom never breaks her cycle of getting up at around seven, so her breakfast is long over. She takes a lot of naps on our couch or in the sun on our porch, though. Just as my foot touches the first step, I can hear Dad's voice pouring from the kitchen downstairs.

"Elaine, I know how much ya love her, but Eve's got to get outta there herself, alright?" *Stay and listen.*

"You don't get it. He *hurt* her. Like, proper hurt her. She showed me. Heck, he hurt the kid." *I knew it. It wasn't a one-sided blush.* "You should've seen the look on his face when he came into the bar yesterday."

"I know, Honey. But there's nothing ya can do instead of speaking to Eve."

"I can call the Sheriff. Or beat up that prick myself."
I can just picture Dad's face right now. Head turned
away, eyes squinting at all the mentions of violence.
"And then what? This town's small. Everyone will
know you called Dan in or…hurt him. And he'll call
you in on those *buddies* of his. The whole lot of them
ain't afraid to lay their hands on a woman and I
can't have that. I know you're worried. You've got a
good heart, which is why I love you, but I'm worried
about *you*."

When Mom and I got home last night, I went
straight to bed. I was lying there with my eyes open,
staring at the ceiling above me, like Abel did a
couple hours earlier. I simply couldn't sleep. Mom's
normally good at hiding her feelings, but yesterday, I
felt her worry and I knew it wasn't about Abel not
having any *good* friends, but about him and Eve
being stuck with an alcoholic. *Why hadn't I just asked
Abel about his cheek?*

Abel

"Dude, it's your turn." Alan slaps my arm. I shake my mind awake and grab the vodka bottle from his hand and take a sip, swallowing hard. *Getting drunk at eleven. What a Saturday.* The gang has gathered in James' room in his parents' basement. "War Pigs" plays on his record player, the air is dense with smoke and old clothes fill the ground. He sits on the couch we've been calling his new throne. *A king needs a throne.* It used to be a truck at the junkyard, but since he stopped telling us to meet there, he needed an alternative. I'm sitting on the floor in front of the couch, resting my back on it. Alan and Glen both sit on the floor in front of us.

"How come Pussy Man can use your throne?" Alan whines.

"Piss off." James The King orders. "He's not *using* it." Just leaning against it. "Plus, he's allowed to." *Cousin privilege at its finest.*

I wait for the burning in my throat to disappear and hand the bottle over to James and return back to my thoughts of last night, reconstructing the scene.

I see Dad's TV glowing, airing an old Football game, I know Dad is too wasted to follow. There's crap laying everywhere. Old takeaway boxes on the table, dirty socks on the floor, empty cans. Lots of them. Everywhere.

"Why can't you just be like James?" He spits.

"Why would I want to be anything like that bastard?" He's my cousin and the only friend I've got, but even I know how messed up he is. Still, I can't seem to let him go.

Dad and I are six feet apart from each other. He's sitting on our couch, surrounded by more cans. I'm standing in front of him. The table's between us. *Good.*

"Unlike you, James is a good, hard-working young man. Lending a hand to your uncle at the garage whenever he can. Doing as he's told. And what 'bout you? Ain't got nothin' accomplished. You're a disgra-"

"I haven't fucking accomplished anything 'cause you don't let me go to fucking school!"

He gets up. *He can still do that? Probs to you, Dad.*

Mom's standing in the doorway to what we call our kitchen, barely resembling an actual kitchen. We've got a fridge, oven and a gas stove. That's about it, but we manage. I see the light of Dad's TV reflecting in her eyes. In her tears. *Fuck, she's crying again.*

"You listen to me and you listen to me good!" He's stumbling around the table. Three feet. *Don't back off.* Two feet. One foot. I smell the booze coming out of his mouth and deep inside him.

Sticky, sweaty, rough. That's how his hand feels on my wrist. They also feel familiar.

"School is for boys who don't know how to get their hands dirty. For wimps. I will *not* have my son grow up to be a pussy."

"Oh, so James a pussy? Is that right, Dad? Cause I'm *pretty* sure he goes to school, given he's not having a puff somewhere downtown." He doesn't need to know, I'm the one he's having a puff *with*. His grip tightens. *Got him!*

"You need to man up." *Way to avoid an argument.*

"Man up and start living in the real world where real men do real work!"

Right, cause you're the one providing for your kid and wife. Not Mom switching workplaces to finance your addiction, hardly leaving any money for a proper meal.

"I'm not a man. Fuck, I'm thirteen. I'm a kid!"

Mom sobs. *Why won't she just get out of here?* She locks eyes with me. I break the connection to lock eyes with Dad. *Get your hand off me.* I pull back and shake his arm off. He's drunk, so I know he isn't very tough and strong right now. Still, the slap that follows stings like Tiger Balm. Mom gasps. *Say something or get the fuck out.* But she doesn't hear my thoughts.

"You will learn to be a man." *Don't break eye contact. Get on his level. Though I wouldn't want to get so low.*

"You're fucking pathetic." *Have the last word.* Jacket, keys, shoes.

"Where you goin'? Huh!?" *Ignore. You had the last word.*

"Well, you better not come back tonight!" *I will, but you won't know. By the time I'm back, you'll be long passed out on the couch.* I shoot Mom a look. Apologetic, loving. She shoots back. Understanding, loving.

Close the door. Don't bang it or he'll come running after you. Given he's still able to run.

It's still early evening. Friday, meaning band-night at Hell's Saddle, meaning Elaine is already at work. *My savior.* Though I might need to have a joint with

James first and share the mutual hate towards my dad, though I never got why James has got something against him. Sometimes, I think he hates my dad more than I do. I like to imagine it's because of his marks on me.

"Are you out of your mind?!" *There you go. Speak up, Mom. If you won't get out, then at least get involved.*
The gravel is crunching underneath me. Jeffrey, our neighbor in the trailer next to us, is shouting at his dog.

"Stop barkin' ye critter!" His Mastiff always wakes up the whole trailer park whenever there's shouting coming out of our home sweet home. I know he'll be at the bar later. Band-night's his favorite. I also know he's going to pretend he didn't hear anything. Whenever Mom works the bar after a fight, and Jeffrey's there having his rounds of beer or playing security guard, he never mentions anything to anyone as long as it's not urgent or critical. It's just a matter of time till he comes over to throw a fist at Dad. Jeffrey's a good guy after all.

Chapter Five

Dan's never hurt Eve before. I've seen bruises on
Abel a bunch of times before. Never on Eve. When I
was eight, him nine, I was sitting at my favorite
booth in the bar – the one closest to the door, so I
could see who comes in or check the clock above the
doorway – drawing a picture for Mom to hang up in
the back. Tracing a green crayon over the white
paper. It was still early, so there were no guests.
Mom had the jukebox quietly playing "Riders on the
Storm" and was going through a list of the Whiskey
delivery that came in this morning. This was way
back, when I wasn't yet called "Protector of The
Jukebox". Today, it's my job to switch it on
whenever a band is done performing or there is no
band to begin with. I hold that responsibility very
close to me.

Eve was looking through the bottles Mom brought
in. Abel was in the booth behind me, leaning over
my backrest and staring over my shoulder.

"Hey Pony!"

"Leave me alone." I was even more annoyed with him back then. "Don't you have a gang to hang out with?"

"They're stupid." He sounded unbothered by them, like the gang wasn't a part of his life. I knew it was, though. I've seen them hanging around downtown, jumping from place to place like little bandits. And whenever he was with them, he was different. He did stuff he never would've done if he were alone. He acted all tough and grown up. I've always hated it and I especially hate the fact that he still hangs out with James, Alan and Glen.

"Watcha doin'?"

"Drawing, can't you see?"

"What's that?" He pointed at the red orbs drawn between the branches of a thick and green tree. I looked at the spot his finger was pointing at, then his finger, his hand, his wrist and arm. And there it was. Red and on display. It looked like one main big part, four thinner, longer parts on one side and another thin part on the other side.

"Pony?"

"Uh...they're apples."

"Hm. They're too big." He pulled his hand back.

"Well, this tree bears the biggest apples in all Folkspine's surrounding." I sounded like Dad saying it.

"Show me." I turned around to face him. A bright smile spread from one side of his face to the other. *Just a kid.*

"What?"

"Show me the tree. You said it's near Folkspine."

"No way! It's my own special tree." *Mine and Dad's.*

Chapter Six

Go downstairs and join them in the kitchen.

"Mom?" She looks up at me standing on the last step.

"Honey! You're awake. Your Dad and I were just-"

"Talking?" I finish for her. Mom looks at Dad, Dad looks at me. His eyes are easier to read than hers, partly because he doesn't try to hide his thoughts or feelings. *Or just isn't very good at it.*

"You slept alright?" *Way to avoid a conversation, Mom.* I nod, lying. When I finally managed to fall asleep, it didn't last long. I woke up a bunch of times, turning from one side to the other or watching the moon through my window while trying to either ban the Brennan family from my mind or figure out what happened.

"There are still eggs on the stove. They're cold, though." Hence the lack of smell.

"Thanks, Mom." I walk past my parents and instead of grabbing eggs from the stove, move over to the fridge, open it to grab the Sunny Delight and drink straight from the bottle.

"Sweetie, get yourself a glass."

"Oh, come on, Elaine. This ain't Hell's Saddle. Let the kid drink from the bottle."

Chug, chug, chug.

"Hell's Saddle! What time- Twelve?!" *Gotta work on my sunlight interpretation.*

"I gotta go. I've a job interview." She gives Dad a quick kiss on the lips.

"You're applying for a job?" I question after swallowing.

"No, someone finally applied for Hell's Saddle. Thank God." *Thank You, Lord.* Mom grabs her jacket from our coat stand, looks through the kitchen window to check the weather and quickly puts it back. *Give the woman a break.*

"Finish your eggs, will you?" Now it's my turn for a kiss on the cheek.

"Yes, Sheriff, yes!" I salute. She fetches her purse from the kitchen counter right next to Dad's old cowboy hat, opens the front door and lets it fall back into the lock with a bang.

As expected, silence fills the kitchen afterwards. Dad eyes me from the side and I give him the full high eyebrows, head-tilt look. In response, he claps his hands together.

"Well, the critters ain't takin care of themselves, eh? Gotta go, Squirrel." This is a nickname I can happily live with.

"It's twelve. You've got nothing to do till one. Since I live here too, I know your schedule, Dad." Get up at five, check the barn and then the fence in case Trixie – our horse – kicked it broken again. If yes, take her to her stable in the barn so she doesn't break out (she never does anyway, but Dad says you can never know what's going on in that head of hers). No matter what, feed Trixie, then Jewel. Follow by milking the mommas, feeding them and giving the calves their bottles. Once everyone's fed and milked, fix the fence – if necessary. Then, move everyone over to the meadow. Empty barn equals time and space to clean out the dung. Load the dung, so the county's other farmers can come get some for their fields. Then, go back to the meadow and check on Trixie. Clean out her stable and check for dung in the meadow. After that, do some other maintenance around the farm. Congratulations, you've got lunch break till one.

"Smart kid." He nods with a proud smile, like I just recited the routine to him.

"So, what *were* you guys talking about?" I say as I move over to the stove to fill a plate with eggs and bread. I feel Dad's eyes staring me in the back of my head, so I turn around to face him.

"Oh, come on. Please, Dad?"

"I really shouldn't." Normally, he would have given in by now. He isn't exactly stubborn like Mom. I walk away from the stove, back to the fridge, fetch the ketchup and spread it in lines over my eggs.

"Besides, I think ya already know." Dad continues.

"Well, I don't." The fridge closes, but I don't sit down to eat my breakfast. *I need to finish this conversation first.*

"Well, what *do* ya know?" *What do I know?*

"I know that Eve came in last night looking worse than ever, that she's been crying, Jeffrey knows something and Abel got slapped across the face."

Dad's eyes drop. He doesn't like it when someone's being upfront about "unholy topics" like that. Says it's not nice for a good Christian to go around taking violence so lightly.

It is to one's honor to avoid strife, but every fool is quick to quarrel.

Proverbs 20:3

I continue with my list. "And now, that Dan apparently hurt Eve too." I can feel my tongue and throat drying out, so I take another sip from the Sunny Delight, cherishing it for a couple seconds before pushing it down my throat with a loud gulp.

"He can't go to school." Is all Dad says after a while.

"Well, yeah. He's a grown man." I respond.

"No. I mean Abel. He can't go to school. Dan won't let him."

"That's bullshit." *How have I never noticed?* Abel kind of talks a lot – only after meet-ups with the gang involving pot or whatever they do – but he's never shared any school stories. Besides, the school I go to is the only one in town and I have never seen Abel in the halls. But I do have the pleasure of passing James every once in a while.

"Alex."

"No, Dad. It *is* bullshit." He doesn't argue and for a moment, we both just stare at each other.

"Yeah. It really is, Squirrel."

"What did Eve say about it?"

"Said she's too afraid of Dan to contradict. Said he thinks school is just for…not for men." *Meaning pussies.*

[52]

"Can he do that? Like, legally forbid him to go to school."

"Not sure, honestly. I've never had to check it, thank God." He looks up at the ceiling. "Yesterday, Eve tried to talk some sense into that airhead of a father, though. First time she ever even addressed the whole school situation. And he…" He's looking for a different word for slapped or punched or hit or pushed or whatever it is that Dan did. "Slipped up."
Good one, Dad. God's proud of you.

"Well, we *could* tell the Sheriff." I remind him of what Mom said. "And Eve…" I try to wash down the frog in my throat with more juice.

"Just like ya Mom. And I love you both." He gives me a pat on the head. "Which is exactly why I don't want you two to get involved. That Brennan's dangerous. I know how their minds work." *My thinking.* Dad knows Dan from stories shared at Hell's Saddle and then at home by Mom. And he knows the bar's history too. "I couldn't forgive the Lord if anything ever happened to you."

"I love you too, Dad." Is all I answer.

"Can we drop it now? I'm getting' sick." He always does. Whenever anyone talks about violence, sex, drugs and whatever, he starts to physically get sick. One time, he was over at Hell's Saddle having a drink with one of his farmer friends. He told Dad about how he saw two guys fighting in an alley the week before. How one ended up with a smashed-in nose and the other with a broken rib. Dad had to get up and go puke in the toilet. Mom told me about it the next day at breakfast.

"No, really. You should have seen him. He looked like someone just punched *him* in the guts." She let out a laugh.

"It's not funny, Elaine. You know I can't deal with stuff like that."

"Yeah. We both know. Which is why we love you." She looked over at me and I smiled in agreement – and because it *was* kind of funny. Turns out the two guys were fighting because the one that ended up with the broken nose was gay and tried a move on the other. Dad went to church that day to ask the Lord to forgive the guy. Or that's what he told me.

"Okay. Sorry, Dad."

"It's alright, Squirrel." He offers me a one-sided smile and I return a full one.

"Now go eat your eggs. See ya outside." He grabs his cowboy hat from the kitchen counter, but doesn't put it on. Can't enjoy the sun with a brim around your head. He's had that thing for as long as it's been able to fit on his head. I know it was once white, but now it's kind of beige brown. It's also worn and torn, but he will not, for the love of God, buy a new one. He leaves the kitchen with it to go sit down in his rocking chair on our porch.

"See ya!" I answer before he quietly closes the door.

Chapter Seven

On weekdays, I do my homework after school, help
Dad at the farm and then head to Hell's Saddle. On
Saturdays, Dad and I take our weekly walk and
when we're back, I help him with the farm again. On
Sundays, church is the top priority – of course.
After finishing my eggs, which taste great when
they're cold by the way, I clean away my plate and
head back upstairs. Drained as I was last night, I
didn't take a shower. Sleep and worry still stick to
my body, so I head to the bathroom to take a good
cold one.

I take off my socks, pants and panties. Only my shirt
left. I lift it up and look down on me. *Haven't grown.
Good.*

I hop into the shower and let the cold water touch
my skin and mind, washing one of them clean while
leaving the other with dirt in the cracks. I clean my
important parts while trying to neither look nor
touch them too much. I never liked the words boobs,
tits, pussy, vulva, vagina, whatever-the-fuck. And I
like the actual body parts even less.

When I'm finally done with the shower, I dry myself and go back to my room to dress. Since it's hot as Hell out, I choose my denim shorts and a plain white t-shirt that hangs loosely over my body. Mom said I'm starting to grow as a woman. I haven't noticed yet and to be honest, I don't want to. Most importantly, I don't want people like James to notice. The thought of two hills of fat growing underneath my skin makes me physically sick. This is *my* tummy's flaw. I've always felt a slight cringe at the thought of my naked body and the thought of it changing into something curvy is even worse. I shake off the thought and focus on something else. Like the wooden cross Dad got me for my twelfth birthday. It rests hanging from my neck like always. He carved it from a piece of an apple tree, *our* apple tree, and drilled a hole into the top. He then put it on a thin leather band which he knotted up in a way that somehow makes it possible to adjust the length. I have not understood this magic yet and I think I never will. I always pull it as tightly as possible so the cross sits nicely and high on my chest. I touch my neck to feel for it and give it a squeeze. Next, I put my light brown hair into a ponytail, comb my bangs and put on a cap. After pulling my ponytail through the hole in the back, I'm ready to go. Before stepping out the front door, I fetch my mud-covered boots and pull them over my feet.

Outside, I see Mom's car left the spot we parked it in last night, leaving slight tracks in the dry dirt. Dad's still sitting in his chair with his hat resting in his lap, rocking back and forth, eyes closed against the sun and humming a tune.

"What's that?"

"Good Hearted Woman." He answers, not pausing his rocking or sun refuel.

"Should have known."

Every year, on Mom and Dad's anniversary, they both go on a date at Hell's Saddle. Even though Mom's working every day, even on their anniversary, Dad still finds ways to make their special day a really special one. He gets all dressed up in his best jeans, clean boots, white western button-up, cowboy hat and his father's bolo tie. He comes into the bar, scans it for Mom and once he's got her, steals her away. Eve and I manage the bar for the time being, which includes one live or jukebox performance of "Good Hearted Woman" and one drink each. Dad takes Mom's hand, taps his hat and forces her onto the dance floor. They jump up and down and sway side to side like teenagers who have just fallen in love. If their anniversary falls onto a Friday, Dad gets up on the stage, grabs the mic from whoever's this week's lead singer and gives his best performance. He needs a few deep breaths – where anyone else would just push back a shot or two – to find the courage, but when he does, everyone cheers at him. He always sounds off-key and just straight up bad, but Mom loves it. Same goes for Eve, me and the rest of the bar. Every regular knows the date of their anniversary – fourteenth of December by the way – and patiently waits for the couple of the hour to get together and perform their yearly scheme. We've even had to endure some years, in which Goodfellow-night was more cared for among Folkspine than any band-night.

"You're definitely a better dancer than singer…or hummer."
Dad opens his eyes and chuckles. I join him.

"You ready to go?" I ask after the silence between us has settled back in. The squeaking of his chair stops and he checks his watch.

"It ain't one yet." He's scheduled his lunch break to last up until one at noon, which is when I'm normally done with homework on a weekday and can get out to help out on the farm or go for a walk slash ride with Trixie. To keep a routine, the same timetable counts on weekends.

"I know, but we can always need a head start, right?"

"It's like ya already run the place." He brings his hands down on his thighs and heaves himself out of his chair. "Alright, Squirrel. Git!" He puts on his hat and I realize he's become almost unrecognizable without it.

"Right on!" We stomp down the step from our porch and let our boots hit the dirt.

Chapter Eight

The trail connecting Main Road and our farm leads
to our barn and the meadow. You move from our
house, past the barn on the left and the meadow
further down on the right, until you've reached Main
Road and turn left to go to Folkspine's downtown.
Dad and I follow the trail until we're standing in
front of the barn. He throws me the keys and lets me
unlock the gate. After I'm done, I toss the keys back
to him and open the barn, revealing empty stables on
the ground. The hayloft's right on the top, holding
Trixie's and the girls' main food supply. I'm not
allowed up there. Dad claims it's too easy to fall
from, which in my opinion is bullshit, given I've
been climbing trees since I was six and haven't fallen
once – which he knows for a fact.

"Where's Jewel?" I question the lack of ear ringing
barking.

"In the meadow with the girls." The girls are all
eighty of our Jersey cows. Right now, they're
accompanied by Trixie, our white and brown
Appaloosa.

"You go get the saddle. I'll search together everything else and meet you in the meadow. Can ya handle that?"

"Sure as Hell I can!" He shoots me an admonishing look at the mention of Hell.

"It's heavy, ya know?"

"Yeah, I know. I can do it." I nod heavily.

"Atta." He grins at me.

I make my way to the opposite end of the barn, across the pathway between the stables on my left and right. Dad is right behind me, the sound of his heavy footsteps following the sound of my light ones. In the far back, we keep all our stuff for Trixie and some of Dad's tools. Right next to the ladder leading up to the hayloft, Trixie's saddle is resting on one of the last stables. I grab it with both hands and pull it from its spot. Dad eyes me, hands out in the open in case he has to help out. He doesn't.

I've got the saddle steadily in my hands and start walking back towards the barn's gate. As I reach it, I can already feel my upper arms burning.

"Be right there, Squirrel!" Dad shouts after me, rummaging through the boxes of brushes and such.

"Uh huh!" Is all I can answer between breaths.

A minute passes and I reach the gate of our meadow. I place Trixie's saddle on the fence, lean against it and try to regain a steady breath while watching the girls. The cows are grazing away on the green grass and daisies while the calves are trying to get some of the milk Dad left for them from their mommas. After taking some deep breaths, I place my palms in front of my mouth and holler.

"Hiya critters!" The ones that stop grazing and drinking moo in response. Jewel comes running up to me from the other side of the meadow, barking and letting the hot air fly through her beige coat. She crawls underneath the fence and I open my arms for her to jump into. I laugh as she licks my face.

"Hiya, Jewel." I greet her with a kiss on the head. In the distance, I see Dad leaving the barn and struggling to lock it behind him. He always makes sure the barn is locked at all times. Not even Mom owns a key. Dad's the only one. He walks towards us, hands full of brushes and tiny tools, shoulders packed with a saddle pad and bridle. Jewel jumps out of my arms and runs up to him, circling him as he tries not to fall over. Once he's caught up to me, he puts the stuff down and gives Jewel a scratch behind her ear.

"Did Trixie kick the fence tonight?" I ask, inspecting the wooden planks surrounding the meadow.

"Not that I know of. But if she did, she didn't break it this time."

For as long as I can think of, Trixie's been kicking at her fence at night, breaking it down sometimes. We keep her in the meadow in case she wants to walk around and graze. Most nights, she just stays in her stable, but she often wanders along the fence under the darkened sky, kicking at it. Dad has had to repair parts of the fence a bunch of times by now. And since he's pretty old-fashioned, he refuses to install a proper iron bar or wire fence.

Trixie has never broken out. She creates an open door, but doesn't walk through. Dad questioned some of his farmer friends about it, but none of them had a clue what's going on in that head of hers. *If she wants to break out, then why would she stay in the meadow after breaking the fence?*

Chapter Nine

After getting Trixie cleaned up and saddled, Dad gestures at me to get on her back. As I put my foot in the stirrup and swing my leg over Trixie's back, Dad keeps his hands in front of him in case he has to lend them to me. Once again, he doesn't. I grab the reins and click my tongue at Trixie to get moving. Since I've gotten too big for her to handle us both and Trixie's momma, Tara, died a few years ago, Dad and I haven't been able to ride together anymore. We still take our weekly route through the woods and take turns riding Trixie, but it isn't as fun as it used to be. I've been begging Dad to expand our farm with a second horse, so Trixie wouldn't be so lonely anymore and he and I could properly go riding again. I think he's still grieving Tara's death and doesn't want to feel like he's trying to replace her. To him, every animal on our farm is like family. This includes every single cow, Trixie and Jewel. And it definitely used to include Tara. She was Dad's first horse and the first animal to live on this property, way before Dad expanded it to be a proper cattle farm. This was back when his family moved to

Folkspine, Colorado, from somewhere in Montana –
I think. He doesn't really talk much about it. I know
Dad lived in Montana before moving here with his
parents, and I know Tara has always been his
companion. Well, ever since Dad was a teenager.
I've seen pictures of him in his teenage years,
standing next to her, same cowboy hat as today
covering his head. He was always weirdly positioned
in the photographs. Like he was too far on the right
or left, like something was supposed to be next to
him, but isn't shown in the pictures.
But nowadays, without Tara, he looks a little less
happy than back then. Even when we're taking our
walk together, which I know is his favorite part of
the week – next to church on Sundays.

I always get to ride Trixie first as Dad walks in the
front to lead us through the woods to our tree. We
switch roles for the way home. Dad leads Trixie over
our dirt trail and moves right onto Main Road,
distancing ourselves from Folkspine. After a short
while, we leave Main Road onto another dirt trail
and enter the woods. We move along the quiet river
meandering its way through the county's nature,

mountains in the distance, the hot sun beaming above us through the tree tops. Over the years, Dad and I have perfected the art of comfortable silence. Especially within nature. We both admire the green around us, listening to Trixie's hoofs against the rocks and dirt. No live performance at Hell's Saddle, no portion of Mom's eggs, no poem and no book can compete with that feeling of peace and safety. I know Trixie's going to follow Dad blindly, so I lean back on her steady back, keeping my feet in the stirrups, and watch the tree crowns changing above us.

Once I spot a tree with tiny green orbs between its leaves, I sit back up. The apple tree. *Our* tree.

Since it's still summer, the apples are far from edible and hardly even visible. Still, I'd recognize our tree if it were standing in a forest full of other apple trees. I know every branch, just like Dad. We discovered it a couple years ago, when I was old enough to go on rides with him. He took me to the woods, not quite knowing where to go. The chill autumn air was surrounding us and then, there it was.

Nature's fortress, strong and steady, bearing the biggest apples me and even Dad have ever seen.

Back then, I was too little to ride a horse on my own, so Dad and I both sat on Tara's back. We got off and knotted her reins around one of the old branches. This was the first tree I ever climbed, but with Dad's helping hands, I made it to one of the bigger branches sixteen feet above ground. Dad followed after me. He told me to stay right where I was, so I wouldn't fall, as he climbed around the tree picking apples for us.

"I can't believe God forbid Adam and Eve to eat something as good as this." He said, chewing on the watery, golden flesh.

"Mom never told me Eve can't eat apples." I answered, juice dripping down my chin. Dad almost choked on the piece he was working on in his mouth.

"No, not that Eve." He coughed between laughs. We were both sitting on the same branch, he closer to the stem so his weight doesn't force the branch to give out underneath us.

We've been visiting, climbing and eating ever since. On my tenth birthday, he carried a huge backpack on our ride through the woods. I was old enough to ride on a horse's back on my own. Tara was already gone, so we took Trixie out to the woods and Dad was leading us. Whenever I asked him about the contents of the backpack, he just said "You'll see." Never again have I experienced my dad as obstinate as he was that day. I heard him giggling to himself like a little kid with every step we got closer to the tree. When we reached it, I saw a foundation of planks sitting between the branches in the tree's crown.

"Ya old man and yourself will be building us a treehouse." He said, standing in front of the tree, spreading his arms in a T-pose. I jumped out of the saddle as fast as I could and ran over to inspect Dad's work from up close.

"Dad, oh my God!" He suppressed a clearing of his throat, but only because it was my birthday. On any other day, he would've had me recite Exodus 20:7. *You shall not take the name of the Lord your God in vain, for the Lord will not hold him guiltless who takes his name in vain.* But he kept quiet while probably apologizing to our Father internally. When he was done, he addressed me again.

"Happy birthday, Squirrel." He smiled at me proudly. I turned back around and jumped into his arms, like Jewel always does.

We got started right away, as Dad pulled out hammer and nails from his backpack and pulled more planks out into the open. He's been hiding them underneath fallen leaves and sticks. Since I was just ten, I wasn't *really* able to help, but Dad made sure I still felt useful, asking me to hand him his tools as he was balancing on the already installed planks.

Now, almost three years later, we're standing in front of our little home in the woods. The planks are colored in a faded red, which once used to match the apples.

I climb down Trixie's back and knot her reins on one of the lower branches. Dad watches my hands, checking if I tie the knot correctly. Satisfied with my work, he then gestures towards the wooden ladder leading up to the tiny house.

"Lady's first."

I cringe a little, but smile at him and start climbing up. Dad used to help me get up during the first few months after finishing our project, holding my waist on both sides, making sure I didn't fall. He doesn't have to do that anymore. *To be honest, he never had to, to begin with.* Once my feet stand on more or less solid ground, I lean over the edge of the foundation, watching for Dad.

"You coming up?"

He's still standing at the foot of the tree, looking up at me, arms crossed and beaming face.

"What is it?" I ask, though I know what his answer is going to be.

"You've grown so big, Squirrel."

"Then get on my level and come up!"

Inside, Dad and I sit down on an old mattress we found in our attic at home. Dad built some shelves for the treehouse, which now bear most of my notebooks, pens and chocolate bars. I often come here alone to write poems or read the book I'm currently working through – right now, it's "Bridge to Terabithia." But when I'm here with Dad, we enjoy the silence or talk about nonsense, like "Dad, did you know my math teacher has a pet snake named after Dolly Parton?" or "I've heard there was a werewolf in the woods last night. You better stay cautious, Squirrel, or he'll come get ya!"

I've had a good few laughs with Dad up here. *He doesn't seem it today, though.* We're not talking, but I can feel he's got something on his mind.

We're in the middle of eating some of my chocolate bars as I break the silence.

"Dad?"

"Yes, Squirrel."

"What are you thinking about?"

He folds the chocolate's wrapper in his hands.

"I know you've got something on your mind. You can't hide from me." He grins down at the wrapper, but with worry in his eyes.

"It's just…you're such a great kid. And you're so loved by your mom and Eve and everyone at the bar and me."

"Okay, but how is that a bad thing? You can't be sad about that."

"I'm sad because there are kids out there who have no one to properly love them."

"Is this about Abel?" I think back to our conversation this morning. *Time is relative and after a band-night, even twelve p.m. counts as morning.*

Dad nods.

"Eve loves him, right?" I ask.

"Yeah, but not enough to get him out of that trailer."

Pause.

"What trailer?"

"Ya know, their trailer. Home." *What?* His eyes widen as I squint mine in confusion.

"What?" I verbalize my thought.

"Oh…" He covers his mouth with his hand. "You weren't supposed to know that."

"And why's that?" My heart rate quickens. "Did Mom tell you not to tell me?"

"You gotta understand, she doesn't want you to get too involved."

"I can't believe it." I'm standing up now, looking down at Dad.

"Squirrel, I know you're angry." He reaches out to me.

"Damn right, I'm fucking angry." *But why?*

"Don't use that language, please." *I'm sure God will forgive me for saying* fucking *once.*

"Are you angry because we didn't tell you or because they have to live in a trailer?" *Do you have a secret history as a therapist, Dad?*

[73]

"God! I don't know, Dad. Because you didn't tell me. And cause they- cause Dan…"

I hate Dad's worried look even more than Mom's.

"Sit back down, kid." He pats the empty space next to him on the mattress. I hesitate, but eventually do as I'm told. He grabs my hand and looks me in the eyes, which calms me down on the spot.

"We can't control the people around us, but we can control how we deal with them. Neither Eve nor Abel can change Dan, but they can choose to live a life without him. They just have to be brave enough. Without him, they'd be able to go get a proper place of their own, ya know? But that's just not up to us and definitely not up to you."

Abel's face from last night flashes into my head. Not Eve's, who I've seen stressed and dejected all night. But Abel, who, besides everything, had smiled at me in the blue neon light.

Chapter Ten

We ride home in more silence. Well, Dad rides and I walk. It's like every other Saturday, only today, the silence is off. It should sound like it always does. That's the routine. Dad rides Trixie, while I walk beside her, and we both listen to the silence around us. But right now, there are unspoken words in between, disturbing the sacred silence. I want to talk more about Eve and Dan and Abel, and Dad wants to do the same, but the conversation simply doesn't happen.

Back on the farm, we see the Flying Fishbowl parked in front of our porch. We take Trixie back to her stable and Dad trusts me with taking off her bridle, saddle and saddle pad.

"I'll go see what Mom is up to. See ya inside?"

"Yeah, see ya."

He leaves the both of us alone and steps through the meadow gate towards our house.

Trixie stares me in the eyes as I loosen the bridle around her head.

"What do you want?" I ask her.

She responds by nudging my shoulder. I take off her bridle and step back to face her. "What is it, girl?" She whinnies and I hear Jewel in the distance barking in response. Trixie always stares at me whenever she feels like something's off. Last time she did it the day before a history test. I was so nervous about messing it up that I hadn't been focused all day and ended up putting the saddle on backwards and knotting her reins the wrong way. But today, I did everything right. Still, she continues eyeing me as I take off her saddle, which I place next to the bridle on one of the bars forming the stable. Lastly, I take off her saddle pad and place it next to the bridle and saddle on the bar.

"Trixie, everything's fine! You can stop staring now." A neigh shoots across the meadow. "Okay, I'm gonna ignore you now, if that's alright m'lady." I bow to her and turn to grab the saddle from the bar, holding it steadily with both hands, just like this morning. *Gonna have to go twice for the bridle and saddle pad.* I take a mental note.

I pace across the meadow, passing some of the grazing girls. I place the saddle on the fence to open the gate, step through and close it up again. I retrieve the saddle from the other side of the fence and make my way across the path towards the barn. *Shit, Dad's got the keys.*

I try not to snap my back as I put the saddle down on the ground. After having lost the weight, I take some time to pant before making my way towards our house, where Mom and Dad are probably catching up over a cup of coffee. The door's open, so I step inside and take off my boots.

"I really have to think about it. I'm not sure I want someone like that working my bar." Mom's voice mixed with the smell of coffee fills the air inside. "Someone like what?" I ask her, stepping into the kitchen, where both my parents are leaning with their backs against the counter, a cup in one hand each.

"Already done, Squirrel?" Dad asks, looking at his watch.

"Keys, please." I say pointing at his pocket.

"Oh, right!" He takes them out and lets them jingle through the air before landing in my hand.

"Someone like what?" I ask again looking at Mom.

She puts down her cup and looks at me. Serious.

"The…person that applied for the job at Hell's Saddle."

"Yeah, what's up with them?" I toss the keys from one hand to the other, playing with them.

"They're…" She looks over at Dad for help. "How do I explain it, John?"

Now it's Dad's turn to put down his cup.

"Well, she…" Dad pauses, looking for an explanation. "He is a sinner." The keys in my hands stop moving. Silence fills the room. My gaze wanders from Dad to Mom and back to Dad.

"I'm not following."

"A sinner just like Eve, who ate the apple, remember?" Dad offers to explain.

"Yeah, I know what a sinner is, Dad. You always make sure I never forget." I shake my head from side to side. *I still don't get it.* Mom takes a deep breath. *Is it lecture time again?*

"Honey, do you know what a transvestite is?" She asks me.

"I don't think so?"

"Elaine, don't." Dad reaches out to her.

"No. She has to know at least something. Especially if she – I mean he…" Mom readjusts her eyebrows and sighs, as if this conversation is so exhausting. "If they will start working the bar."

She fixes her eyes on mine, but no words come out of her mouth.

"A transvestite is someone, who disobeys the Lord." Dad offers and Mom nods at his explanation.

"These people got the devil in them, alright?"

"Sounds like a perfect addition to Hell's Saddle. Not sure Jeffrey is going to be happy about sharing his title." I joke, but no one even breaks a smile.

"Alex, listen to me. *If* this tranny will start working the bar, then I need you to be careful and stay away." Mom orders.

"But why?" *I'm still not getting what she's trying to tell me.*

"Because they're perverts." Her voice breaks a little. Dad moves closer to Mom and puts a hand on her shoulder.

"Your Mom's right. You best be careful around people like that."

"So…" *What is a transvestite, though?*

Dad turns back to me like he just heard my thoughts. *Therapist style.*

"You don't have to get it. You just have to know it's a sickness and you don't want to contract it, so keep a distance." Dad never gives orders like that. "Let's all just pray for them at church tomorrow. Have them be saved by the Lord." *Why would they need saving?*

"Okay, Dad."

"Atta." He smiles at me from across the kitchen. I don't mimic his upturned lips.

"I gotta go." I say, holding up the keys.

"Right. Be right there for the second feeding round!" Dad shouts after me, but I've already put on my boots and stepped out, closing the door behind me.

Chapter Eleven

Dad and I get to work on the farm for the rest of the afternoon. I put away Trixie's gear and he feeds her and the girls. Next, we check in on every single calf and when there's nothing left for me to do, I go search for Mom. I find her in the kitchen, collecting her purse, keys and whatnot. *Hell's Saddle's calling for her.*

"Can I come?"

"You really gotta get yourself some friends." One might be hurt by hearing their own mother say such a thing, but not me. Not with Elaine Goodfellow as a mother. I know she means it as a joke, though we both also know it's probably the truth. But I guess I missed my only chance of making friends at school, when I said I'd like to switch lives with Abel fucking Brennan.

"Why, when I've got you and Dad." I tell her. "Besides, Trixie and Jewel are my friends."

Mom rolls her eyes at me, but tells me to meet at the car at five. I run up the stairs towards my room, skipping every second one. *Notebook.* I walk towards my desk and grab my going-out-notebook from the top drawer. I keep most of my notebooks at the treehouse, but this one always stays in my room. Given it's not stuffed into my bag or clutched to my chest when I'm out. *Can't risk forgetting random bursts of inspiration, so I write them down on the spot.* I've also got a notebook just for found notes and one that serves as a diary. Mom jokes, I'm starting to go crazy over my organizing.

Okay, what else? A pen? No, Mom's keeping some at the bar. Better shoes! Preferably ones without dried mud.

I own two pairs of cowboy boots. One for working on the farm and taking walks and one for Hell's Saddle, school and church – "going out" as one might call it. Whenever James sees me in the halls, though, he comments on them. Last time it was "Will you ride me like a horse in those?" which wasn't very creative, to be honest. I was making my way to my locker to grab "The Silver Chair"– the best book in the Chronicles of Narnia series, by the way – when he, Alan and Glen passed me. I did wonder where Abel was, but I didn't give it a second thought. *How have I never noticed, he doesn't go to school?* James was walking ahead with Alan and

Glen following like dogs. James made the comment,
Alan laughed – praising the leader of the group – and
Glen shot a glimpse of an apologetic look at me.
Almost too short and small for the human eye to
catch. But when Alan snorted like a pig between
laughs, Glen couldn't help but break a smile.
I pitied them. All that insecurity and having to
compensate for it by picking on the loner. Plus, it's
super weird for a seventeen-year-old to hit on a
twelve-year-old like that. Pity turned into anger and
made my blood boil, so I wanted to kick the fertility
out of his nuts. But I didn't give him the satisfaction
of letting his comments get to me and both parties
passed each other without a second word – one of
them leaving a trail of smoke and the smell of pot
behind. Dad tells me to just ignore James while
Mom advices me to stay away from him or punch
him in the face the next time. *I'm more comfortable
with Mom's idea.*
I run back downstairs and grab my clean boots
standing next to the ones covered in mud – and
probably dung too. I put them on and head out of
the house towards the Flying Fishbowl, clutching

my notebook to my chest. Lack of chest. *Praise the Lord.*

"That was two minutes." Mom's standing next to the driver's door, smiling at me with her arms crossed. Almost like Dad did earlier at our tree. We get in and take the same route as last night. Only this time, we head back towards Hell's Saddle.

"So, have you made up your mind about the job application?" I ask after a while.

"I don't know, Honey. I really need the help, you know?" *Who* doesn't *know?* "If I had another employee, I could maybe take some nights off and spend time with you and your dad."

"And Eve wouldn't have to stress herself at work so much, right?"

"Right." She turns her head to smile at me.

"What's his...uh her?" I can't make up my mind. Mom shrugs her shoulders like "I don't know either."

"What's their name?"

"Taylor Beckham." *Huh.*

"Not exactly a boy's or girl's name. Kinda like me, right?"

Mom slams on the brakes as we reach a red light. My head slams forward.

"Don't ever say that." She's trying so hard to sound calm. "You are nothing like that deviant." *Deviant.* I repeat the word in my head a couple times and every time, the sound it makes in my brain makes less sense and stings worse. *What's up with Taylor that they're so bad?* I nod in silence and we don't speak for the rest of the way as I look out the window and wonder.

After parking the car on the street in front of the bar, Mom fully turns towards me.

"Taylor's working tonight. It's just a test to see if he fits into our bar and can do the job right." *So, it's a man?* "I need you to stay with me or Eve or anyone you know tonight, yeah? Don't go off anywhere with him on your own. Understood?"

"Understood." *I understand what she just said, but I don't get it.*

We get out of the car and step in front of the bar. Right where Grandpa and Dan's father used to stand when the picture was taken. Mom takes her keys from her pocket and unlocks the door. Stepping inside, I get the eerie feeling I always get seeing the place like this. No music, no laughter, no colors. Even though it's still bright out, Mom flicks on the big light. It's uncomfortably white and buzzing. There's no guest, no Jeffrey and no Eve – yet. At least there's no Abel either. It's just Mom and me and she gets straight to work and neatly rearranges all the chairs to their original space. Some are lying on the ground, another one is on top of the stage and Mom even finds one in the restroom. I failed to recognize the mess after waking up last night or I simply got used to seeing the place trashed like this after a band-night.

"Nothing like a busy band-night." She words my thought, mumbling to herself as she comes out of the restroom with the chair in her hand.

I sit at the bar, right where I was sitting last night too. On the last chair on the left. From there – just like last night – I watch her.

Mom and Dad always tell me that I either take over the farm or the bar later. Having my parents trust me with their families' life work makes me proud to be a Goodfellow. Now, I just have to decide if I take after Hell's Saddle, which was brought to life by Mom's father and his partner, or our farm, which Dad's father built after moving to Colorado. *What if I don't even want to stay here?* Either way, I make sure to know how to take care of both places, so I try to keep an eye on either one of my parents whenever they're working and I'm nearby.

Next, Mom grabs the broom from the back and starts sweeping the floors. I realize my skin sticking to the bar counter's surface and go behind it to grab a cloth. I wipe down the counter with warm water and some dish soap. When I'm done, I throw the cloth back in the sink and sit back down, looking for other small tasks to do.

Mom distracts me from my mission as she exclaims. "Well, would you look at that." She gestures at the pile of dust and rubbish she just created. "Seems like I've got something for you, Sweetie."

"What is it!?" My eyes open wide in excitement, knowing *exactly* what it is.

"Someone left a note." She confirms my suspicion. She picks it up and immediately hands me the folded piece of paper. Mom's my number one supporter when it comes to collecting notes. I glue them down in my note-notebook and try to figure out the story behind it. It's fun to try and find out about Folkspine's secrets, though – sadly – most notes are incredibly boring, like:

Groceries

Eggs

Laundry detergent

Cigs

I'm way more excited about the mysterious ones like:

Yk where, 11

prepare

Ps. Bring me a sixpack

I always tell Mom about my finds and what I think they mean. Sometimes she helps, given she knows all the gossip of Folkspine. _Of course she does. She owns the best bar in town. And drunk people talk._
We never figured this one out. The only clue we had was that I saw James accidentally drop the note when he was searching through his pockets. We nearly smushed our brains trying to piece together non-existent clues, only to call it a day and meet on the terms that James probably met up with a girl _way_

too old for him, to get drunk and probably do other stuff. Like Uncle Dan, like Nephew James. Unfortunately for him, he never got to give his girl the note. This was two years ago. When James was about fifteen. I wonder if they still see each other, having sex in James' basement or the junkyard or wherever people like James hang out to stick their dick somewhere. Dad would freak if he knew I know about sex. He'd give me a lecture on responsibility, losing my purity, disappointing God, waiting until marriage, blah blah blah. And I'd end up telling him that Mom broke the birds and the bees to me. She told me it's all about love and trust and to never abuse sex. To cherish it in your soul and body and only to give it a go when your soul and body, and you and the other person, are in connection with each other. She didn't miss out on contraception. Now, I just hope I don't end up like Mary and get pregnant out of – more or less – nowhere. On second thought, I'm sure being a saint is somehow lots of fun.

I take the note from Mom's hand and she continues sweeping the floor. I unfold the paper and begin to read.

Mom, im ~~soray~~ *sorray*

~~do~~

It looks like the writing of a five-year-old. Some lines are way too long, others way too short. Not to mention the grammar.

"What's it say?" Mom asks, still focused on cleaning the wood underneath us.

"Uh…nothing." Something about it feels off. The long and short lines, like a kid's. But "Mom, I'm sorry" sounds so damn serious.

The bell chiming behind me breaks my train of thought.

Chapter Twelve

"Hey, Loves." I turn around to face Eve looking *way* better than yesterday. Her dark hair is already pinned back, revealing her face, which doesn't look like she's been crying.

"Hiya Eve." I wave at her with a genuine smile. Mom breaks her staring contest with the floor and focuses on her best friend.

"You feelin' better, Babe?"

"Yes. Thanks for the chat yesterday." *The* chat. The "My alcoholic husband hurt me and our son" chat. Must've happened after closing, when I was sleeping in the back.

Mom smiles half satisfied, half worried. Both women then focus entirely on their work, with only one goal. Getting the place ready for later. "Later" meaning eight p.m., when Hell's Saddle opens up and will greet its first guests of the night.

Eventually, I move towards the jukebox and turn on "Sandman." Mum sings loudly as she swipes down the tables. Eve is right in front of me, behind the bar counter, and rinses some leftover glasses from yesterday while humming along. I enjoy this almost as much as Dad's and my silence in the woods.

Usual silence. Not today's.

At some point, Mom turns to Eve.

"Oh, by the way. I've had a job interview this noon.
He's coming in like half an hour to do some trial
work." I turn around to face the clock hanging above
the doorway. Seven.

"Thank fuck finally!" Eve claps her hands together
above her head.

"Eve." Mom sounds monitory.

"Whoops. Sorry, Love." Eve apologizes to me and I
wave my hand, indicating there's nothing to worry
about. *Sorry, Dad.* I turn to Mom.

"Mom?"

"Yeah, Honey?"

"Why do you suddenly keep saying *he* when later
today you also said *she*? You're confusing me." The
cloth in her hand stops moving over a table.

"Cause that's what transvestites are. Confusing."
And before I'm able to ask, Eve's voice shoots
through the air.

"He's a tranny!? Oh my God, Elaine! Are you aware
that's the most exciting thing that happened all
week?" Being the owner of Hell's Saddle, Mom

knows all the drama, but Eve is the one holding the title of *Gossip-Queen*. *It's sad that most drama around here surrounds her family.*

"Calm down, girl." Mom answers like she's talking to one of our cows. "I'm not even sure I want him working here."

"Oh please, Elaine. You always need extra hands."

"I mean it, Eve." *Oh oh. Mom's in boss mode.*

"Just calm yourself, alright? And keep your distance, please. I already told Alex to do the same." I nod at Eve.

"Alright, alright." She then leans in to me.

"I've never seen one in real life, you know?" She whispers. I shake my head in response and whisper back.

"What is a transvestite? Mom won't tell me."

"Well, Love. They are-"

Mom provocatively clears her throat and raises an eyebrow at Eve, who, in response, recreates the distance between us and gets back to work.

It's then that I realize I'm still holding the note in my hands. I fold it back together and stuff it into my back pocket, so I can glue it into my note-notebook later. I'm still waiting for a burst of inspiration for a new poem or diary entry, though. I collect those ideas in my going-out-notebook and then execute them in the correct notebooks at home or in the treehouse. I keep most of my poem-notebooks there and my diary at home underneath my pillow.

At some point, I reopen the notebook and lean over the counter to grab a pen from the bar to write *Find out what a transvestite is.* As if the multiple mental notes I already took don't mean anything.

I spend the next couple minutes doodling across the pages. At one point, I try to capture Mom drying glasses. Eve is somewhere in the back, so Mom is my only muse right now. Which I don't mind. I've got a real pretty Mom, even with her hair down. I color her hair with an orange neon marker. Looking at the finished product, I realize I've made it look like she is on fire. *Well, I'm a poet and not a painter.* I flip through the pages until I find the right one, containing my current list of poem inspirations. So far it reads:

<u>Poem ideas:</u>

~~Eve, Serpent, apple~~

~~Sound Of Silence~~

~~"Stop the skin mountains"~~

I add a new idea underneath:

Mom, fire, hair

"Another idea?" Mom asks me, eyeing the page without trying to read it. She knows I hate it when people look at my notebooks, which is why she appreciates it even more when I read her one of my poems.

"Yeah. I'll write one about you."

"Can't wait." She says, knowing I'll read it to her, once I've got it. We smile at each other.

It's then that the bell behind me chimes. *Taylor? No.* I know who it is. The bell always chimes differently for *him*. Not like an announcement, but more like a song. I turn around to see Abel standing in the doorway, as predicted. The clock above reads seven twenty.

His eyes find mine first. I turn back around towards my notebook and quickly close it. I *especially* don't want him to see.

"Hey." He always sounds so polite, which gets on my nerves. Like he's trying too hard not to be like his father.

"Hey Abel." Mom greets him with a big and empathetic smile. At the sound of her son's name, Eve sticks her head through the beaded curtain.

"Abel, Love?" She gets out from the back and walks towards him for a hug. "You alright?" She says as she pulls back and cups his face in her hands.

"Yes, Mom. I'm fine." He calmly reassures her. When he sees me looking at the both of them, he shakes her off.

"Well, then why are you here? Go help your father with chores." Eve tells her son and Mom and I share a glance at each other.

"He's passed out on the couch." Abel dryly answers.

"Jesus." His mother raises her palm towards her forehead.

"I was just out and walking by when I saw you guys inside. So, I figured, why not join?"

"Great." I mumble to myself as I look back down at my closed notebook.

"Hey, Pony." He shoots back with a smirk in his voice. *God, he makes me sick.*

"Hm." I respond.

"Aren't you guys lovely?" Mom grins at the both of us.

Chapter Thirteen

Abel sits down at the bar counter, leaving one empty chair between us. *At least.* Mom pours a glass of Sunny Delight each and places them in front of us. "Thank you, Elaine." He sounds genuine and kind, as always. Which makes it hard to hate him, but not impossible.

"Thanks, Mom." I copy and raise the glass to my mouth, swallowing the familiar taste.

"Oh, and Abel." Mom focuses her whole attention on him. I watch them both. I watch Abel. I watch his dark brown eyes, focused on Mom. His moles. One underneath his left eyebrow, another one on his ear, another one on his neck... *Focus. But I can't.* I notice his jaw, sharper than it should be, since he's still just thirteen. His brown hair. The same color as Eve's. Dark and cold, but inviting. All messy, like a bird's nest. *There it is again.* The sting in my chest. The unexplainable jealousy.

"I've got someone new trial working tonight. If you plan to stay a bit, then please keep your distance."

"Okay, but why?" He asks just as confused as I, but more cool about it.

"Dad says they've got a sickness." I tune in.

"What sickness?" He asks me. Brown eyes. *On me.* I now see the moles on his right side. One in the inner corner of his eye, one right on his stupid jaw.

"Don't know. Mom won't tell." I raise my eyebrows at her.

"You do as you're told and stay away from Taylor."

"Yes, chef!" We both salute at once. It actually makes me crack a giggle at him. He gives me the most genuine smile I've ever seen. *Shit.*

"Good," Mom says, "because here he comes."

Right on cue, the bell behind me and Abel chimes. I turn around to see…*a girl?*

She's got pretty dark curls framing her face, eyes painted gold, red lipstick on plump, dark lips. She's wearing dark blue denim pants that close tightly around her legs and a tight red top. She looks different from Mom and Eve, though. Less curvy. But she's got breasts just like them. Then, she parts her lips to speak with a smile.

"Hello." *Huh?* Her voice is deep. Not quite like Dad's, but similar to Abel's. And she sounds kind, just like him.

"Hiya." I wave at her.

"Oh! Hey, kiddos." She waves back at me and Abel. *Cute.* He smiles and waves at her.

"Taylor! Right on time, I see. Good." Mom greets her.

"Ah, Miss Goodfellow!" Taylor answers.

"Please, it's Elaine." She waves the newcomer off.

Eve doesn't say a word. She's gone behind the bar after letting go of Abel and is now squinting at Taylor, looking her up and down.

"Ignore her." Mom says as she waves Taylor toward the beaded curtain. They both disappear behind it. When they come back, Taylor's got her hair pushed back with a white headband, revealing a broad forehead and strong eyebrow ridges. The black apron that's now sitting around her hips matches the ones Mom and Eve are wearing. Mom leads her behind the bar counter, so that Taylor's now standing next to Eve, who takes a step to create some space between them. Mom reenters boss mode.

"Eve here will show you how everything works around Hell's Saddle. I gotta go and grab some stuff from the back." She shoots Eve a sharp look, pointing her middle and pointer finger at her own eyes, then at Eve's. Abel's Mom reacts by throwing her hands up – not in surrender, but mockingly. Before disappearing behind the beaded curtain into the back, Mom shoots the same look at Abel and me, more worried and loving, though.

I give both the women some space by grabbing my notebook and pen and moving towards my favorite booth. I place the stuff down on the table and move further to the jukebox to put on another song. After the intro of "White Room" fills the air around us and Hell's Saddle regains some of its magic, I hear Eve saying "And that would be our jukebox. Alex here is the protector of it, so you better stay away from the machine." I turn to her direction and shoot her a joking look. "We got bands performing on Fridays, though. But I guess Elaine already told you." She continues, trying so hard to keep a professional voice.

I turn from the jukebox and skip towards my booth, bobbing my head to the music, when- *Pause.*

My notebook is open. Abel's sitting there, carefully flipping through it.

"Hey!" I stop the skipping and bobbing and run towards the booth to snatch my book from his hands.

"Woah Jeez." He looks up at me. "I'm sorry, Pony."

"It's Alex!" I shoot back. *Why can't he get that?* Eve looks up from whatever she's been explaining to Taylor.

"You alright, kids?"

"We're fine, Mom!" Abel shouts back. He locks eyes with me.

I have never been able to hold his brown stare for more than three seconds. I counted it. One, two. *Oh, come on Goodfellow. That's all you can do right now?*

"Yeah, we're fine!" I surrender and let myself fall into the booth.

"What is that?" He points at my notebook.

"A notebook? I really hope for you, you didn't read any of it."

"I can't read, Alex."

"What?"

"I can't read. I don't go to school." *Shit. I fully forgot that.* "I thought you knew that." *Well, I didn't up until yesterday.*

"Oh! Yeah, of course I knew. I just… forgot. Sorry." *I feel bad.* We're silent. No noise except Eve's voice and the music. *Great, now it's weird.*

"Elaine looks like she's on fire, though." He breaks the silence between us and I internally thank him for it, though I normally prefer it if we don't speak. "Yeah, I know." I don't like to admit it when I create a bad piece of art. I normally tear bad drawings or poems apart. "Stop the skin mountains" was one of them. I think it went something like this:

Stop the skin from mountaining.
Keep your Earth the way it is.
Keep it neat,
Keep it shallow.
Stop the skin mountains.

Inventing a new word just for the sake of art didn't really work for me. Plus, I know I can do better. I just wrote it in an act of nightly confusion. Just when I shake off the cringy feeling I always get when thinking about the mountains, an inspiration shoots through me, tickling my brain. Before I know it, I've opened my notebook to add:

Night sky skin (stars, moles)

When I regain control over my brain, I read over what I just wrote. *Shit.*

"What'd you write?" Abel leans over the table.

"None of your business." I keep my head leaned towards my notebook so he doesn't catch me blushing. *I'm Alex Goodfellow. I don't blush.* I'm still wearing the cap from this morning and Abel quickly pulls it from my head. I look up in surprise, not changing my expression.

"Aha! You're smiling. Must be about me then." He mocks, waving my cap in the air around us. *Why's he so confident out of the sudden?*

"Haha, you wish." *Very suave, Goodfellow.* I snatch my cap out of his hand. Just as I'm about to put it back on, I see a disappointed look on his face and pause.

"What?"

"Huh?" He's just like Mom when I pulled her away from her thoughts last night.

"You were thinking."

"Uh, therapist much?"

"Got it from my dad. Spill it, Brennan." I demand.

"No, I'm just…jealous?" *What now?* He *is the jealous one?*

"What about?" He doesn't answer. One, two, three seconds lost in the brown.

"What about, Abel?" I repeat.

"Will you teach me?" Finally, he speaks up. *First time I've felt glad about that.*

"Teach you what?"

"How to write. And read. Mainly write, though."

"Oh." I don't know what to say. *What does one say when a thirteen-year-old asks something like that? "Of course I will, Honey." But he's a Brennan, remember? Just like James, just like Dan, just like Dan's father. But somehow, Abel is nothing like them.*

"Why don't you ask James? He goes to school and you hang out all the time anyway."

"He's a dick. And stupid too." He's right. I've heard the teachers sharing concerns about James' grades at school.

"Fair enough." I couldn't bear the fact that someone as immature and sadly unintelligent as James would be teaching Abel. "Alright. I'll do it."

"Wait, really?" His face lights up again. *There he is.*

"If it means you'll leave me alone." *If it'll make you keep lighting up?*

"Oh my God! Thank you, Pony!" He's all jumpy like a kid. Because he *is* just a kid. "Alex." He corrects himself.

"Don't worry 'bout it." I finally put my cap back on.

Chapter Fourteen

After a short while, Mom reemerges from the back, a box full of bottles in her hands. Living on a farm automatically makes you strong. I'm still waiting for the day, Trixie's saddle doesn't burn my arms anymore.

Mum sets the box down on the counter and announces "Refill!" She takes a moment to look over the liquid drugs. "Man, they really emptied a lot last night." She mutters as she pulls out the bottles, one by one. Then, she organizes them on the big shelf behind the bar, while Eve and Taylor watch. At some point, Eve grabs one of the bottles. "Didn't Jeffrey's booth empty one of those on their own last night?"

"I thought they only had beer." I scootch in.

"Oh, yeah. Well, at first." Mom answers.

"Speak of the Devil." What follows is the chiming of the bell and Jeffrey's heavy footsteps. "Taylor, this is Jeffrey. Our most loyal regular, Devil of Hell's Saddle and unofficial security."

"Evenin'." He taps his hat.

"You're early tonight." Mom says, looking at the clock above him. I lift myself from my booth to check the time. Seven fifty.

"Oh, don't worry. The Devil ain't here to empty ya taps 'n bottles." He begins scanning the bar. "Just lookin' for..." his eyes fix on Abel's head and he points at him with a "You."

"Uh?" is all Abel responds.

"Jeffrey?" Eve steps up. "What is it?"

"Stay put, Eve. Everythin' good. Can I steal him away for a chat?"

"Uhm...sure." Eve responds.

"Actually, I was asking the little one." Jeffrey turns to me. "Ya two lovebirds."

"What!?" We scream at the same time.

"Haha, come on now. Git!" He nods his head at Abel, who gets up from our booth- *my* booth. They both walk outside with a chime of the bell. Everyone in the bar falls silent. Even the jukebox seems to decrease its volume. Mom looks at Eve, Eve looks outside in confusion, I join her, and Taylor isn't quite sure where to look. Mom breaks the silence with a loud clap.

"Back to work, please. We've got ten minutes before we open up!" Taylor and Eve turn their attention back to work, though Eve still ends up checking the windows revealing Abel and Jeffrey outside.

I watch the both of them. They're not arguing. Just talking. Well, Jeffrey's talking and Abel is nodding his head. At some point, Jeffrey touches Abel's shoulder. *Fuck.*

The normal chime mixes with the melody of Abel's chime as they reenter the bar. Eve looks up at her son and then at Jeffrey.

"Everything alright, you two?"

"Yes, ma'am." Jeffrey taps his cowboy hat again and Abel stays silent as he walks back up to the booth to sit back down opposite from me. He looks…*sad?* He has looked worried before, or angry, but he has *never* looked sad.

"Okay, that's it." *Shit. I said that out loud.*

Before I know it, I've got my hand around Abel's wrist. *Carefully.* He's wearing a jacket, so his arms are covered. *But with Dan as his father, you can never know.* I'm leading him out of the booth and towards the beaded curtain while I try to ignore the feeling of everyone watching us. Even Taylor. Mom and Eve giggle at each other, but I ignore that too.

We disappear behind the curtain and I take a right into the lounge. The blue neon light is still off.

I turn Abel towards the wall and grab both shoulders with my hands.

"What is going on?"

"Pony- What?" He's startled.

"You've been acting weird. All confident and upfront all of a sudden. And now, sad. You never look sad. I know Dan did something and you're gonna tell me what it is. What did he do?"

"I-" He breaks off. "Okay, the confidence might be the alcohol."

"You drank?" *I knew it. He's just a Brennan after all.*

"With the gang, yeah. We hung out before I got here." He admits in guilt.

"Seems like you've been *hanging out* a lot lately." I remember the smell of pot that surrounded this very place last night. "That's not the point, though." I shake off the anger. "What did Jeffrey just tell you? I know you guys are neighbors. You live in the trailer park, right? And I know for a fact, Jeffrey lives there too." *Thanks, Mom, for never shutting up.* "What did he hear?"

"How do you know Jeffrey knows?"

"I'm trained in piecing together clues." *Thank you, note-notebook.* "But that's also beside the point."

"Okay, okay! Dad hurt Mom."

"More specific, Brennan." I lock eyes with him. One, two, three.

"Jeffrey told me he saw Dad…choking her." *The turtleneck.*

"What else?" Four, five. *New record.*

"Uh…called her a whore." My grip tightens on his shoulders. The look in his eyes shifts. Smaller pupils, raised eyebrows. *Shit! I scared him.* I remove my hands from his shoulders.

"Sorry 'bout that."

"It's fine." He rearranges his shoulders. For a while, we just stand there. It's now that we both realize the noise on the other side of the wall. Muffled music, some glasses clinking, chatting. Hell's Saddle's open and already getting busy. Abel's focus shifts from the wall back to me.

"Alex, I uh…" He doesn't continue.

"Yeah?"

"Thank you." My heart skips a beat.

"What for?" *Stay calm.*

"For checking in."

"Of course. Eve's like family to me. So…you are too." I admit. To him and to myself.

Without a word, he pulls me in for a hug. *He pulls me in for a hug?* Hugs are off limits for us. Now my heart doesn't *skip* a beat, but beats almost twice as fast. Instinctively, I close my arms around Abel's back. His hair tickles my nose and I breathe in old cigarette smoke. And I don't mind it as much as I thought I would. And I realize I've been wondering what it would be like for us to hug. I wait for him to pull back. When he does, his mouth stands open in realization. So does mine. We stare and blink at each other. My arms feel weird, having touched something they never have before. The smell of cigarettes still stinging in my nose.

"I'm sorry." *Are those tears in his eyes?* "Fuck. Men don't cry, right?" He tries to chuckle the tears away.

"Uh, they absolutely do. Men who don't are pussies. Besides, you're not a man. You're just a kid." I reassure him. "And don't be sorry."

He swallows to gather himself and nods.

"You wanna go back in?" He points at the doorway.

"Do *you*?"

After he nods, I walk us back out, turning left into the bar. We enter red air, filled with chatter and the smell of booze.

"Amazing how quick this place can change, right?"

Chapter Fifteen

Eve glances over at us as we take our seats by the bar. No empty chair between us. I'm surprisingly okay with that.

I finally notice the slight red marks on her neck. I also notice that Mom saved my notebook from the booth, which is now occupied by men, and stashed it behind the counter. *Thanks, Mom.* She didn't have to do that yesterday, as I always keep my going-out-notebook at home during band-nights. No time to be creative and too much risk of losing it.

Jeffrey is standing at the jukebox, a beer in one hand, the other tapping along to "Oh My Darling Clementine" which looks really cute actually. I chuckle to myself. With his eyes, he's carefully scanning the place. The Devil at work. Eve is calmly tapping some beers in front of us.

Saturdays are always rather chill as most of Folkspine is still trying to cure their hangover from last night. Mom is showing Taylor how to mix a drink and Abel and I are enjoying the safety of Hell's Saddle.

I watch Taylor's hands pouring one liquid after another into a glass. Her hands are strong and her nails are painted in a beautiful hot red, matching her top and lips.

"She's kinda pretty, isn't she?" Abel leans closer to me. His breath tickling my right ear. *There's that skip again.*

"Oh, please. She's like twenty-two." She definitely is younger than both our moms. "Way too old for you."

"I didn't mean it like that. She's a neutral pretty. Besides, she isn't even my type." *Then what is?*

"Yeah, that'd be weird since you're thirteen. But if your cousin can hit on a twelve-year-old at the age of seventeen, then I guess you Brennan's got some issues with age." It came out as a joke, but I *did* mean it. *This whole Brennan thing is confusing the shit out of me.* On the one hand, Abel is almost constantly surrounded by the family fuck-ups. But on the other hand, he himself doesn't seem like such a fuck-up. Except when he's out with the gang.

"Hold on." He backs off a little, giving me space to breathe, and looks me directly in the face. "James?"

"Yes! God, why is everyone so surprised about that?"

"I'm not surprised. He's my cousin...sadly. So, I know the guy." There's a ton of worry in his eyes. "What did he do?"

"Made a comment? What he always does by the way." I answer.

"To you?"

"Well, yeah. He does it to me, but basically every other girl at school too."

"I don't care 'bout the others right now!" *Jeez. Calm down, Brennan.* "What did he say?"

"Uh...something about me riding him like a horse?" It's not a big deal, though. He's always said stuff like that and it never really meant anything to me. But the look on Abel's face makes me reconsider.

"Okay." *That's all?*

"That's all?"

"Yeah, for now. I'll punch him in the face later." He's joking. *Is he?*

"I can handle myself, okay?" I do. I'm just waiting for James' next comment, so I can knock the pea he calls his brain out of his cranium.

"Fine. I won't argue with my teacher." *Right. I almost forgot.*

"So, how is this going to go?" *I actually haven't thought about that yet. It was just an impulse that I said yes. I wanted to help him.*

"Uh…I'll come back to you on that. I've still got my own schoolwork to care of."

We both take back our position. Me watching Taylor, mesmerized by her unusual beauty. And Abel watching me watching her.

It's annoying, but I let it happen.

Chapter Sixteen

First your womb,
Then your house.
Forever a home,
You and your spouse.

With fire on top,
And flames around.
Lighting my way,
By the sun crowned.

I couldn't wait until getting home. I had to clear my
mind and the thing that helps me most is writing.
Sitting there with all those people around me and my
thoughts spiraling around each one. I couldn't
handle the circling.
Like, why'd Dan hurt Eve?
Why won't Mom explain what a transvestite is?
If Taylor's sick, why does she look completely fine?
And Abel.
I *had* to disappear into the lounge and get to writing.
When I get home, I'll just copy it down into one of
my poem-notebooks. Normally, only the first idea

for a new poem gets its place in my going-out-notebook. Not the whole poem – not ever. At least up until now, but I guess the routine's broken today anyway. So, why not break another branch of the routine tree? As long as the stem still stands, I should be fine.

What remains the same is the blue neon light shining onto the paper, onto the poem. I'm sitting on the couch, right where I was sitting last night too, right where I fell asleep. I add "Phoenix" as a title to the top and flip through the pages until I've found my poem ideas to cross another one off the list.

Poem ideas:

~~*Eve, Serpent, apple*~~

~~*Sound Of Silence*~~

~~*"Stop the skin mountains"*~~

~~*Mom, fire, hair*~~

Night sky skin (stars, moles)

I close the book with a bang. I came here to *stop* thinking about him- everyone. *Get it together, Goodfellow.*

I get up from the couch to let Mom know I finished her poem and pretend my mind is focused on something other than Folkspine drama. *Turn left, through the beaded curtain, search for Mom.* But I can't find her. The only thing that catches my attention is Taylor's red lips, parted in an argument with a guest. *Great first day of trial work. Plus, more drama.* She's standing right in front of a man I don't recognize and holds a full drink in her hand. The man looks past her towards...Mom. *There she is.* Standing behind the bar counter.

"No! I will *not* take my drink from this tranny!" He shouts at Mom, who's now taking a couple steps towards the both. *Boss mode if I've ever seen it.*

"Leland, just take the drink or get the fuck outta here." *Apparently, he's Leland.* She sounds calm, but her swearing lets me know she's stressed or pissed off as...well, as fuck. I look towards the jukebox. Jeffrey's gone. *Where is the Devil when you need him?* Leland takes a step towards Taylor and smacks the drink out of her hand, which turns the glass into shards across the floor. My first instinct is to get a cloth to clean it up.

"You are crazy, Elaine! Letting someone like that work your bar, especially while kids are around. I mean, come on! Letting *him* into the place your father worked his whole life for?" Mom draws in a quick breath.

"Get. Out." We don't have a lot of guests right now, but everyone who *is* there is staring. Either to gloat or to check if anyone needs to throw a fist. We've got Jeffrey as the Devil, but that doesn't mean everyone else just lets stuff like this happen and waits for him to clear the situation. *Note: Don't mess with the owner of the only Honky Tonk around.*

"Gladly. And if you don't kick this imbecile out too, then I ain't coming back and you've lost a regular."

"Oh, boo-hoo." She mocks him. *Way to go, Mom. Who needs the Devil when we've got you?*

Eve is behind the counter, kind of backed into a corner, looking scared of Leland. Or scared of the man he is.

"And you!" Leland turns towards her. "What're you lookin' at, huh?"

Mom places herself in front of Leland. The bar counter behind her and Eve behind that.

"Whore." He looks past Mom and spits at Eve. I'm still standing in the doorway to the back, beads all around me. They feel protective.

A slap shoots through the air and some guests gasp.
Worried eyes fall onto Mom and when the
realization hits that it isn't Leland who slapped
Mom, but Mom who slapped Leland, there's some
Oohs and Aahs. Now, Leland's the one with the
one-sided blush and is taking it surprisingly well.
"You come in here, you drink your fucking drink
and you leave. That's how it goes. You do *not* call
my best friend a whore or harass my employee." At
this sentence, she faces Taylor. "You've got the job."
Taylor nods, fear still in her eyes.
"She *is* a whore! Probably into all that kinky stuff
with those marks around her neck." He smirks at
Eve, who's still standing in her corner, stiff and with
terror in her eyes. *And Abel?* When I left to go to the
back, he was still sitting at the counter. But he's not
there. Instead, he's...coming out of Eve's corner.
He's been with her the whole time.
Now, he's moving past her, out from behind the
counter, past Taylor and joins Mom and Leland. He
gently takes Mom's arm and leads her next to
Taylor. *What's he doing? Leland is twice, thrice his size.*
"Abel, what?" Mom asks.
"Abel!" Eve shouts, still in her corner.

He looks bigger now, older. Not like Dan or James. *They both lack his maturity.* He raises his arm, makes a fist, thumb on the outside. *He knows how this goes.* I know it because Mom taught me. The bell chimes, but no one bats an eye at the door. Abel pulls back and lets his fist come crashing straight into Leland's nose, who stumbles a few steps back and lands into Jeffrey standing in the doorway.

"Ya go for a smoke *once!*" The Devil says as he grabs Leland by the shoulders to turn him around to face him. "What's going on here? Ya look…" He pulls Leland to the side so he can face Abel. "Ya did this, kid?"

Abel nods silently, chest rising and falling quickly.

"Good work, son." There's pity in seeing how much Abel's face lights up at the word. "Alright, Leland. Time to git!" Jeffrey's still holding him by the shoulders, forcefully. Not like I did with Abel's shoulders earlier. He turns Leland towards the door, which another guest is holding open, and pushes him out onto the street.

"Come back and the Devil will take proper care of ya! Got it?" Jeffrey doesn't wait for an answer and smashes the door shut.

Chapter Seventeen

Hell's Saddle breaks into a cheer, Eve's shoulders
fall and Mom runs towards her for a hug. Regulars
come running up to Jeffrey, who's proudly patting
Abel on the shoulder. He however, still looks off.
He's breathing fast, looking towards our moms, then
at Taylor, who's got tears in her eyes, and then at
me. I lock eyes with him.
One, two, three. That's all it takes for me to know.
Or all it takes for me to know what I *don't* know.
Either way, I finally move from my spot between the
beads with my notebook still clutched to my missing
mountains. I push through the crowd of clapping,
hollering and stamping men and once I've reached
Abel, I grab his arm and pull him back through the
crowd towards a more open area.
"Pony?" I keep my hand on his arm as one of them
shakes. I can't say if it's Abel's arm at the
adrenaline, or my hand at...*what?* Fear?
But there's no time to find out, because before either
one of us can notice, I've got my arms wrapped
around Abel's body. *Skip a beat. Then, twice as fast.*
How is this *the new routine?*

One of my hands is still grabbing the notebook. But the other one touches the fabric of Abel's worn-out leather jacket.

"That was fucking great." I lean into his ear, but I don't whisper.

It is now that I notice how quiet the bar has been for the past few seconds. And I only notice because the noise, the clapping, the cheering suddenly loudens as he hugs me back. And we both ignore the whistling directed at us – it's safe to say, every regular at Hell's Saddle knows us two and has been eyeing us whenever we're in the bar at the same time. We're tighter now than when we were hugging earlier. When we pull back, I feel his eyes on mine, but I can't meet them. Instead, I take his right hand in mine to inspect it. *Pretty roughed up, but his thumb did a good job of protecting the rest of his fingers.* I scan the bar for more wounds, not letting go of his hand. Jeffrey: None. Mom: None. Eve: None that are new. Taylor: An open, bloody cut in her hand. She's holding it up to inspect the red dripping down. *Must've happened when Leland smacked the glass out of her hand.* I walk us toward the bar counter, place my notebook on top of it – *I don't care about that right now*

– and lead Abel and me towards Taylor. I grab her hand with my now free one to pull both of them through the beads into the lounge. None of us say a word. Before disappearing into the back, I glance towards Mom and Eve, who are still checking in on one another. *Good, they didn't see us.* We turn right into the blue.

"Here, sit down." I let go of their hands, gesture towards the leather couch and go back into the hall. When I come back with the first aid kit in my hands, I see them both sitting there as ordered. Abel right where he scootched over to last night and Taylor right where I was sitting.

"Alex, you really don't need to. I'm fine." *Pony.* He starts to push himself off the couch.

"Shut up, Brennan, and let me help you." I snap and he sits back down. *We've done this before.* I kneel down in front of them and open the first aid kit. I fetch one of the dressings and hand it to Taylor. "Press this onto the wound. I'll look at it in a sec. You good?" She nods and I realize she hasn't spoken since I came out from the back.

Then, I turn towards Abel, looking down at me. *There's that brown.* And this time, I meet it. But just for a short moment. I clear my throat to return to my mission. Which means taking another dressing, opening the bottle of alcohol and putting some on the dressing.

"Give me your hand."

"Pony." *There you go.* "I said you don't have too. I'm fine."

"You're not fine!" Even I am surprised at the crack in my voice.

"Okay." He nods. "I'm not. Go ahead." He surrenders and stretches his hand out towards me. I take it in my left and tap his knuckles with the dressing in my right. He flinches at the contact and presses his eyes shut. *What a baby.* I chuckle at the thought.

"It's not funny, Goodfellow." But again, I hear him smiling.

When his open knuckles are somewhat clean, I throw the dressing to the ground.

"Where'd you learn this?" He asks with his hand still surrounded by mine. It's cold to the touch. With the red almost gone, I notice how pale it is too. I flatten out his hand in mine, reading it. Analyzing it. The old bloody crust around his nails, he always scratches or bites, the open wounds, the mole on his thumb. Like a poem. Rough on the back, soft palm. *I wonder-*

"Pony?"

"Uh..."

"Where'd you learn this?" He repeats. *Right.*

"Well, I live on a farm." The amount of times Dad pierced a nail through his finger while fixing the meadow fence. The amount of times I fell from Trixie. The amount of times Mom stumbled over Dad's tools because she didn't watch where she was going.

"Fair enough." He takes his hand back from mine to inspect his knuckles. At the loss of contact, I notice my heart feeling a little heavier than usual.

"Man, that fucker had a hard ass nose." He shakes off the pain in his hand.

Taylor finally makes some noise. She's...*laughing*? Abel and I take a quick look at each other, then at Taylor.

"You good?" It's Abel's turn to ask the question.

"Very, actually." She smiles at him. It's genuine and kind of child-like. "Thank you. No one has ever broken up a fight that involved me before."

"Well, I was uh…protecting my mom." He explains himself. "Eve?"

"Yeah, I know. But still."

Abel takes a second to think. "I should also have done it for you, though. He shouldn't have talked to you like that. He's a-"

"Shithead." I finish for him. We take turns looking at each other.

Now all three of us laugh, and for a second it feels like I've found something. Something I can't and don't want to share with anyone.

I then take Taylor's hand in mine. It's bigger than Abel's, but similar to his. Somewhat rough and soft at the same time, but darker and intentionally painted red at the tips. I don't wonder what *her* fingers would feel like interlinked with mine.

I take off the dressing from her wound and grab a new one, which I drench with alcohol.

"This'll hurt." I say before applying alcoholic pressure onto the light palm of her hand. She takes it like a pro, not like Abel. After having cleaned away the blood, I see how deep the cut actually is.

"It's pretty deep. Put some powder on it." I sound like my dad when he's patched me up. It's amazing how good wound powder works on humans too. And it's funny when he acts like I'm a cow to distract me from the pain.

"You *are* good at this." I smile at the compliment. A proper patch up and bandage later and she looks good to go.

"There you go." I slightly trace my thumbs over her palm.

"Thank you…uh."

"Pony." Abel interrupts.

"Alex." I correct. "And ignore him. He's particularly stupid."

Abel clutches his heart and Taylor chuckles at him. There's something elegant in how she holds her unaffected hand up to her mouth.

I get up from the floor, collect the trash and dressings on the ground and throw them in the bin next to the couch. Like on commando, they both scootch over to each side of the couch, giving me space to fall into the middle. I do so with a heavy sigh.

"Jesus." I say just now realizing what has just happened.

"Yeah." They both agree at once.

Abel punched a regular in the face for harassing his mom and he didn't look like an amateur while doing. Also, Taylor got harassed and this might be my only chance to find out why. I look straight ahead as I address her.

"Taylor, can I ask you something?"

"Sure, little one." *Like she's always been working here.*

"What's a transvestite?"

Chapter Eighteen

"What's a transvestite?" I ask, sitting between the girl I just met and the boy I'm supposed to hate.

"Oh." She seems startled. "Well, uhm…are your parents Christian?"

"Yeah." It sounds more like a question than an answer.

"And you? Are you Christian too?"

"I guess." I answer, clutching the wooden cross dangling from my neck. "Yes." I reassure her and myself.

"You know how God made all His children in His image?"

"Genesis one twenty-seven." Even I am surprised by how fast the answer shoots out of my mouth. Also, this is the first time Bible study has actually come in handy. *Thanks, Dad.*

"Exactly. Well, His image of me is wrong. He made me the son of Adam when I was meant to be the daughter of Eve."

"Okay?" *Not sure if I get it now.*

"Let me phrase it this way." She takes a deep breath in. "I was born a boy. With boy parts."

I look at her confused and Abel steps in with an explanation.

"She was born with a dick." He then turns to her. "Right?" And she nods.

"Oh!" I exclaim and scan both their faces. Taylor smiles, but I can see in her eyes that she's also on alert. Abel, on the other hand, looks almost emotionless and simply waits for her to go on. So, she does.

"But I didn't want it. And when I grew older and didn't get a proper chest, like your Mom," she turns towards Abel, "or your Mom…I just felt off. And I wanted to change. My Mom made me jealous, my sister made me jealous, the girls at school made me jealous. I wanted to be like them so bad." *Wait.* "I had to get out. You gotta know I grew up in a very Christian family. Here in Folkspine, actually. But they didn't like people like me, so I hid. And when I couldn't handle hiding anymore, I left, became the woman I am and now, I'm back."

"So, you grew…boobs?" I ask her.

"Haha! No, no. These are fake, Honey." She lifts up her red top to reveal a bra stuffed with fabrics.

"That's fucking cool." Abel finally speaks up. "You like redefined the laws of God." I know he's an atheist, so it's weird to hear him talk about God. *But he's got a point.* He's sitting at the edge of the couch now, beaming with light again. I, however, push myself further into the soft leather.

"Thanks, but it also makes me a sinner." She pulls her top back down.

"Everyone sins, so who cares? If God fucked you up, you fuck Him up."

I register them both laughing, but I don't really hear it. I only hear the blood rushing through my ears. Pumping twice as fast as usual... again. Only this time, it's different. This time, it's bad.

"Does it work the other way too?" They both pause and look at me.

"What do you mean?" She asks.

"Like... if God made a daughter." The words burn my tongue and I order my body to keep on talking, but the question doesn't come.

"Can she turn into a son?" Taylor takes the words out of my mouth and I nod.

"Sure. I wouldn't see why not. I've met lots of people like me on the road after leaving Folkspine."

[133]

Leave Folkspine. "And some of them were born like you, but turned into someone like…" She gestures at Abel.

"Abel." He helps her out.

"Right."

Someone like Abel.

"What made you leave Folkspine?" I ask.

"The people." *Figured so.* "They haven't changed, but I have. I still get worked up about stuff like today, but I'm stronger now. I know what I want and I will not let anyone take that." Abel and I both smile at her. It's like we've always known each other, like there wasn't a time before this moment. Like Abel is the part of me I wish to be and Taylor is the part of me I never knew I had.

"But you loved them, right? Your family, for example." *I need to know this.*

"Of course. But love for others doesn't make you happy. It makes you survive where you are, but it doesn't make you live. To live, you need only yourself and love for yourself. Once you've got the hang out of that, you can start loving other people." I take her in. Her words, her face in the blue, her voice. And it's like I'm seeing God. God in the body of a sinner, but still the God that loves His children. He loves Taylor and I see it in her eyes, even if she doesn't know. And He's speaking to me through her. So, I listen.

"You kids." He continues as she places her bandaged hand on my thigh and the other on Abel's shoulder. "Can I ask one thing of you?" We both nod without a second of even considering the other option. "Break out if you feel trapped. No matter who built your cage. Your parents, other adults or yourself. Never love your master." We nod in silence. "Don't listen to God. If He says you're wrong, He's wrong."

And maybe it wasn't God speaking, but the Devil in disguise. Maybe I wanted God to tell me He loved Taylor. So, I'd know He'd love me too.

Abel

In all the years I've studied Alex's face, I've never
even once seen this expression. When Dad became
disgusting, Mom stopped working as a hairdresser
and took the job at Hell's Saddle as it offered a
higher wage. I've spent my time at James' or at the
junkyard with the gang. But when I'm not with
James, Alan and Glen, I hide downtown watching
the city or at Hell's Saddle watching Alex.
But in all those years, I haven't seen her *this* beside
herself even once. She's right between me and
Taylor and when she's not looking at either of us,
she's staring straight ahead with something hidden in
her eyes. I must know the blue of her eyes like the
back of my now bruised hand. Normally, she's very
certain and upfront. She knows what she wants, she
knows who she likes – me excluded – and she's not
afraid to show that. But most of all, she always
knows who she is. She knows she's Elaine's and
John's daughter, she's a proud Goodfellow, she's a
loyal Christian – to some extent – and she's a poet.
She knows her passion is shaping sentences that flow
like the creek near the woods, and helping her

parents at work. And she knows she's good at both. Alex never had to tell me any of those things. *Not that she would've shared anything with me anyway.* I've analyzed her face, like my father's, like my mother's, like my cousin's. I know when Dad is about to lay his hands on me, I know when Mom is about to break apart, I know when James is pissed off at Alan or Glen. And up until now, I thought I knew what Alex was all about.

Chapter Nineteen

Back in the red, the people have gone back to their routine. Jeffrey's having another beer, this time at the counter. *Guest mode.* Mom and Eve are working and the rest of the guests have taken back their seats to laugh, share stories and drink. "Truckin'" is calmly playing on the jukebox.

"It's like-" Abel starts.

"Nothing happened." I finish.

"That a good thing?" Taylor asks.

We all share a look, shrug and part ways. Taylor joins the moms behind the counter, I sit down in my seat at the far-left corner and Abel sits down on the right, next to Jeffrey.

"Saved your notebook again." Mom addresses me while working on a drink behind the counter.

"Thanks." I clear my throat, waiting for a lecture about disappearing with Abel and Taylor, *the deviant.* At some point, she must've noticed we were gone. Mom keeps on wiping the counter, rinsing glasses and tapping the occasional beer.

"You're pretending." I say, realizing she won't address the elephant in the room.

"Damn straight."

"I'm sorry. You were all busy checking up on each other and everything was so chaotic and they were both injured and I wanted to help and they-"

"Alex." She interrupts. "Don't worry. You did the right thing after all. If I were you, I would've done the same." But she looks serious, even without facing me.

I think back to this morning when Mom and Dad were talking in the kitchen, which feels like ages ago. I think back to how Mom wanted to help Eve so bad.

"You've a good heart." Now, she gifts a genuine smile.

"Half of it is yours." I gift one back.

"Oh! By the way, I finished your poem."

"Will you read it to me later?"

"'Course." And I will. Because I love her and want her to know and nothing speaks love louder than a poem.

"Elaine?" Taylor scoots in from the side.

"Oh, Taylor. You okay, Sweetie?" *Sweetie? Is Mom warming up?* "I'm so sorry. Leland shouldn't have."

"It's fine." She waves her off and it really seems like she means it. "I wanted to thank you."

"Of course. I protect my employees. It's how I always ran the place. And since you do a good job, you're part of the team."

"Thank you." Taylor repeats. She then turns towards Eve.

"How are you?"

"Fine." *Yeah, Eve still needs some time to warm up.* But she actually does look fine. "Abel here handled it like a pro." She turns towards him and Jeffrey with a smile.

"Kid's got it in 'im, eh? He'll be the next Devil. I can sense it." *Imagine me running Hell's Saddle and Abel being the new Devil.* Jeffrey nudges Abel's shoulder with his. He looks kind of flustered. On both cheeks, which I'm glad about.

"Thank you, Love. I know what you did there."

"Sure, Mom."

Mom and I both watch them, checking for signs of telepathic exchange. Abel and I keep our seats at the counter, occasionally glancing over at each other. It's way quieter and less busy than last night, so my mind can wander from person to person and moment to moment. This time, I let it. I don't run to the back to distract myself with a poem. For some reason, I feel like I *have* to sit down with the intention of brainstorming and not with the intention to distract my mind from deviant thoughts.

I grab my notebook from behind the counter, flip through it until I've found the right page to cross out: *~~Find out what a transvestite is.~~*

I flip further to add something to my list of poems:
Break the cage

After a few seconds of reconsideration, I correct it to:
Break the ~~cage~~ fence

Book Two

The Gun

"And he'll give you that smile, and you'll know that, even if just for a few hours, the world can be a home."

Kala, Colin Walsh

1986

Chapter Twenty

"Did Jeffrey tell you to fight back?"

"What? When?"

We're sitting in our booth, going over the school notes Alex prepared for today. Hell's Saddle is still the same – except for the fact that band-night got switched to Saturday. Of course, Alex freaked out when she heard Elaine announce the switch.

"Mom! You can't do that, come on!" She complained.

"Yeah, I know we've got a routine."

"Then why'd you switch it up?" It always fazes me, knowing there are people out there who rely so deeply on a routine.

"Jeffrey heard some regulars complain that the bands only play on Fridays." *He needs to start getting a loan for his dedication to this place.* "Said they still got work to do after a long week and can't come here. Saturdays just fit their schedule better."

"I think the place gets full enough." Alex mumbled to herself. I was just sitting there to listen and take in the information.

"True. But with Taylor joining us," Elaine looked over to her employee, who smiled back at her "we can handle even more guests. Ergo, more profit." I could see it in her face how hard Alex tried to process the change ahead – with no avail.

"Plus," Elaine continued, "I figured, you could officially lend a hand here and there on band-nights too."

This was four years after Taylor joined the Hell's team. She's working good and it was even her idea to ask Alex to work on Saturdays. She knew how much Alex loves this place and how much joy it brings her to be a part of it. *Taylor truly is a gem.* So, Elaine knew exactly how to catch her daughter's attention.

"Like...like work here?" Alex responded while her eyes seemed to pop out of her head.

"Yeah." Elaine went on. "We figured you'd have nothing to do on Saturdays-" But Mom interrupted her by clearing her throat.

"Right." Elaine turned to her and back at Alex. "Nothing except for preparing lessons." She nodded at Alex and then at me. "But besides that, you've got nothing to do. With your homework done and all, and since you never miss a band-night anyway, you could earn some money." Taylor nodded at her boss's offer.

"You're serious?" Her eyes wandered between her mom, Taylor and my mom. "With an apron and all?"

"With an apron." Her Mom agreed, suppressing a laugh.

So ever since then, Alex has been earning herself some extra bucks on Saturdays, never missing a single one.

Mom noticed how I looked over at her, my eyes bigger than anticipated. She simply shook her head left and right. Not so much to draw attention from the others to her motion or my face. I asked her about it later and she told me it wouldn't be a good idea for me to work at Hell's Saddle too. Which pissed me the fuck off. Not because of Mom, but because I know Elaine wouldn't want me to work at her bar, simply because of my bad reputation.

Thanks, Grandpa. Thanks, Dad. Thanks, James.

So, that's all that changed about the place. The lights are still the same, the old red leather booths and the framed picture next to the stage with

Grandpa nowhere to be seen, which doesn't bother me at all since he died way before I was born – alcoholism. The bands still play once a week – on Saturdays now – and Jeff still throws a fist every once in a while, with me occasionally joining him. It's fun "working" with Jeff. I can be at Hell's Saddle, watch Alex work, we can chat with Taylor and Jeff and me and throw people out. It makes me feel useful. Like my destiny might not be to end up like my dad. People dance, drink, laugh and fight. The women work the counter, tapping beers, mixing drinks, taking orders and protecting each other. Mom's hair is the same, still short and ash and Elaine's is still on fire. However, Alex and I have changed. My hair is longer, growing way past my collarbones, while Alex's is way shorter. She's lost the bangs and ponytail and let Mom cut her light brown hair into something resembling John in "The Breakfast Club," but shorter and less cheesy. Which confuses the fuck out of me because I think Judd Nelson was kind of hot in that role.

The bar's still closed, but when we made our teacher/student contract, Alex insisted we study at

Hell's Saddle. Of course, she wrote the contract and then read it to me. I was actually surprised to see how quickly she made up her mind about how our private lessons would go. It didn't even take her a month to prepare everything after I practically begged her to teach me. I'm even more surprised by the fact the lesson's been going on for six years now. I asked her a couple times before if she even wanted to keep going, because she's taught me all I needed to know to teach myself, but she insisted she'd help me study. She said it was because I was too much of an idiot to teach myself, but her eyes said something different. So, I didn't protest and happily attended school every Tuesday and Friday, as ordered. After six years, we've both got the contract memorized and Alex often draws references to it, when I end up breaking a rule – which I do a lot, happily. She gets all pissed off at me for it, but every single time, I see her suppressing a smile. It's cute.

Dare I say, Alex Goodfellow might have stopped completely hating my being, which truly is a wonder and a blessing in of itself.

The Goodfellow/ Brennan private lesson contract

In terms of schoolwork, the student is to do whatever the teacher says.

The student shall never criticize any poems that are being analyzed, no matter who they're written by. In return, the teacher shall lay down all hate and annoyances towards the student during lessons, to fully concentrate on the work.

The main focus will be: reading, writing and analysis of literature. If there's spare time, the teacher will bring forth other subjects such as: history, physics, math etc.

The lessons will be held at Hell's Saddle, Folkspine, before opening. Every Tuesday and Friday the two will get together and examine the teachers notes. On Fridays, the teacher will give the student homework to do over the weekend and to present on the following Tuesday. This serves as a verification if the student is able to turn the learned lessons into something of his own, like a text, essay, poem etc.

Lastly and most importantly, there will be no emotional connection whatsoever between the student and the teacher, no matter if during lessons or in their spare time.

Signed 08/22/1980

Alex Goodfellow, teacher   Abel Brennan, student

This was after she taught me how to write my name and basic words like "student." We broke the last rule pretty quickly, but we tried. *Well, she tried.* I didn't give a rat's ass about the rule.

We were sitting right where we are now, when she was reciting words for me and I wrote them down. When she told me to write coconut, I ended up with cock-o-nut. She slid from the booth, grabbing the floor, trying to breathe between tearful laughter.

"She okay?" Taylor asked from behind the counter where she was cleaning up the bar. I didn't think it was *that* funny, but seeing her like that, I couldn't keep myself from joining. Alan and Glen would've laughed their asses off too. But I preferred laughing with Alex and pushed the thought of the both of them out of my mind.

"When Taylor was trial working. You know, Jeffrey came into the bar and had a talk with you."

"Oh, *that.*"

"Yeah. You told me he told you Dan hurt Eve. But there must've been more."

"That was, what, six years ago? Why are you asking this now?" We're sitting over her school notes and my notebook. Alex insisted on buying it for me, so I got the *right* one. Whatever that means.

"I don't know. Just came into mind."

"Well, yeah. He did. But I didn't need him to tell me to fight back. Fighting back is in my blood. It's what I do."

"Okay."

"Are you okay, Pony? You're being weird." Even with her hair down and short, she's still Pony.

"Yeah. Back to reading." She taps her pen on her school notes. We're covering literature today.

"I don't want to read. I want to write." I complain.

"You can write when you're alone." *I will.* "Right now, we *read* literature."

"Yes, Miss." I joke, staying true to our first rule, but she's not smiling. Like I said the wrong thing. *Fuck.*

Mom's laughing behind the counter with Elaine. After I punched Leland in the face for calling her a kinky whore, she's been more relaxed. Like she knows I can and will throw a fist for her. Dad hasn't laid his hands on her since. Jeff would've told me if otherwise. He's the one who told Dad what went down at Hell's Saddle and I'm glad Dad finally knows I can break noses. He's still hurting me sometimes, but I swore to myself, I'll only use my fists to protect the ones I love and I'm not on that list.

Jeff and I, however, have actually become something like buddies. If Dad fucks up again, his trailer is always open for Mom and me and I'm not sure he knows how much that's appreciated. Sometimes, when I can't sleep at night and see his light is on, I go over to his trailer and knock. He lets me in and we chat over a beer. At first, he wanted to be reasonable and offered me a Coke or something, but since I'm nineteen now, we gladly share the taste of beer. He calls me "son" a lot and I try not to interpret anything into it, but sometimes, when I'm walking through downtown at night, I think about it and get a weird, heavy feeling in my chest.

Anyway. He calls me "son", I call him "Jeff" and we're the Devils of Hell's Saddle. Well, Jeff's still the Devil and I'm his right-hand man. He's gotten a bit older. Crazy what six years can do to you. His moustache is fully white, not brown *with* white like it was back then and he's always covering his bald spot with his cowboy hat now.

Since hitting the infamous P, I've been shaving the patchy stubble that won't form into anything proper. So instead of pretending I've got a beard or whatever, I just shave it.

Not sure *when* Alex hit the P, but at some point, she must have. Her face is kind of pretty now. I mean it always was, but we're both teenagers now, so I feel allowed to think it. She'd punch me in the guts if I ever told her that, though. Something about her face is so unique, I couldn't describe it. Maybe the fact, she sometimes gets misunderstood for a boy by the drunk guests.

"Ey kid, will ya make me a beer?" A guy once asked her on a band-night. And she gladly raised a glass to the tap and filled it like a pro.

"You'll be a fine bartender once ya grow up to be a proper man." She didn't say a word to correct him. She didn't even pull a face. Just smiled, nodded and told him to enjoy his drink. When she registered me watching – questioning even – she simply looked away and pretended to be busy.

Now, she's sitting right in front of me, in teacher mode. There's not a speck of makeup on her face, as far as I can tell, and she looks like a poem. Not sure if she's hiding anything close to a chest under her T-shirts and flannels, but she's doing a pretty good job. Pretty good job hiding them, making me curious and confusing me with her John – Bender, not Goodfellow – impersonation.

Literature, Brennan. We're doing literature.

Taylor comes in with a chime. "Greetings, Loves." Working at Hell's Saddle has had an impact on her vocabulary, so she tends to copy Mom or Elaine. *I love her for that.* She's been getting so much more confident too. Half of it is thanks to Jeff and me, not to mention Alex, and the other half to Mom and Elaine. They're both still weirded out by her, but she's a part of the team and treated as such. Alex tells me that John, however, remains stubborn as ever. She always looks down when telling me about what her dad said regarding Taylor's "kind."

"God's only mistake."

From what I heard, John's a good guy. But man, sometimes I just want to smash in his fucking face for talking Taylor down. I can still feel Leland's nose cracking underneath my knuckles. The feeling creeps me out, but then again it reminds me of the hate rooted in Folkspine and how good it feels to fight hate with more hate.

"You listening?" Alex snaps me back.

"Uh! Yeah, sorry."

"Forget it. Class dismissed. We ain't getting anywhere today." She admits and leans into her seat with a sigh. She waves Taylor over.

"Beckham!" There's some envy hidden inside of me whenever Alex calls Taylor by her last name. But that's stupid, of course, since I'm not the only person on the planet with a last name. *I've got the worst one, though.*

"Ah, the local lovebirds." She giggles, walking over to our booth.

"You are so Jeffrey." I shoot back and she clutches her heart in sarcastic anguish.

"Sit with us, T." Alex insists. "You've still got time before your shift."

"It really *is* like she already owns the place, ain't it?" Taylor asks me and I shrug with a smile. She sits down in front of me, next to Alex. I see Mom glancing over at us. It pisses me off, she still does that.

"Literature, huh?" She leans over our notes, revealing a window showing the fabrics in her bra. I look away. "How's it going?"

"Well, he's pretty good actually." Alex leans into Taylor. "I don't like to admit it, but some of his poems are better than mine."

Really?

"Aw, look. He's lighting up again."

"Shut it, T." I demand and she throws her hands up in surrender and both girls laugh.

I never thought of myself as a poet. I wouldn't even dare to call the stuff I write poems. Compared to Alex's, they're nothing special.

"Taylor, Honey. Can you come over a sec?" I hear Elaine shouting from behind the counter.

"Well, duty calls. Talk to you two later, if you're not busy being tangled up." She gets up and Alex throws a pen after her. The comments come from all over town ever since Alex and I started sharing the same booth. When I walk past James downtown, he throws a "On your way to meet the wife?" at me. I try my best to ignore him, since I left the gang. Taylor isn't any better and Jeff always pushes me with questions like "So, ya and the little one, eh?" I always shrug him off.

After a while, I face Alex to meet her eyes.

"You really think so?"

"What?" She holds the connection for three seconds. She always does that, I counted it. But even if just for three seconds, locking eyes with Alex and getting lost in the open blue, feels like I'm flying straight out of this shithole of a town and into freedom.

"That my poems are good?"

"Sure. For someone looking as stupid as you, you're doing a pretty good job."

"Jeez, thanks." And I mean it.

Chapter Twenty-One

The first thing she gave me to read out loud was one
of her poems. And I'm glad the first poem I ever
read came from my favorite poet. Now, years later
and after reading almost every poem she ever wrote,
I know her writing style. I've analyzed it like I've
analyzed her face. I'd probably recognize one of her
poems hidden in a library stacked and stacked with
other artists' works. And I'd recognize her face in
Hell's Saddle at every band-night and every
Goodfellow-night.

I never once asked about the meaning of any of her
poems, no matter how curious I was. It's none of my
business and if Alex wanted me to know, she'd tell
me.

After making our contract and me slowly starting to
be able to read small sentences she wrote, she
handed me her open poem-notebook. At first, her
notebook organization confused the shit out of me.
Why would anyone need that many notebooks? I always
fill mine with everything. School stuff, poems, letters
I could or would never send to those they're
addressing, etc. And when one notebook is full, Alex

simply buys me another one. I've been trying to pay her back for years now. I don't know from what money. It's not like I didn't try to get a job, but no one wants to have the Brennan boy working for them, especially without any graduation. That goes for Elaine and it goes for everyone else too. I couldn't work at the stores I helped James steal from and I also couldn't help out James and Uncle Ramy at the garage – simply 'cause James doesn't want me there and I definitely don't want to be there too. But still, I want Alex to get something back. *Anything.* But she always shrugs it off with a "Don't worry 'bout it."

So, the least I can do is try and obey the rest of our rules and Alex makes sure the first one is always top priority.

"Read this."

"That's way longer than any of the stuff I've read before!" I complained a lot back then and still do. Still, at the end of the day, I do what she tells me. Because I'm so pathetically thankful she'd spend her free time teaching the son of the town's fuck-up what the kids learn at school.

"Rule number one." She reminded me. "Besides, I want this to be the first poem you'll ever read."

"But why?"

She shrugged her shoulders. "It's about your mom, so I figured it'd only make sense you read it."

"You wrote a poem about my mom?"

"I write a poem about everyone I love." *Maybe-*

"Now stop asking questions and read."

Forbid The Rotten Apple

Nude inside,

Painted outside.

Before the crumble,

Before the rotting.

All those reds and she picked the only brown.

For from this seed,

In her womb grew a fresh one.

Red and reflecting.

Should've fed the rotten to the Serpent.

Should've picked a red.

Should've left with her seed.

It took me a few tries to read it out loud. When I got it right, I read it in my mind once more. Capturing it with its meaning. Sometimes I lie awake at night and recite the poem in my mind. Sometimes, I end up crying into my pillow at the heartache Mom's life gives me. Also, I'm an atheist but I still get the reference. Folkspine is a small Christian town and Pastor Raphael does his best at making sure it stays that way.

"Alex, this…" Her eyes widened, but she managed to look ashamed at the same time. I couldn't think, so I just stared at her.

"Thank you." She quietly answered, taking the notebook back.

"Has she read it?"

"Nah. I only let Mom read my poems."

I took a moment to reconsider saying it. "And me."

"And you."

It was that day that I decided I want to read everything Alex has ever written. And I want to write, too. And I want to write *with* her.

After a while, I go over to the jukebox to pick "Old Time Rock & Roll." Alex eyes me, checking I don't pick Metallica again and nods in approval when the song starts. When we became study buddies – though it sometimes still feels like we're strangers – Alex started to allow me to pick a song if I'm being extra polite or do my homework good, like I'm a child. It's actually kind of funny and I enjoy feeling like an actual child for once. She's the evil Protector of The Jukebox and nobody messes with that. Except for me. Most times she hates the music I choose because it "doesn't fit Hells Saddle's *joy and warmth.*" Like the place isn't literally called *Hell's* Saddle. Jeff and I dig the music, though. And cause he's the Devil and loves the music, Elaine is fine with my song choices. And if Elaine is fine with it, Alex has to be too, even as Protector of The Jukebox. One time, I picked out "Creeping Death." Hearing the intro, Jeff immediately shot up from his booth to scream "Which one of ya glorious bastards put that on?!" When he saw me standing next to the jukebox, he pointed straight at me and announced "That's my son!" to the whole bar. He was pretty fucking drunk that night. At least that's what I tell myself. *Why can't Dad be more like Jeff when he's drunk?*

Alex gave me a warning look, but I recognized the worry in her eyes when Jeff called me his son.

"Okay, you win this time." She was waving her finger in my face and I pretended to bite into it. She pulled back and went on while I smiled at her.

"But in the future, you'll pick something that doesn't make my ears fall off."

"And doesn't last almost seven minutes?"

"And doesn't- Jesus, really?" I nodded. "And doesn't last *that long*."

"Got it." I smiled wider at her and she turned away. So now, I'm careful with my song choices. *I don't want to lose my jukebox privileges.* Alex still isn't one-hundred percent fond of most songs, but since I turned it down a bit and Jeff still gets up every time to shake a leg, she tolerates it. Maybe she's just glad my face lights up whenever I can pick a song. But maybe that's just my wishful thinking.

It's reached a point where even I recognize it when my face "lights up," as the girls call it. I try to keep my mouth from breaking into a smile and my eyes from widening, but being at Hell's Saddle with T, Mom, Elaine and especially Jeff and Alex…I just can't help it.

Hell's Saddle is my Heaven and that's coming from an atheist.

Alex puts away her school notes and I close my notebook as if on command. She lies down on her side of the booth, legs dangling over the seat, and groans.

"What's the time?"

I look above the doorway.

"Seven thirty."

"Ugh!" The last half hour before opening is always the longest.

"Mom!" *Dang, the girl can shout.*

"Yeah, Honey?" Her Mom shouts back.

"Is there stuff for me to do?"

"Aren't you guys doing lessons right now?" My Mom scoots in. At first, I wanted to hide the fact I've been having exclusive private lessons from Mom, but how could I hide that when we literally study at her workplace? When she saw us reciting the alphabet and me writing it, she asked what was going on. Alex told her, while I remained silent. I think Mom's actually really thankful for Alex. Almost as much as me.

"Ain't fun today." Alex answers her.

"Sorry, Honey. We're all done here."

Another groan later and Alex addresses me.

"Brennan?" My last name is a curse, but it sounds like a symphony coming out of her mouth.

"Yeah, Pony?"

"You wanna do something?" *Come again?* We never "do something." We're study buddies. We haven't even been at each other's homes. We meet up at Hell's Saddle, study, chat with Taylor, she helps our moms and then we part our ways. That's how it goes.

"Huh?" I sound fucking pathetic when I'm confused like that.

"You know. Like, get outta here and do something."

"Shouldn't I get to my homework? Which you didn't yet give me, mind you." It's Friday after all.

"Ah! Thank you, kind Sir, for reminding me. Lemme think..." She's not thinking. I can hear it in her voice.

"Okay okay, here it goes. Homework for today: Hang out with me." My heart never skips a beat. *Why did my heart just skip a beat? Is Alex Goodfellow asking me to hang out?*

[169]

"We…*are* hanging out."

"Get your ass out of this booth." She sits up, grabs her notes and walks towards the counter to store them behind it. I'm watching her, frozen in time and space. "Brennan. Rule number one." *The student is to do whatever the teacher says.*

"Lesson's over, remember?" *In terms of school work.* I tease, knowing damn right I want to hang out with her.

"It's homework so it still regards school. Now git!" She copies Jeff. "I want to show you something."

I get up, store my notebook with her notes and catch up with her.

"Oh, Jeffrey is gonna *love* to hear about this." Taylor whispers to Mom and Elaine as the three watch us leave the bar with a chime.

Chapter Twenty-Two

Outside, the warm autumn wind surrounds us. It's still light out, but the sky is slowly starting to change color. I pull down my sweater's sleeves and Alex pulls up the zipper on her hoodie. She leads me past Elaine's Flying Fishbowl – *can't believe she still drives that thing* – and walks down Main Road. I follow her. *Should I walk beside her?*

Her stride is confident, she knows exactly where we're going.

"Uh, Alex?" She doesn't turn around. "Pony?" And she faces me. *There you go.* What happened to *"It's Alex. Has always been. Will always be."*

"Where exactly are we going?"

"You'll recognize it when we're there. Come on!" She waves at me to come walk beside her and I do so. *Why are my arms so stiff? Where does someone put their arms when walking? And why is everything so silent?*

"So…Taylor, huh?" *Way to go, Brennan.*

"Yeah, we're still not doing small talk." *Should've known.* "Just enjoy the silence."

I *did* read "The Sound Of Silence." It might actually be one of my favorite poems she ever wrote.

"For there's beauty in silence. For of connection, it is the science." I quote her and she turns to smile at me. And in that moment, I think she's right. Silence *is* the science of connection. Normally, Alex talks like a book, just like Elaine does. She didn't use to, though. It only started when we began with the lessons, broke the last rule and grew a little more comfortable around each other. "What do you mean, you don't listen to Parton? Not even Springsteen? Jesus." Or "Taylor said she used to go to church every Sunday. I've never seen her there, though. Have you? No wait, you're an atheist. Why do I even speak to you then?" But now, she's apparently all about silence.

So, I'm walking through downtown, like always. But this time, it's with Alex Goodfellow. The Alex who spent lots of long years hating me. She asked me to hang out and I accepted. *Like, why wouldn't I?* We walk past the hair salon Mom used to work at. But this way leads out of town. To my luck, we're distancing ourselves from the trailer park.

Thank…whoever, it's in the opposite direction.

We exit town, but keep following Main Road. I've got a thousand questions, but I won't ask a single one. Because *this* silence doesn't feel like a threat, but like safety. At home, silence means "the calm before the storm," but here and with Alex, it feels like there will never be a storm to come. I keep on glancing over at her, but hidden behind the hair framing her face, I can't analyze her.

In the distance, I see a trail leading away from Main Road and towards a property so big, I can only dream of living there. As we get closer, I recognize a barn. *Is Alex taking me to her place?* Seeing the barn, I know this has to be her father's farm. The Goodfellow's are the only people in Folkspine that own a farm, so this must be it. I look over at her, but there's no change of movement in her body. We get closer to reaching the trail and... *walk right past it?*

"You didn't think I'd take you to my house, did you?" She breaks our silence.

"Of course not." I lie.

"Good. Because it's way better where we're going."

Half an hour later, the sky has changed into a painting of dark blue and orange. I'd love to look into Alex's eyes to see the sky's reflection in them, but we're still walking. There's something eerie about walking through the woods as the sun's about to set, but I don't give a single flying fuck about mountain lions or getting lost right now. Leaves scrunch beneath us as we walk on a trail leading through the trees. Then suddenly, the trail stops right in front of a broad stem. The trail doesn't go around it – it stops.

"Ta-daa." Alex presents the orange leafed tree like a child presenting a pillow fortress – which I've seen movies about, but never got to experience.

Without a second word, she starts climbing up a ladder leading up. I can't quite see into the crown, as the woods' shadows cover us. I'm still standing on the trail, looking into the dark for Alex and a couple seconds later, the tree starts to be lit up by fairy lights. Resting in the crown of the tree is a tiny treehouse and Alex stands right on its platform. She's surrounded by tiny dots of yellow light. *A painting for the Gods.*

"You coming up?" *No need to tell me twice.*

Without a word, I move from the trail, up the ladder and join Alex on the platform. Then, she disappears into the tiny house.

Inside, there's a mattress on the floor and shelves all around filled with books. Notebooks.

"What is this place?"

"Don't you recognize?" I take a second to look around and think. It's then that I realize the smell of fallen apples on the ground and the red orbs hanging between branches.

"This is your tree."

"Mine and Dad's, yeah." She sits down on the mattress and pats the spot next to her. I join her, keeping a certain distance so our knees don't touch.

"Why'd you take me here?"

"Because."

"Pony?"

She rolls her eyes and groans. "I wanted to come here, but I didn't want to come alone." *So, she picked me as a companion?*

"What do you do when you're up here?"

"Eat chocolate, read, write, do my homework, prepare our lessons," she shoots me a look and goes on "think."

"So, those are all your notebooks?" I look around the small room.

"Most of 'em. Some are in my room at home, but the rest, I keep here." She pushes herself up from the mattress and walks towards one of the shelves. She grabs a handful of notebooks and sits back down next to me, close enough to have our knees touch. *Another skip.* I try to ignore it.

"Ah! The infamous note-notebook." I say reading the handwritten title on the book at the top. Kind of cute she designs her notebooks herself. On this one, there's a sticker of Sherlock holding a magnifying glass.

"Got a new mystery?" She never engages me in her note riddles, but I enjoy watching Alex and Elaine leaning over single notes or the ones glued into the notebook. The last time they did it, their mystery turned out to be unsolvable. "No, that doesn't make any sense. I don't think Jeffrey even knows where to buy crack. Can't be him." "I give up." It's real fun watching Alex get worked up over stuff like that. Also, Jeff knows very well where to get crack. Which is why he too shares a hate for Leland. Leland is also the one who used to provide Alan. Bad business, bad outcome. I shake away the goosebumps forming at the memory of Alan.

"Nah, town's been kinda boring lately." *I wish. Try being a Brennan and calling life boring.*

She opens the book and flips through the pages. It doesn't seem like she wants me to engage. More like she really wanted to come here and just do her thing of looking through her notebooks. Like she just wanted someone to be with her, in silent company. So, I don't say anything. My body's tense as I eye her from the side, watching her hands flip through the pages, stopping at some and skipping others. And once again, I don't mind the silence.

She flips through grocery lists, phone numbers with hearts behind them, appointment dates etc. She starts at the front of the book and works her way through it. She stops at a page covered in red question marks surrounding a single piece of paper. For a moment, she looks at it and before she can turn the page, I grab her by the wrist.

"What's that?"

"Don't know. Never figured it out."

It can't be.

"Abel?"

I'd recognize that anywhere.

"Brennan. What's going on?"

[177]

I knew it. He always went out at night, saying he'll help his brother at the garage.

"You're hurting me."

When he came back, there was never a speck of dirt on him.

"Abel."

Yk where, 11

prepare

Ps. Bring me a sixpack

"Abel, my wrist!"

"Shit!" Her hand's pale at the lack of blood circulation. I recognize the mark on her wrist. How many times I've had to look at that myself.

"Fuck, Pony. I'm so sorry." *Not like him, not like him, not like-*

"Sit back down." I didn't even realize I got up.

"No. I gotta-"

"You're not going anywhere. Please." She's so calm. So low-key.

"Sit the fuck down, Brennan." *There goes low-key.* She gets up to grab my hand and pull me down on the mattress with her.

"What is going on?" We're across from each other, knees touching. One, two, three in the blue.

[178]

"Okay, take a deep breath." Four, five, six. She's holding it.

In and out.

"Good." Both her hands hold both of mine. *In and out.*

"Now, what's going on?" *What is going on?*

"That...note." She nods. *In and out.* "Dad...he wrote it. I recognize the handwriting."

"Anyone could've written that."

"No, you don't get it. I collected anything Mom and Dad wrote. I tried to teach myself how to read and write. I burned their handwriting into my brain."

"Okay. But what does it mean?" *That's what I'm trying to figure out right now.*

"He hid something. When I was younger, like *way* younger, before Dad became...you know." Before he stopped drinking anything, but beer. Alex nods. "He used to leave. Like, randomly got up at ten thirty, grabbed his jacket and told us he was off to help his brother in the garage. When he came back, his hands were clean. His jacket was clean, his jeans. You don't work at a garage and come home looking like that. But he was fucking drunk."

"Sixpack."

[179]

"Exactly." I feel my breath slowing down on its own.

"So, you ever found out where he went?"

"Definitely not the garage. When Dad left for a couple times and I started to grow suspicious, I asked my uncle if the two of them got their work at the garage done. Mom told me to stay out of Dad's business, but I didn't give a shit."

"Of course you didn't." Alex smiles at me. I take another deep breath and smile back. Now *she* lights up. *Damn.*

"So, what'd he say?"

"That he hadn't seen Dad in days."

"Jeez." She squeezes my hands.

"Yeah." I look down toward her fingers wrapped around mine. I take her left hand in both of mine. It's the one I hurt. I trace my thumbs across the back of her hand. I see her taking a few deep breaths.

"I'm so sorry about before."

"Don't worry." She always says that. But I *do* worry. All the time. "You're not like your dad and I know that. You never will be." How do I *actually* burn something into my brain, because this is something I never ever want to forget?

"Do you want to figure out what happened?" *Not alone.*

"Will you help me? Please?"

"If you stop looking at me with those puppy eyes of yours." *My what now?*

"Sorry."

She removes her hands and gets up with a jump.

"New rule: No more apologizing." She leaves the tiny room and walks towards the ladder.

"You can't just update the contract!" I shout after her.

"I wrote it! I can do whatever I want with it!" She shouts back and I get up to follow after her.

"Turn off the light, will you?" I search for the fairy light and switch it off, covering us in a darkness I never knew I could comfortably live in.

"Where are we going?" I ask. "I can't fucking see."

"Just follow my voice!"

I'd follow that voice anywhere.

Chapter Twenty-Three

"So, you really don't have any clue that could help us solve this?" I ask her, switching my vocabulary to detective mode. Which is stupid because I don't feel like joking and playing pretend right now. We're walking back the way we came, through the dark forest. Tonight's full moon creates a slight silhouette of Alex. She walks confidently, avoiding every branch or stone in our way. I, on the other hand, almost stumbled over two times by now. Of course, she made fun of me. Which was nice, because for a moment I could pretend this was just another Friday night. But on any other Friday night, I would be scanning the bar with Jeff, or doing my homework for Alex, or walking around downtown until late at night so I knew Dad would be asleep when I got home. At least, I wouldn't be high or drunk with the boys anymore. I left that part of my life behind *that* day.

"Uh…there actually is one."

"Well, what is it?" We're walking side by side, arms occasionally touching. My body doesn't feel so stiff anymore.

"Okay, I didn't wanna tell you, but James dropped it. Like way back when he was fifteen or something." He's a full ass man now at twenty-three which creeps me the fuck out. *But wait.*

"Wait." I actually pause walking. Alex pauses a step in front of me.

"So, it's his?"

"Well, I always thought he wrote it and wanted to give it to a girl or something." *Yeah, that would've actually made a lot of sense.* "But turns out I was wrong."

"Dad gave it to him?"

"Seems like it, doesn't it?" *But why would he?*

"But why would he?"

"That's what we're going to figure out now." She starts walking again and I pace up to walk beside her.

"No."

"What?"

"We are *not* going to James'."

"*You* wanted to figure out what was going on back then."

"That was before you told me that son of a bitch owned the note once."

"Uh, your poor aunt?"

"Fine. Son of a gun then." I pause to take a deep breath. "This isn't funny, Alex. I'm being serious." My hand lands on her shoulder and turns her towards me. We both stop walking and I find the moon reflected in her blue.

"If it will make you happy, I will talk to James and try to find out what was going on. You go back to Hell's Saddle and I fill you in on the *drama* later since you want to find out so bad."

"It's not that I want to find out so bad. It's that, given your expression, some serious shit must've went down. Even if you don't know what. I know you can feel it."

"It's fucking dark. You can't even see my expression."

"No, but I *hear* it."

I sigh in surrender. "Okay. We'll find out what happened. You can come with me, but you will wait outside. I'll go in and talk to James. Got it?" She takes a few seconds to think it over.

"Okay. Lead the way then."

I never wanted to go back there again. And I definitely didn't want to bring Alex along. *Should we stop at Hell's Saddle and ask Jeff to come? Would that make me look weak?*

"You're awfully quiet." We've left the woods and made our way back on Main Road towards downtown.

"*You're* the one who wanted to enjoy the silence." I copy her strategy.

"Yeah, but you're not quiet so we can enjoy the silence. You're quiet because you're thinking." *How does she do that?*

"I don't know what to do and I don't know what I'm gonna say to him and I don't want you there." *Lie. I want her there. I just don't want her near James.*

"Happy?"

"No."

"Well, sorry." She tries to interrupt me breaking our rule. But then again, I don't give a single flying fuck about the rules. "But I don't think you know who you might be dealing with." I go on.

"And you do?" *Why's she angry?*

"Given he's my cousin, yes."

"Okay. Then tell me about it. Your plan, I mean."

Try not to get kicked in the guts?

"I don't have a plan. All I know is, we- I mean *I* have to be careful. James can snap pretty quickly."

"I punched him in the face once."

"What?"

"When he was still in school. He groped me," *What?*

"so I knocked his lights out." *Now, there's no reason to find that hot, but…*

"Didn't know you had it in you."

"Well, I'm my mom's kid." Though Elaine has never actually fought anyone, not that I know of, she always stands up for herself and those around her.

"And you don't survive in this town if you don't fight back."

Folkspine really must be fucked up if even Alex has to throw a fist eventually. *I'd throw mine for her anytime.* I clear my throat.

"Well, guess I gotta kill my cousin now." It comes out as a joke, but I'm not sure it is. When Alex told me, James asked her to ride him, I did go over to his place and punched him in the face. I never told Alex about it and I thought James had learned his lesson.

Well, I *hoped.* Now that I know he didn't…

"Ah yes. Very careful and suave."

Now it's my time to groan. "Ugh! I just don't know what to do." Right now, I want to go over to James' to make him regret laying his hands on Alex and not to find out what my dad did. I don't give a shit about Dad right now.

"You've got a goal, right?" She's so calm again.

"Cut off his hands."

"No. You will go in there, calmly talk to him, not get into a fight, find out what your dad did and get outta there. I told you I can handle myself. I don't need a man to protect me." *She's right, she doesn't.*

"Okay."

The gravel's crunching underneath us as we pass the trail leading up to Alex's place. *Maybe another time.*

Chapter Twenty-Four

"You ready?" *No.*

I haven't been here in years, I haven't talked to him and I don't want to. The only words we share are comments of annoyance when walking past each other. "Still alive?" "Fuck you, James."

I left the gang to stop hanging out with him, but after having Alex remind me of my goal, I'd rather talk to James, than not know what shit Dad has been hiding. I just hope I won't snap looking James in the face at seeing the hands that touched Alex.

We're standing in front of my uncle's and aunt's house. Their bedroom is dark behind the window and since it's maybe nine, nine thirty, they're not asleep. They're probably off somewhere smoking pot and having sex in my uncle's car, like fuck-up teenagers.

"Do I have another choice?"

"We *can* go back to Hell's Saddle." I know she doesn't mean that. She's bluffing. And I let her win. "No, I want to find out." She smiles at my answer. I hold Alex by both shoulders and move her away from the front door and towards the facade. The street lights finally make it able to properly look her in the blue.

"You stay right here, yeah?" She rolls her eyes at me, breaking the eye contact. Three seconds.

"Pony, this is serious. This isn't kids messing around. This is adult stuff." I lightly shake her.

"Yeah yeah, okay." She pushes me off, gesturing towards the front door.

James must be inside, since his bedroom in the basement *is* lit up and I recognize "Motorbreath" playing from his speakers. *Pisses me off we both listen to the same music.* But that really is *his* song.

Just as I lift my hand to knock, I think back to him in his room, probably high or drunk or both, having the music loud enough to blast through closed windows. *Yeah, he won't hear the door.*

"Uh, where are you going?" Alex is about to follow me as she sees me walking away from the front door.

"I'll do this like I always have, when we were kids." When I still hung out with my cousin to listen to his records, have the occasional smoke and talk about tits. Well, he did. I listened.

I go over to the basement window, right above the sidewalk, crouch down and knock hard, three times.

I see him inside. He does look way older now, but he's also still the same. Lying on his old dirty couch between dirty clothes, smoking and probably thinking dirty things.

I knock again, harder this time. He looks up at the window, eyes squinting. I give him a wave, no smile. He gets up with a lot of effort and makes his way up the stairs and I get up to tell Alex to stay at the wall. She nods and I position myself in front of the front door. Waiting for him, I feel my pointer fingers picking at the skin on my thumb and its cuticles, peeling off the blood crust from the last time I scratched at it.

James opens the door with a stumble. *Drunk.*

"Jesus. You're still alive." *What a greeting.*

"Very funny."

He continues with a slight mocking grin. "Didn't think I'd ever see you here again." *My thought too.* His hand reaches out to move it through my hair, but I pull back. His grin falls and he moves his hand towards the buckle of his belt.

"What you want? To punch me in the face again?" *Sounds good.* He takes a puff from his cigare- joint. *And high.* How did I not smell that?

"No. I want a talk." He looks me up and down. I do the same with him. Blonde spikes, ears pierced, chain around his neck, old white T-shirt. It's a shame the guy looks actually cool. Still, I *do* want to punch him in the face for all the shit he did. Especially to Alex.

"Fine." He holds the door open for me. I glance to the side to meet Alex's eyes before stepping in. She nods.

The inside looks like it always has. Messy. *How can someone be lucky enough to live in a house and deface it like that?*

He leads us to the kitchen, but I stay in the doorway, leaning against it. James opens the fridge.

"Beer?" Like we're still buddies.

"No thanks." He scoffs and grabs one for himself, opening the can on the spot. He takes the joint from between his lips to chug down the beer, throwing the empty can on the kitchen counter. *An actual kitchen with a kitchen counter.*

"Puff?" He asks after swallowing.

"No." The joint lands back between his lips.

"Pussy." *Apparently my second name.* I take a deep breath in.

"I didn't come here to get wasted."

"So, what do you want?" He crosses his arms, not like a pouty kid, but like a defensive adult. The joint slowly goes out.

"Like I said, to have a chat."

"Let's go downstairs then." He moves past me, bumping my shoulder on the way, and walks down the hall to the basement stairs. I follow.

The further we get down, the louder the music gets. Inside, a wall of smoke and the smell of pot hits me. It's weirdly nostalgic. The room's exactly the same, the music, the old couch, old cans in corners, metal posters everywhere and Alan's graffiti of a dick with tits in the corner – kind of sweet to see he too didn't cover it up. James walks over to his record player and turns it down. He lets himself collapse onto his couch, searches for a lighter and holds the flame against the joint. Like before, I'm just standing there. On the last step.

"Fuck man. Just get in. Don't act all weird and polite." Focused on the fire in his hands, he doesn't look up.

I move towards him, over cans of beer, porn magazines and dirty – probably crunchy socks – to sit down on the couch.

"So, go on. Have your chat." He takes another slow puff on the relit joint and holds it in for a few seconds before letting it out with a sigh.

"Can you quit the smoking for a second?"

"Come on, I just relit it." I shoot him a look. "Fine." He leans forward with a roll of the eyes to rest the joint on the brim of his full ashtray on the table in front of us.

It's now that I realize, I still don't know what to say to him. James leans back, shuts his eyes and waits.

"Did Dad ever come over to help Uncle Ramy?"

Don't know what to say? Just be upfront.

His eyes reopen, revealing red instead of white.

"What?"

"Like, years ago. Dad used to sneak out. Said he'd help at the garage, but came home drunk instead."

"How should I know?"

"We'll *you* always helped out, so I figured you would've known. Ramy told me Dad never came over, though."

"Well, then he didn't." He sounds annoyed.

"So, you don't know where he went? Like in the middle of the night."

For a moment, he doesn't answer. When he does, though, he sounds almost sober.

"When was this?"

"Uh…" I think back to what Alex told me. "I think you must've been fifteen." For a second, I see his eyes widen. His movement stops. There's not a single breath coming from him. Then, he clears his throat and repositions himself on the couch. He forces his voice to sound deeper.

"Yeah, no idea. I was pretty high back then." *And what are you now?*

"James. You know something and you know I know." *Because I've analyzed you like I've analyzed Dad, Mom and Alex.*

He doesn't say anything. He doesn't tell me to piss off, he doesn't insult me. For the first time, he's silent. *No, that's wrong. He's been silent like this before. Back then.* And this is not a silence I can enjoy.

"Here." I lean over to grab the joint from the table. "Gimme the lighter." He hands it over without a word and I hold it against the joint, relighting it.

"I'll have a smoke with you." I hesitate, but eventually close my lips around the joint and pull the air into my lungs.

The whole motion comes naturally to me, though I never wanted to have another joint again. Especially not with my cousin.

I hold it for a few seconds and let it out with a cough. James watches me the whole time. When I'm done, I hand it over to him and he takes another puff himself. For a moment, we sit there in more silence, feeling the pot work its way through our blood, like we did back then. We'd probably still be doing this on a regular basis if I never left the gang. Though it'd just be me and James now. No Alan and no Glen.

"Dude, that shit's strong." I say with an involuntary laugh, feeling a little off.

"Mexico." He answers. Next, he takes a deep breath in – not from the joint.

"You won't tell?"

"What, Dad?" He nods in response. "I don't talk to him." I reassure him, he nods again and after a few more seconds, he begins to crush my world.

"When I was fifteen, he started coming over here. When Mom was out with her girlfriends and Dad was working at the garage." I see him swallowing hard. "Then, at some point, he started to meet up with me out of town. The woods…" He takes a long pause. "Or the junkyard." *Oh.* "We always had "our spot" and our time. Eleven on the dot. God forbid I came late for even just a minute." He presses his eyes together.

"So, you two got drunk together?"

"He got drunk. I stole sixpacks from my dad and brought them with me."

"So, you brought him beer." I take a deep breath in and out with relief.

"No. Well, yes. But I…" He looks at me, expecting me to finish for him, but when I don't, he takes another breath in. "I brought myself."

My heart starts accelerating. I don't interrupt him in the silence that follows and wait for him to go on.

"He always told me to "prepare." The first time he came over here, he barely got it in. So, from then on, he told me to start working on myself before he came over. Said it'd be easier for the both of us. When Mom almost caught us once, he simply told her he wanted to come over to have a chat with my dad, but hadn't found him and asked me where he is.

After that, he told me to meet up some place else. And I did."

I think carefully before asking. "Why?"

"Because I was scared." He almost laughs at my question. "He said he'd tell on me. Tell my dad that *I* forced myself on top of *him*. That *I* pinned *him* down." He sits up straight to finally look me in the face. "You know how Dads are, right?"

"Fucking scary." Is all I can say.

"And scary while fucking."

I take a sharp breath in and a deep breath out.

"Hand it over." I point at the joint in James' hand and take a deep, long puff, cherishing the smoke inside my lungs like a hug from the inside. After letting it out, I hand it back to him.

Chapter Twenty-Five

We finish the joint in silence while Metallica keeps playing. It's the first joint we've shared in years and I'm starting to get why we did it so often. I pretend not to notice how my body feels like a pebble that's been sitting in the creek for years and years, its edges being rounded by the cold water. When there's no pot left, we both take a moment to reflect.

"Fuck man." Is all I can say. *What should I say? Think? Do? Feel?*

"Yeah." We both pause for a minute and it feels like we never split apart. I still feel pretty down-to-earth. Not sure if that's a good thing.

"Does he still…" I don't want to say it.

"No. After I turned eighteen, he stopped. Said it wasn't fun anymore." *That's years. Long years. That bastard.* And I feel so fucking guilty for feeling lucky that I wasn't Dad's next victim after James. *Was James the only one?*

"I got addicted at that time. I didn't know where to go and what to do except getting high or drunk or both. Anything that took me out of my body." It's hard to remember James before drugs entered his life. In my mind, he's always been using. But he *did* lose control over it when he was around sixteen or something.

"Yeah." Suddenly, I don't have the urge to punch him anymore. Sitting next to me, high and drunk, isn't the James he pretends to be. It's the kid he never really got to be. Underneath inked skin, underneath all the smoke. There's the kid I used to spend my childhood with. As cousins, as friends. He's not a junkie. He's a fuck-up, yes. But because someone else fucked him up.

"James, I-"

"I'm sorry, you know." I let him interrupt me because this is probably the first time he has apologized to anyone. "I did some pretty messed up shit and said some other shit and was just…shit. And on that day, you know, I was so messed up. I shouldn't have." *Did he forget how messed up I was?*

"No, I get it." And I *do* get it.

"Really?" *Just a kid.*

"Really, man."

"I'm glad you're here. Still here, you know." I don't know if *I* am.

[199]

"Yeah." Is all I can answer. And then I remind myself and switch the tone in my voice. "By the way, if you come near Alex again, I'll mess you up."

"Alex?" He sounds genuinely confused.

"The Goodfellow's kid?" The farmer's daughter, Protector of The Jukebox, town's princess.

"Right. The cowgirl. She fights back good, though." He nods and I shoot him a look, like I mean it.

"Got it." He throws his hands up and nods again, harder this time.

"Good." I nod back and push myself off James' couch.

"Thanks for…having a chat." He sounds so small.

"Of course."

"Will you come back?" The question catches me off guard.

"Do you want that?" *Also, do I?*

"Yeah, man. We're cousins."

I stare at him, not knowing what to say. To be honest, I've missed him. But I also know very well why I decided not to hang with him anymore and I think that was the right decision. So, I just smile in response and slowly make my way up the stairs, down the hall and out the front door, flying over the dirty carpet. *Not* that *down to earth.*

Outside, the cold night slaps me in the face. I take a few breaths, feeling into my body.
Alex is crouching on the sidewalk right next to James' window. She jumps up when she sees me. "Cracked the case, Watson?" she asks with a grin and a bad British accent. I look at her and start walking down the street. Suddenly, everything hits me all at once. The pot, what James said, what Dad did, his blood rushing through me and me not being able to stop it. *I can't go home. I can't go anywhere. I definitely can't stay where I am or reality will catch up with me. I can't be with Alex right now. I need to walk. Left, right, left, right. Move forward.*
"Abel?" She's behind me. *Grey sidewalk, muffled Metallica, yellow streetlight, full moon.*
"Brennan." *Left, right, left, right.*
"Hello?!" She touches my shoulder from behind. I turn around quickly. Her wrist in my hand, again. Tears in eyes. *My* eyes. "Shit. Abel, what happened?" Turn back around. *Left, right, left, right.*
"You smell horrible." She tells me from behind.

"Did you smoke?" *Can't answer.* "Abel, please. Please talk to me." *I can't.*

"Sorry. I'm...high. Can't talk."

"Okay. But that's not it."

"Gosh, stop analyzing me!" *Right. Definitely my right to say something like that.*

"I'm not a poem!" Salted water stings my eyes before dripping down my chin.

"Well, maybe you are." My heart aches a little at the sound of her cracked voice. I didn't want to scream at her. *Is this how Dad feels? Does he ever regret it?*

"What?" I turn around to meet the blue and I don't know why. I don't want her to see me like this. It's more that I want to see her.

"Forget it."

"No. What?" I ask again.

"Maybe you are a poem." She repeats. Three seconds.

"Whatever." I turn back around and keep walking. Again, I don't know why. It's like I'm working against myself. I want to stay with Alex, I need it. I need the mutual understanding that the world is fucked, even though I haven't fully been able to figure out what Alex's issue is. But I turn away from her and the blue and walk away.

"You act so fucking strong all the time, but you know deep down you are just a sad kid no one has ever properly loved!" She shouts after me, but doesn't follow. And I can't blame her, but my mind keeps repeating *Walk with me, Pony.*

"My mom loves me." I try to convince myself.

"Not enough to save your soul from the Devil in your home." *Please, don't talk about my dad right now.* Because it makes me see his face. I see James and, though I try to fight it, I see Dad and James – together. Then, I see my mom and our trailer and I imagine the amount of cans that are scattered across the floor and I imagine him snoring on the couch while Mom picks up his mess. And there's that boiling in my blood that makes my skin crawl because I know it's his blood and I've been begging the universe for different blood, but it stays the same. Brennan, through and through, is rushing through my veins and pounds at my head until my brain shakes left and right inside my skull and I can't fight it anymore.

"Well then fuck you, Alex!"

[203]

"What?"

"You heard me! Fuck you and your perfect little family! Go back to your farm or the bar you love so much, where everyone loves pretty little Alex. The *lovely* girl from next door! I told you not to come with me. I told you this is real life shit, but you didn't listen. You're so full of yourself!"

Silence creates a wall between us. Between the brown and the blue.

"You don't mean that." Like a sledgehammer. And she's right. I don't. I just don't know where to put the earthquake inside me.

I keep walking, the distance between us growing. Again, I want to turn around and walk up to her. But I leave.

Stop walking, dude.

When I finally do stop and turn around, Alex is right there. In front of me. And close.

"You don't mean that and I can hear it." *Pony.* "And I didn't mean what I said." I see through my tears into her eyes. *How can blue be such a cold color and still warm me up from the inside?* "It's okay." Her arms open to take me in. I keep my arms close to my chest and Alex closes hers around me. Her face in my hair.

I sob into her like a little child crying to his mother when the boys at school were mean to him. And she holds me. And it's the first time in my life, that I'm crying without being scared of my dad finding out. Because Alex surrounds me and between her arms, nothing and no one can reach me.

"I'm such a…" *Bastard. Idiot. Fuck-up. Child. Asshole. Wimp. Pussy.* I try to think between sobs. *A Brennan.*

"No, you're not." Her arms close around me even tighter and suddenly, someone else's skin tightening around me doesn't mean the end of the world.

For a moment, we stand there. Right in Folkspine, underneath streetlights and the moon. Me crying into Alex and Alex letting me.

After what feels like eternity and not long enough at the same time, I let go. My instinct tells me to turn away so she doesn't see my red eyes, from the weed and from the salt. But I don't. I look at her. And she looks at me.

"Want to talk?" She calmly asks. Three seconds.

"Another time, if that's okay." Four.

"Of course." And she smiles at me. Five.

"I'm so sorry. I- I crash out. I don't know what to do with myself and then I turn-"

"No. You're not him. I promise you. I've told you earlier today and I still mean it."

"Sorry." I sound weak in front of Alex, and I only give a small fuck.

"Rule." She reminds me with a smile.

We start walking again. I don't know what time it is and I don't care. Our arms brush each other and we walk. I don't know where, but I keep walking.

"Abel?"

"Yeah, Pony?"

"I know you have some serious shit going on right now and I don't want to bother you with my own shit..." *Please do. Anything that takes my mind off things. I've opened up, now let me see you.* "But there's something...uh I mean if that's fine- I mean if you want to go home and sleep or be alone then that's- "

"I don't want to be alone." I really don't.

"Okay." And then "Let's go to my place."

"Your place?" I ask, not sure I heard her right.

"Yeah. I mean, we *could* go back to Hell's Saddle, but I don't think being around drunk adults day and

night is any good for you. Plus, you're high and I
ain't sure if Eve would like to see you like that."
Word and word. "Besides, I want to show you
something."

"Again?" I joke.

Chapter Twenty-Six

We walk back to where we came from. Towards the woods and the tree and the tiny house in the top. We close up to the farm, but don't walk past it this time because Alex turns right onto the dirt trail. I'm standing at the junction between the trail and Main Road, while Alex strides ahead.

"Come on!" She walks backwards and shouts at me. I hesitate, but eventually move my foot from the pavement of Main Road to the dirt of the trail. It feels like I'm invalidating her privacy, but she lets me and so I trust her that she trusts me.

The moon's hanging high over the barn on the right and I question the whole night. Maybe I'm just high, but maybe Alex and I are *actual* friends and not just study buddies. And I'm walking up to her place, catching up on her. I don't walk up to people's places. I don't get invited. The only places I go to is Hell's Saddle and our trailer. The list used to contain James' and the junkyard.

There's a fence on the left, but in the dark, I can't see what it surrounds.

"What's in there? In the fence, I mean." I ask.

"Right now, nothing. It's our meadow for our horse and the cows."

"Please tell me the horse has got a name." Given the hundred times "A Horse with No Name" was played at Hell's Saddle, I wouldn't be surprised if their horse was nameless too.

"Trixie." Alex answers after a quick laugh. "She kicks down the fence at night, so now she sleeps in the barn with the cows. She didn't use to do it so often, but we can't take risks."

"So, she'd break out?" I ask.

"No, I don't think so. Dad still wants to keep her in the barn." When we pass the barn of the right, I hear loud, high-pitched barking coming from inside.

"Quit it, girl! It's me." Alex shouts and at the sound of her voice, the dog stops.

"That's no cow and no horse."

"It's Jewel. Loudest dog in all Folkspine, I'm telling you." She clearly hasn't heard of Jeff's Mastiff. We distance ourselves from the barn and walk up to a house. A proper two-story house, flag on a pole next to it, white porch with a picket fence around. The dream. I don't see the Flying Fishbowl anywhere hidden in the dark, so Elaine must still be at Hell's

Saddle. *What time is it?* Alex confidently walks up the step to the porch and then to the front door. She fetches a key from her pocket and unlocks the door with a twist. The door opens wide, revealing darkness behind it. She steps in and flicks on a warm yellow light.

"Take off your shoes." She orders as she takes off her own and places them on the side in the hall. I follow after her, stepping through the door and do as I'm told. Seeing my Chucks resting next to Alex's cowboy boots in the warm light gives me a weird feeling of home. Like if I were on vacation right now. Of course, I've never been on vacation, but I used to pretend a lot as a kid.

"You want a drink?" Looking down at our shoes, I hadn't noticed Alex disappearing into the next room. I follow the new light and her voice into the kitchen. *Another actual kitchen.* Alex doesn't wait for an answer. When I come in, she's already grabbed two glasses from a cupboard and opens the fridge for a bottle of Sunny Delight, filling both glasses with the orange liquid. She reminds me of Elaine just now. She hops onto the kitchen counter and takes one of the glasses in her hand. I walk up to her, take the other one and awkwardly stand in front of her. "Thanks." I feel like I've just been invited to the White House. *How can I feel uncomfortable standing in Alex's kitchen? I'm still high and have just cried into her not even an hour ago.* I still feel some of the dried salt sitting in the cracks under my eyes.

She gestures towards the kitchen table behind me and I copy her motion to hop onto it. We're facing each other now, legs dangling from the edge of our seating place, glass of Sunny Delight in our hands. I wait for her to drink first. I was raised in a trailer, but I still have manners. When she does, I lift my glass towards my lips and let the juice flow inside. The sweetness hits me like a shock. I've forgotten how thirsty joints make me, so I can't help but chug the whole glass down.

"Jeez. Want another one?" She asks concerned.

"Nah, I'm fine." I lick the remaining juice from my lips.

And then we're silent again. I take some mindful breaths, taking in the feeling of sitting in a kitchen, in a house with a porch, across from Alex, who supposedly is my friend now and who had just endured one of my break downs.

"Can I ask you something?" She breaks the silence first.

"Go on."

"Why *don't* you hang out with James anymore?" Her head is down, facing the glass in her hands.

"Is that a serious question?"

"Well, yeah. You've been friends for so long. Why not anymore?"

"Because he's an asshole? You know that."

"But you're cousins."

"Alex. The guy steals booze and cigs on a daily basis and he harasses people all the time, including you. Plus, he's basically never sober. I've got the same crap at home. I don't need that in my free time too."

I don't need to tell her about the gun.

"Hell's Saddle ain't exactly full of sober people either."

"That's different."

"Why?" *Because Mom and T are there. Because Jeff is there. Because you are there.* I don't answer.

"Did something happen between you two?"

"What? Like, today?"

"When you stopped hanging out."

"Why do you even want to know that?"

She's quiet for a moment and I patiently wait for her.

Then, she lifts her head to meet eyes with me.

"Because I wonder how you could be strong enough

to leave your family behind for your own good."

1982

Chapter Twenty-Seven

When James was nineteen, he held his first gun. I was just fifteen back then and Glen and Alan were his age. Dad's hate towards me was almost a daily routine by then. The occasional slap, grabbing my wrist, throwing stuff at me. I was used to it and knew how to handle situations with him. The routine was simple and still is. Keep distance – if the distance decreases, stand your ground – keep eye contact, check on Mum, have the last word, don't smash the door shut. Simple. I was already living in terror day and night and the gang was my escape. Back then, we were still complete. Looking back at it, it's kind of weird for a bunch of nineteen-year-olds to hang with a fifteen-year-old. But we were a group and I felt included, which I was desperately hanging onto. I was just nine when they started experimenting with drugs at thirteen. They dared me to a puff or a sip, and I happily did anything they gave me. It made me feel like one of them. One of the adults, even though they were still just kids themselves. When the gang first formed, the boys were eleven. Before that, James and I didn't have any other friends except each other. At first, we were all just jumping around downtown, playing bandits and Sheriff. Of course, James was the Sheriff. Looking back at it, I don't think that was a smart move, because even if we were just playing pretend, James already didn't have a good concept of justice. Over the years, James started stealing as we watched in awe. First it was candy, then porn magazines, then booze. They often sent me forward as a distraction so James could commit his acts of theft. We got drunk in his room or backyard and as the years passed, we got high too. We moved from downtown and his place to the junkyard out of town. Here, we now had our own realm with James as king, a truck as his throne. Alan was like the knight, Glen the jester and I was just happy to be included. When the boys were about sixteen, we suddenly stopped going there. James refused to meet up at the junkyard, and I now know why. We retreated back to James' place and downtown and did our business there. Suddenly, one random night, James ordered the gang to meet back up at the junkyard and, as always, we obeyed. Alan couldn't stop yapping about how excited he was to finally get back in the realm.

"The King's back!" Alan shouted through the trees as we walked up towards the junkyard. We could pretend to be in our kingdom in James' room, but the junkyard felt more real. We were happy to get back. The moon was standing high and beaming in its full glory. I looked at it in awe, wondering how many fates it had already seen spread out. Glen and Alan were walking ahead, with me following a few steps behind. I could see how their arms brushed against each other in result of how close they were walking together. When James came into view, their distance grew. He was sitting on the hood of the old broken-down truck. His throne. Six packs were resting on the hood right next to him. It was hard to see, but with squinted eyes, I could see one was already emptied and two were still full. He had a cig in one hand, casting a slight light on his face, and a can in the other, taking turns consuming the drugs. When he saw us coming closer, he got up. He wobbled for a few seconds before finding his step, gave Glen and Alan a dab up and ruffled through my hair. He always did this when he was drunk or high or both – which was basically all the time.

"Welcome back, boys!" He greeted us.

"Long lives The King." Alan jokingly bowed.

James tossed each of us a beer and I opened it with little hesitation, because I was expected too.

"Why'd you call us here?" Glen asks after emptying his can and grabbing a fresh one.

"Got a lil something for you." James gave the pocket in his jacket a pat. He didn't seem to mind the questioning glances passed between us three. He didn't seem to mind anything.

We were standing between countless cans of beer and I knew each and every one came from him. The whole place felt eerie. There was a fireplace near the truck, black and grey with old burned down wood, embers still glowing, cigarette butts all around. The gang hasn't met up at the junkyard for a while and the last time we went here, there was definitely no fireplace.

"Have you been coming here?" I asked him.

"Make yourselves at home." Was all he had to say and today I can finally piece the puzzle together.

"Dude! This was *our* spot." Alan exclaimed. He was always the louder one of him and Glen. Glen was kind of like me, a bit shy and just wanting to fit in, with the only person he felt he could hold on to. For me, it was James. For him, it was Alan.

"Sorry guys. Needed a place for my own. I'm The King after all."

"Not cool." Alan threw his empty can at James.

Our realm had reminded him of my father's sins. Another emperor had attacked James' kingdom, took his crown and made James his jester. I suppose he started coming there again after the horrors stopped. I can only imagine how many hours he's spent sitting at the fire, getting higher and drunker by the minute and smashing junk to even tinier pieces. I imagine he was probably crying too, though he would never admit that. He's real about the whole "Boys don't cry" motto.

"So, what do you have?" Glen asks impatiently. "Crack?"

"Right! We haven't had Crack yet." Alan complained.

"Relax. It's not Crack." James answered. He loved to tease the boys like that. It didn't affect me much. I'd do whatever drugs he gave me and that was it.

"Man! We gotta get some Crack."

Thanks to Leland and himself, Alan died of an overdose two years ago.

After a couple more cigarettes and a hell lot of beers and stunts around the junkyard later, James told us to go follow him. That day, he was probably the drunkest I've ever seen him. I had a weird feeling inside my stomach ever since we arrived. Something wasn't right. Not with James. He led us across spare parts of old trucks, refrigerators and other crap people just threw out. After a couple climbs and steps, we arrived at a sort of clearing. James had placed some moldy empty beer bottles on the hood of another old truck. He stood in front of it, turned around to face us and put his hand in the inside of his jacket.

"You ever pulled the trigger before?" He asked us. No one answered. We didn't believe he actually had a gun. That was until he pulled it out and pointed it towards us. The moonlight reflected in its metal casing.

"Dude!" Alan backed off and Glen stepped behind him.

"What the fuck?" He said from behind Alan, gripping his back like a little kid.

"Get off!" Alan shot back at Glen and added a "Ya pussy." Because that's what James expected him to say. So, Glen reemerged at the order.

I stood still where I was. Slightly behind Glen and Alan, on their right.

"Chill. It ain't cocked."

Alan suppressed a chuckle at the word cock.

"Where'd you get it?" He then asked James, stepping closer to inspect the handgun while his fear turned quickly into amazement.

"Stole it from my old man, duh. Figured we could do some aiming." He pointed the gun at the bottles.

"You're drunk." I said, concerned about James' condition while holding a gun.

"And?" Alan questioned me. Glen hesitated, but nodded.

"Maybe he shouldn't play around with a gun right now?" I told him.

"I ain't playing. We'll do some practice, that's all." How is it that the youngest of a group of four is the most reasonable one?

"Who wants to start?" James addressed us all.

"Me, duh." Of course, Alan. He already stepped closer to James, holding one hand out, expecting the gun to land in it. James pulled it away from Alan.

"Nah. I think lil pussy man should go first." Glen's back straightened, but when he realized he wasn't addressed, he just looked all confused. Instead of handing the gun to Glen "the pussy," James moved towards me. He took his other hand to the barrel of the gun and stretched his arm out towards me. I looked at it. Gun at my eye level with its grip right in front of me.

"I'm out." I turned from him to walk back home, or whatever that place is called.

"No." When I turned back around, I was facing the muzzle.

That day, I learned to never turn my back on a guy holding a gun, even if that guy is your own cousin – maybe especially then.

"Dude, what the fuck!" Glen stepped forward, but Alan stretched out his arm in front of him.

"He will go first." James said through gritted teeth.

"Fucks wrong with you?"

"I want you to go first." He pushed me.

"I ain't touching that thing." To this day, I can still feel the face I pulled right then. Disgust and anger. "I want my cousin to grow up to be a man, alright. One little shot and then you can go home."

"Why?"

"You need to be able to defend yourself." He said, almost begging.

"From what?" I shouted back.

He didn't tell me back then, but today I realized what he meant. And I realized that I should be thankful for what he did. I should thank him for loving me so much that he stole a gun from Ramy and wanted me to shoot it. He knew Dad's keeping a gun in our trailer. He knows where it is and I know it too and now I know he wanted to prepare me for the moment my father laid his hands on me in a different way, so that I'd be able to create holes through his body. And now I know, he probably put on an act of having us all gather at the junkyard, getting drunk and then making it seem like we all should pull the trigger. He didn't want to meet me under four eyes and casually teach me how to shoot a gun because he knew I'd ask questions. And how

should he explain my father is a rapist and a
pedophile?

"Come on man." He flipped the gun, facing the
muzzle away from me, and shoved the grip in my
hand. He moved out of my way, so I had a clear
view of the bottles in front of me.
I stood there, gun in my hand, James and Alan
watching my every move, while Glen stared at my
face.
I reminded myself of how the men in Dad's movies
handled a gun. I cocked it and thought. A thousand
thoughts passing through my brain each second. I
could prove to the gang that I'm a man, I could
make my cousin proud. I could decock it and drop it,
I could show Glen how to be better. I could take the
chance, I could save myself. The gang couldn't be
my escape anymore. How could a bunch of drunk
teenagers be better than my drunk dad? It was only a
matter of time before they started losing themselves
too. At least that's what I thought. This was the
breaking point of our friendship. I promised myself
in that moment, no matter what happened, I
couldn't be with them anymore. They were fools and

their leader was an addict playing with guns. And if I can't be with the gang anymore, then there's no escape for me. Nowhere else could I find what the gang has been giving me. But today, with Alex, that thought might've evaporated.

But back then, I was sure I lost all that was good in life. I lost the illusion. The illusion of a friend group that loved each other through and through. That meant happiness and comfort and safety.

So, I didn't aim at the bottles, I didn't decock it. I lifted my hand and pushed the muzzle to my temple, locking eyes with James.

He went pale on the spot, pupils dilating and nostrils flaring. Alan stood still, didn't move a muscle. James and I locked eyes and his looked like those of a deer in headlights. I increased the pressure on the trigger and closed my eyes. But before I could finish, I felt someone rushing at me and slapping the gun out of my hand. It fell to the ground and fired at the impact. I opened my eyes to James flinching, his eyes still on mine. Alan fell forward with a step and I saw that Glen's spot next to him was empty. I turned around to see Glen. He fell to the ground next to the gun after he had stumbled over a rock when rushing towards me.

"What the fuck was that?!" Alan shouted. James turned towards him and then back at me, not saying a word.

"I was defending myself, like you said." My eyes were locked with James' again. Water started to fill in mine. The disappointment of not succeeding. Knowing this was probably my only chance, because I would never collect the strength to do it again. That day, I almost saved myself. Out of the spontaneity of the action. Before I knew it, I was holding a gun and with it, the power to break free.

"You were killing yourself!" Alan screamed. He came towards us and I thought he would slap me across the face, so I prepared myself for the impact. Instead, he bumped my shoulder as he ran up to Glen to help him up from the dirty floor.

"I'm good." Glen's voice was quiet, the words only meant for Alan to hear. He was shaking all over and Alan held him by the shoulders. James stepped back, watching all of us. His gaze shifting from me, to Alan, to Glen and then to the gun on the ground.

I kept my promise and never came to any gang meetings after that. That day, I realized what the gang consisted of. An addict, an aggressor, a lost soul and a suicidal kid. We weren't a gang. We were stupid boys trying to escape whatever problem we had by feeling like a group. We weren't even a group. James was a loner, but so was I. Alan and Glen were in love with each other, but pretended they weren't. No one ever talked about it and they both ignored their feelings. Later, I figured out that James eventually stopped hanging with the both of them, because they were acting "weird," as he called it. Then, the two of them were seen drunk and making out downtown. The news spread like fire around town. This was three years ago. After Alan died, Glen seemed to have no one. Alan wasn't there anymore to throw a fist for him and James definitely wouldn't take up the role of Glen's protector. Folkspine is a town marked by generations of hate towards anyone who isn't living by the laws of God. Like basically every other gay person in Folkspine, Glen too got into some fights. When he couldn't handle it anymore, he left town. Just like Taylor. No one heard from him since. I often think about Glen and remind myself why I stay hidden like Taylor. I can handle hiding.

After me ditching the gang, Alan dying and Glen leaving, James was all alone. I now know, he would've needed me. His cousin, his friend.

But when I was fifteen, I held my first gun.

1986

Chapter Twenty-Eight

"No, nothing happened between us." I answer, not knowing if it´s the whole truth. "I just realized I didn't want to hang out with him anymore."

"What about the rest of the gang?" She asks me.

"You mean Alan and Glen?"

"Yeah. Why'd you stop hanging with them?"

"I thought everyone knew about them." News spread fast and I know for a fact Elaine heard at work and told Alex.

"I know about them, I'm asking why you didn't hang with them anymore."

"Well, before they became uh…" *How do I say this?*

"Official. Before that, for a while, they still hung with James, so I didn't really want to go near them. You know, Alan was pretty messed up with drugs too. Hence the…overdose." I wait for her to nod and when she does, I go on. "Glen's a good guy, though. Saved my life onc-" *Fuck. Fuck fuck fuck.*

"What?"

"Uh." *Think, Brennan, think.* "A guy held me at gunpoint once, when I was fifteen. Glen tackled him." *Not that far from the truth.*

"Jesus." She seems to believe me and I relax in relief. We fall silent again and after a moment, I question why I'm even sitting in Alex's kitchen in the first place.

"You wanted to show me something." I remind her.

"Oh, right!" She actually forgot about it. She quickly jumps from the counter and I wait for orders.

"Be right back. Stay there."

"Aye aye."

She leaves the kitchen and seems to run upstairs. Her steps grow quieter and eventually, she seems to be walking right above me.

I take a moment to look around the kitchen. The fridge is plastered with notes and old drawings from Alex. There's a framed photograph on the wall next to it. Elaine, John and Alex posing as the peaceful trio that forms their family. The clock on the wall across from me, right above where Alex sat, says it's one.

The stomping above me has stopped and is now coming from the stairs, growing louder. When she comes back into the kitchen, I ask "Don't you have lessons to prepare tomorrow?"

I know she hates breaking her routine and I know she loves going to bed early on Fridays, so she can get up early the next day and prepare her notes for the following Tuesday.

"Yeah. And?" She says while walking past me and jumping back down on the counter. She's got a notebook clutched to her chest.

"It's late."

"I don't care. This is more…" She doesn't finish and we just look at each other again.

"You're a bad teacher, you know that?"

"Shut up." She says with a chuckle and it sends lightning through my spine. I look at the notebook, now resting in her lap.

"Which one's that?" I ask, not recognizing it.

"My diary." *Her diary?* "I want you to read another poem."

"From your diary?" I ask as she's sitting back down across from me.

"Why not your poem-notebook?" It genuinely surprises me that Alex would break her routine of dividing her work into different notebooks.

"Some poems don't belong there. Some belong in my diary." *Hidden.*

She opens the diary and I keep my eyes off it, so I don't accidentally read something I'm not supposed to. Now that I actually *can* read, I wouldn't dare to go through her notes on my own. Especially not after she snapped at me that one time in Hell's Saddle. I still remember the drawing she did of Elaine.

I hear the pages flipping in her hands and when the noise stops, I look back at her. She's looking down at her diary, reading over the written page. *She's thinking.* And she's thinking for a long time. Her teeth come down on her lower lip and I stare, afraid it might start to bleed at the pressure.

"You don't have to show it to me, you know."

"No, I do." She sounds small, fragile and kind of fallen apart – which shocks me. She's always loud, she's always sure, always right, and she never hesitates.

"Why?"

She looks up to meet my eyes.

Alex

"Why?"

Because I need someone to read it and I want it to be you.
And you're still high, so I hope you will read it once and
then forget about it and never even consider analyzing it.
But internally, I wish he'll see through the words and
into my soul. Because he's the only one, I want to
see my soul.

Trixie hadn't stopped kicking her fence and I had
started to realize I was trapped by the wood too. It's
like Taylor said:

"Break out if you feel trapped. No matter who built your
cage."

Now, thinking of Taylor laughing as the woman she
is, and looking at Abel, eyes brown as ever and jaw
sharper than ever, I can't shake the feeling that I'm
about to kick at my fence harder and harder until
there's nothing left.

The first kick was denying the skin mountains and
covering them with Dad's T-shirts and flannels. The
second kick was begging Eve to cut my hair. Now
I'm just waiting for the third one.

"Just do it, Brennan." And so, I hand my diary over to him and he takes it.

And he hesitates, but starts reading. He looks into the depths of my soul and I let him.

Break The Fence

Like the hoofed creature,

Locked in planks and pillars.

Locked by men and God,

For wanting to turn like caterpillars.

We kick,

We tear.

We open,

But we stay.

For I don't know who holds her back.

But oh, I know it's the love that keeps me in.

For me and her could both be free.

But oh, I love the master within.

He stares,

He judges.

He controls,

But he loves.

Yearning like the golden goddess,

She left and turned.

She lived and returned.

For I long just like her.

[239]

Chapter Twenty-Nine

The urge to analyze it. The urge to ask a thousand questions. The urge to hold her close and consume her soul.

"Pony." Is all my vocal cords can produce. My mind is still cloudy, but I read over it again. Again and again and she doesn't stop me. I burn her perception of God, John, Trixie and Taylor into my brain. But most importantly, her perception of herself. I burn every single word into my brain and when I'm done, I hand the diary back to Alex.

She takes it in her hands and closes it. When she looks up from it and into my eyes, there's a view I've never seen before. There's an ocean in the blue. Sea water filling her eyes.

"Oh shit." That was supposed to be just a thought. She blinks and the water presses out of her eyes, rolling down her cheeks. She keeps her eyes closed.

"You okay, Pony?" *Fuck. How do I do this?* I've cried in front of Alex a couple times now. The last time was just a couple moments ago. But now that the roles are reversed, I don't know what to do.

I follow my instinct and hop down the table to take a step towards her. Before I know it, my hands are on the side of her thighs, my thumbs making circles on her jeans. She takes her hands to her face to wipe away the tears and opens her eyes again.

"Jesus." She tries to laugh it off. "I'm sorry."

"Oh. No no, don't be."

She lowers her head to look at my hands and I just now realize what I'm doing. I quickly pull them away and take a step back. My heart racing.

"Thank you."

"Yeah, I don't know why I did that." I shake my head quickly.

"No. I meant, thank you for doing that." *Oh.*

"Oh." *What's going on?*

"I uh…" She sniffs. "I wrote that when I was fifteen." *Thank you for switching the topic. Honestly.*

"Fifteen!?" It comes out louder than anticipated. When I was fifteen, I nearly killed myself. I didn't know you could put unspeakable thoughts into words and create art out of it.

"Yeah. I had the idea sitting inside my notebook for years and at fifteen I finally put it into actual words."

"Alex, this is genius. How?"

[241]

"Well, I went to school, didn't I?"

"Right." The jealousy stings my heart a bit. I take a moment to look at her face and as her red eyes and cheeks become the only thing I can see, I can't ignore the urge anymore.

"Do you uhm…like, do you want to talk about it? The poem, I mean."

"Do you want to hear?" *What kind of a question even is that?*

"Yes, please. If you don't mind." *Pa-the-tic.*

She nods and takes a deep breath in.

"You remember what T told us? When she was trial working and we were all in the back?" I've memorized it on the spot and have never even once forgotten a word.

"Break out if you feel trapped. No matter who built your cage. Your parents, other adults or yourself. Never love your master." I recite.

"Exactly."

"So…you feel trapped?" Sitting in this kitchen, in her house on this property, I can hardly imagine.

"Hm." She nods.

"How?"

She shoots me a look.

[242]

"No, not like that. I really mean: How do you feel trapped? Like, why?"

"It's…hard to say. I can't tell you." *Ouch.* We might just be study buddies after all. "It's just…there's some stuff and I can't handle it living here."

"Here, as in Folkspine? Or here, as in right here with your parents?"

"Both."

And then we're quiet and I think and Alex thinks. And I look at her and I see her lips part for a second. And she closes them again.

"Who trapped you? Who's your master?" I ask carefully and for a second, her eyes widen at how sudden the question shoots out of my mouth.

"Everyone. My parents, God, myself." She pauses and I give her the time to think about what she wants to say. "God gave Mom and Dad the pillars and planks. They built the fence, Dad maintains it and I stay in." My eyes wander to the wooden cross around Alex's neck.

"So, why don't you get out?" I could ask myself the same question. *Why am I still here, in Folkspine?*

"Like I wrote, love. It keeps me in. I love my family and I love God and I love Folkspine."

"Bullshit."

"What?" Again, her eyes widen.

"It's bullshit. I mean, yeah, you love them. But do you love yourself?" *Listen to you, Brennan. Talking big about self-love.*

"Yes. Maybe? I don't know."

"You should be your number one priority." *Where is all of this coming from?* "If you want to get out, then pack your bags and leave. Do it like Taylor did, like Glen did." *And take me with you.*

"You're insane. I could never."

"So, you'll just stay inside?"

"In the fence? Yeah. I know every blade of grass, every flower. It's my home."

"So, you'd rather stay in watching the grass grow, while there's a forest on the other side? You'd rather look at the thick trees waiting for you with unwritten stories, than go out and actually explore the woods?" We stare at each other. It takes three long seconds before Alex answers.

"Jesus. I've made a good poet out of you. Or it's just the weed." She jokes.

"Pony, I'm being serious." Though I *do* feel honored. Not about the weed part, but about me

[244]

being a good poet. My face doesn't light up, though.
We're talking serious shit right now.

"It's not like I don't want to leave. I simply *can't*."

"Why?"

She scoffs at the question.

"I can't just leave. I'm about to graduate, I'll take over the bar or the farm, I need to help my parents, I need to support my church. I have a life here."

"You have a life out there."

Chapter Thirty

The next day, I'm sitting at our booth in Hell's
Saddle. We didn't agree to meet up here today, but
still, I find myself glancing over at the door. Besides,
it's Saturday, so she's working. Which is exactly
why she'd normally already be here.

She'd get in with Elaine and start restocking and
cleaning up for band night. And when the band
arrives and starts setting up, she's the first one to go
up and recommend a song for later that night. Last
time it was "Born In The U.S.A." and I'm hoping
this night it won't be something by Springsteen.

Sorry, man.

"Waiting for your damsel, Loverboy?" Taylor mocks
me as she's mopping the floor, preparing it just to be
covered in beer and sick in a few short hours again.

"Shut up, Taylor." To my regret, it doesn't sound
like a joke. "And she's not a damsel."

"Jesus, alright." The mop stops in her hands. I let
out a sigh.

"I'm sorry, T." I genuinely mean it and she nods
with a smile.

"Wanna talk it out, Love?"

I wouldn't know what to say.

Since yesterday, I've been all over the place. When I
came home last night, I spent nearly hours writing in
the plastic chair in front of our trailer. Once I've
written everything down, all feelings a man isn't
supposed to have and all the poems I could think of,
I went outside for a walk downtown. And when I
came back to the trailer park, I still felt off. I saw the
light in Jeff's trailer was on, so I knocked. Barking
shot through the trailer park and I heard Jeff
screaming "Piss off!" I know he didn't mean me
knocking, but his dog.
"Howdy, night owl." He greeted me and
instinctively held the door open for me. We've done
this a couple times before. He knows it's me when
there's a knock on his door in the middle of the night
and he always lets me in.
I entered his realm and Mastiff jumped at me. When
I started coming over, I asked Jeff if he even had a
name. "Nah. I just call him critter or Mastiff."
"How creative." I answered. So, he's just been
Mastiff ever since.

After calling him off, Jeff quickly fetched every
empty beer bottle lying around.

"Sorry for that, son." He thinks his beer bottles
remind me of Dad. And they kind of do, but I don't
mind because I know Jeff is nothing like my dad.
Plus, Dad only drinks the cheap beer from cans.

"It's alright." I sat down on Jeff's couch. It always
feels familiar and more at home than my own bed.

"Ya good?" He let himself fall back next to me to pat
my thigh once.

"Why wouldn't I be?"

"Ya never come over in the middle of the night
when you're good. And ya reek like pot."

"Touché."

"So, what is it?"

I answered by letting out a loud sigh, indicating that
I either don't know or won't tell him.

"Ya weren't at the bar tonight." He switched the
topic.

"Did you need me?"

"Nah. Nothing happened. And even if, the Devil can
handle himself, eh?" He made a fist in the air.

"Yeah." I know he can.

"The little one wasn't there either." He eyed me from the side.

"Is that so?"

"Damn right." *Maybe he doesn't know.*

"The Beckham said ya went off together." *He does.*

"Damn you T."

Jeff chuckled in response. "Is that what this is about?" He stubbed my side with his elbow.

"Maybe. I don't know. Tonight's been…a lot." Besides everything surrounding Alex, there was also me going back to James' place and finding out my dad's a pedophile rapist. *Yeah, maybe Dad isn't the right word for him anymore. Maybe it never was.*

"Want a beer?" Jeff offered as his way of comforting. I took a second to think, but ended up accepting. Having a beer with Jeff feels different from getting drunk with the gang. It almost feels like I'm sitting next to a father who could be mine, on our porch as the sun sets over the front yard. Something I can only dream of. Something Alex has probably done hundreds of times. Though I've never seen her drink alcohol. I guess she and John treat themselves to a good glass of Sunny Delight every once a while.

So, he got up, fetched two bottles from his fridge, opened them with a lighter and sat back down, handing one over.

"Thanks." I said as we let our bottles collide.

We lifted the bottles to our mouths and pulled our heads back.

And while I let the cold liquid work its way down my throat, I thought of what Alex said to me at the bar. *"Did Jeffrey tell you to fight back?"* And my mind wandered from there to when we were standing outside of Hell's Saddle six years ago. When he held my shoulder after telling me I needed to stand up and not just at home – though I already used to do that even before Jeff told me. He said I should stand tall – if not for myself, then at least for my mom.

And I thought back to Leland's nose crushing under my knuckles, and how it now felt like I gave him part of his serving of an early karma for insulting Mom and killing off one of his customers – Alan. And I thought of the hate I felt for Leland and how pathetically small it looks next to the hate for my father.

"Didn't know ya smoked." Jeff broke my train of thought. "Pot, I mean."

"I don't. Stopped years ago."

"What about today?"

"I went over to James. I needed to talk to him, but he wouldn't say a word. So, we shared a joint until he opened that mouth of his."

"Hm." He nodded. No questions. That's what I love about him. Whenever I talk about my family, he doesn't push me. He just pushes about Alex, which is fine with me. It actually makes me more comfortable to open up, because he isn't so pushy about my family. So, I almost always end up telling Jeff what's on my mind. And the pot mixing with the alcohol and Jeff's comfort made me open up a bit last night.

"I uh…found out some stuff about-" *Who is he? Dad? My father?* "Dan." I stared into my beer bottle. I prefer bottles over cans. Doesn't feel so unreasonable like James' or Dan's drinking.

"It was pretty fucked up. I mean it's all the past," *I hope,* "but still…pretty fucked up. And then I thought back to some stuff I used to do when I was younger, which was fucked up too, so…"

"Tonight's been fucked up?"

"Tonight's been fucked up."

[251]

And that's all I told him. I couldn't tell him anything else. Not about my father and not about Alex. Dan is something I just have to ignore and Alex is something I need to figure out on my own.

I couldn't go any further and I didn't want to. I wrote poems and texts and random entries about it at home. I wrote down what I couldn't tell Alex, I wrote down what James told me and then tore the paper apart, I wrote and wrote until my hand hurt and there were no words left in me.

It's how I try to deal with the unthinkable. Initially, I wanted to learn how to write so I could compose a letter to Mom. And when I did learn how to write, I didn't write the letter. At the junkyard, I would've done it, even without a note to Mom. When I was younger, when I still tried to teach myself, I started writing one, but lost it and never picked up writing it again. It felt too heavy, the words wouldn't come. I would've left her thinking she messed up as a mom. But instead of the bullet, writing kind of ended up saving me. Alex's passion for writing saved me. Learning how to write saved me. Poetry saved me. Though I can't let go of the fantasy. I can't let go of the little piece of metal in my back pocket. I can't let death go but I can ignore it calling me. So now, when I feel like the world holds no home for me, I create a home in my notebook. I write what I wish I said or did, but couldn't.

I told everything I could to Jeff and the rest to paper. And there's nothing I would want Taylor to know. I love her, but I try to keep the people I show my soul to to a minimum.

I appreciate Taylors offer, but decline and I think she suspected that.

"Alright. You know where to find me if you change your mind."

"Thanks, T."

And off she goes to mop the floor. Dark hands with red tips grabbing the stick. And I notice how big her hands look around it and how she still manages to use them so gracefully like she's singing a song with her fingers. I glance over at Mom, rinsing glasses behind the counter. Her dark bob pinned back, eyes focused on nothing but her work. And how happy she seems when she's like that. Elaine is somewhere in the back, sorting through bottles, but I know she's probably squinting her eyes trying to calculate something in her head right now.

Then, finally, the bell chimes. I look up towards the door, only to be disappointed. A group of four men enters the bar. They're holding cases filled with instruments, microphones, cables, boxes and whatnot. It's the band for tonight.

"Evenin' ladies." One man holding a guitar case greets while tapping his hat. He didn't see me.

"Howdy." Taylor jokes at his gesture.

"Evening! Boss's in the back. She'll be here any minute." Mom informs the group. "You remember where everything is?" *Guess they've performed here before.*

"Yes, ma'am."

So, Mum and Taylor get back to work and the men make their way to the stage to set up. When they pass me, one of them addresses me.

"Gotten big, boy." I don't recognize him, but he seems to have seen me before.

"Evening, Sir." I greet him with a nod.

"So polite." He turns back towards Mom with a chuckle. She reacts by raising her shoulders and smiling.

When Elaine reemerges from the back, she places a box of bottles on the counter, greets the band and scans the bar.

"Abel, Honey?" She addresses me.

"Yes?"

"You know where my daughter is?"

"No. Sorry. I've been wondering too." I shrug my shoulders at her and she turns to go behind the counter.

"I'll call home." She grabs the phone and starts dialing. I watch her, waiting for any sign of Alex.

"Where are you? The band's already here." Elaine speaks to the device and I turn my ear towards her direction to hear better. "Call me when you get this." *She didn't pick up.* "And get your ass in here ASAP."

Chapter Thirty-One

The band is in the middle of "The Devil Went Down to Georgia," the air is red, there's chatting and clinking and laughing everywhere. I'm sitting at an empty booth, surprised there even is one at ten on a band-night. Jeff is here too, standing on the table of his booth, giving a performance not only for his buddies, but the whole bar. He taps his boots on the wooden table and sings along like he's telling an actual story. Since it's his song, the rest of the bar claps at him in rhythm. The band knows all this, so they just waited for Jeff to get in so they could give him the spotlight. It's almost like Jeff's tonight's band. I watch him with a bright smile on my face. *Lit up.* He occasionally looks at me with bright red cheeks and a smile so wide and genuine, it makes me want to cry. The three women are all standing behind the bar counter, with the youngest of them still missing. They, too, are clapping along in rhythm. Taylor's red lips are open to a holler, Mom and Elaine are leaning into each other, Jeff is having the time of his life, so is the rest of the bar, there's good music and good booze. It's a perfect Saturday night. But something's missing. Alex is missing and I wish there'd be Springsteen playing so I'd know she's here somewhere. She's never skipped a Saturday to work. More importantly, she would never ever miss a band-night. No matter if she's working or not. Every single Saturday, she ends up at Hell's Saddle. But not tonight. I look around and she's just not here. I've been glancing over at Elaine the whole night to try and see if she's got a look on her face. Anything indicating where Alex could be, if she called at some point when I wasn't listening or if she came in when I wasn't watching the door. But she's acting like nothing unusual is going on. Then again, it's band-night, so maybe she's just too stressed to think about anything, but work right now. *She's perfected bar owner mode.*

When the song ends, the bar breaks into loud laughter and whistling.

"We expect the same from you when we come back next year, Jeffrey." The singer lets Jeff know through the microphone.

"Please, it's *Devil!*" He loudly corrects him while making horns on his head with his pointer fingers. The bar's cheering increases, Jeff sits back down and the band starts the next song. I listen for a second, waiting for Springsteen, Parton or Denver. Anything indicating Alex made a wish to the band. But when "Free Bird" starts playing, I know there's not a chance Alex could've picked that. Jeff almost throws himself off his booth to whistle at the band, to which the singer reacts with a "We knew you'd dig this!" I, however, get up from my booth and make my way to the counter.

"Will you give me some beers, T?" I shout over the noise. *One won't do much for me.*

"Sure, Love." This is not the first time I've asked her to tap me a beer. I never ask Elaine and definitely would never ask Mom, though. Since I'm legally allowed, I've been having some occasional beers at Hell's Saddle. But tonight, I need more than the occasional beer. She turns to the tap and fills two glasses with the golden liquid. I thank her as she places them down in front of me.

"Still troubles?" She carefully asks and leans over the counter.

"Kind of."

"Well then. Hope the beers help." She gives me a wink and gets back to work.

[258]

"Yeah." I say to myself, grab the beers and walk past the counter to the beaded curtain. *I need to sit down on the leather, watch the blue neon light above me and listen to the muffled noise on the other side. And I need to get drunk.* The thoughts surrounding Dan still circle through my mind, James circles through my mind, Alan and Glen, the junkyard. Alex. After not getting enough sleep last night, I'm not feeling like myself. At least that's what I tell myself, the reason is.

And just as I turn right into the blue, my eyes are greeted with another blue. Alex's blue.

"Jesus fucking Christ!" I almost spill the beers.

"You shouldn't swear His name like that." She jokingly lifts a finger and I smile with a sigh. *She's here and she seems okay.*

"You scared the shit out of me."

"Turn around so I can see the stain."

I stare at her and she stares at me and then we break out into a laugh. And just like that, the circling in my mind stops. After gathering herself, she nods at the beers in my hand.

"That for me?"

"Actually, I wanted to get drunk back here. But..." I take another look at her eyes. "I don't feel the need anymore." I stretch one hand out and she takes one of the glasses. I sit down next to her on the couch, not on opposite sides, but so our legs are almost touching.

"Didn't know you drank." I glance over at her.

"There's a lot you don't know." She jokes, but it hurts a little. Then, she raises her glass and I do the same. The beers clink and we each take in the liquid.

"I didn't see you come in." I question.

"Came here straight after school." *It's Saturday.*

"It's Saturday."

"Then I came here right after preparing for *your* school." She doesn't sound convincing, but I don't push further. I know there's no use in it. However, Alex is acting weird. Still, I want to know how exactly she got in.

"How? The place is locked until your mom comes in." I remind her.

"I've got a spare key." She smirks at me.

"That's so unfair." And to that, she chuckles. "Your Mom's been looking for you, you know. Does she know you're back here?"

"Nah. She rushed through the hall a bunch of times,

but you know how she is. So focused on getting to one place, that she doesn't look around when going there." *There's some poetry in that.*

"So, why are you back here and not…out there?" I'm careful with this question. Staying in the lounge and not being in the bar to work or bother the band is not like her.

"Needed to do some thinking and any place else was too quiet." *Exactly. Though Hell's Saddle isn't exactly loud without guests or our moms and T. Well, I guess Alex had her juke and that's all she needed.*

"I thought you liked silence."

"Not when I'm alone." *I get that.*

"I get that."

"Why are *you* here?" Now, it's my turn.

"Needed to do some thinking? Or try and stop myself from thinking." I gesture at the glasses.

"Right." She raises her glass back to her mouth and empties it in one go. I watch her and follow by doing the same.

"Another round?" *I've never seen her drink and now she's trying to chug down beer?*

"You sure?"

"Think I can't handle it?"

[261]

"Another round it is." I answer and she gives me a satisfied smirk. I take her empty glass and get up to leave the lounge.

At the counter, Mom looks at me with question marks in her eyes, but I wave her off. I wait for Taylor to stand in front of me and when she does, I whisper shout a "Hey, T" at her. She turns towards me and leans over the counter. Fabric. I look away.

"Will you make me four?" I ask her with surprising embarrassment. I know how Elaine handles employees and family drinking at Hell's Saddle. Two drinks are on the house, then you've got to pay. So, I put my hand in my pocket, past the familiar small piece of metal I always carry and pull out the last bill I have to hand it over to her.

"Woah. Slow down, boy." She tells me.

"It's not just for me, don't worry." She squints at the beaded curtain. *Does she know Alex is in the back?*

"Alright then." She grins at me and ends up tapping four beers for me. *Does she know?* Taylor is hard to analyze. Maybe because she hid for so long. She places the full foamy glasses in front of me and grabs the bill from me.

"You're a gem." I tell her as I take two glasses in each hand.

"Love you too." She answers as I leave.

Chapter Thirty-Two

"Two each? Man, you really wanna take the edge off, huh?" *As if three beers in total could ever mean that.* I don't answer.

"Want some money for it?" Of course, she knows the rules too. She's already got her hand fiddling in her front pocket.

"Absolutely not." I answer, sitting back down and handing half of the beers over to her. We both put one down on the ground and take a sip from the other. What follows is another comfortable silence. We sit, we listen, we watch, we drink. And I think. The circling is back, but not as fast as before. The booze helps and Alex definitely does too.

"I uh…"

"Hm?"

"James told me some stuff." *No no, wait. This is something between me and my notebook and maybe Jeff.*

"Okay." She's like Jeff. Low-key and calm.

"Dan, he- he did some stuff." *Stop it, man. This isn't for Alex.*

I look down into my half-empty glass. I feel her eyes on my face, but I can't turn to meet them. For the first time, I can't meet the blue.

"Stuff *to* him." *Don't scare her with this.*

"James?"

"Yeah…" I sound weak. Pathetic. *Once again.*

I feel her hand on my leg. She's placed it on my thigh, rubbing it with her thumb, like I did yesterday.

"To *you* too?" The question stings my chest.

"No. He just hurts me, that's all. I mean he hurt James too, but that's a different pain."

I see her nodding. Her hand still on the denim, the heat flowing through it, onto my skin, into my body and to my heart.

I place my hand on top of hers and give it a squeeze. For a moment, we stay like this. I look up to meet her eyes, to get lost in the blue and she lets me. For five full seconds. Five seconds of leaving everything behind. Internally, I'm begging her to say something. Anything. And she parts her lips, takes a breath in, but closes her mouth again.

"You know, I know we're just study buddies, but you can tell me stuff."

"We're not." *Ouch?*

"Oh. Sorry." Again, I don't care about our rules.

"No. I mean, we're not *just* study buddies. You're the first real friend I've ever had." *Say that again?*

"Say that again."

Her eyes widen and she takes a sharp breath in.

"You're my first friend ever."

"We're friends?" And again, I'm weak and feel like a kid. And again, there's sea water forming in the corners of my eyes, but I push it away.

"Yeah." And I nod and we smile at each other.

"And I *will* tell you. When I'm brave enough."

"Of course. I'll wait."

Chapter Thirty-Three

Walking back into the bar with Alex is a form of art in of itself. She's stumbling left and right into chairs and customers. I hold her by the arm to lead her away from the crowd, which is exactly how I expected it to be – impossible. The dance floor is full of moving people, with no end of the mass in sight. The band plays Parton's "Jolene" and I pray to whoever is up above that Alex doesn't recognize the song. But of course, to no avail.

"Dolly! Abel they're playing Dolly!" She slaps my arm a bunch of times.

"Yeah Pony, I know. Come on." I try to lead her towards the door without getting caught by our moms, but she wiggles herself out of my hold and makes her way to the dance floor. She stops right in front of the stage, facing the band and singing along. I see how the lead singer looks at her all confused, so I'm guessing he didn't recognize her like he did with me and won't scream her name into the mic like he did with Jeffrey. Alex really does a pretty good job of not looking like she did years ago. I try to be sensible and serious and pull her away, but something in my mind is telling me to have fun for once. Because for once, I'm already having fun and it's not because of the booze. So, I walk up to her and watch her for a moment to reconsider. *Ah, fuck it.* My hand reaches out to her shoulder and turns her around.

"Hey!" She shouts at me. "Oh. It's you."

"Sorry to disappoint." I feel a smirk on my face.

"Nah. You're quite alright actually." She taps both her hands on my shoulders and rests them there.

"I don't know how to do this."

"Yeah, I figured." She laughs and it takes away the cringe. "Let me."

And just in that second, I feel the singer's eyes on me. And to my luck, he doesn't address me through the mic. But what he does isn't exactly any better. Because the band switches songs. To "I'm On Fire." *Of course, Springsteen. I guess Alex simply looks like she loves him. The band didn't need to recognize her to know that.*

"Oh-" She gasps with wide eyes.

"No." I protest and shake my head.

"Oh yes. It's too late now. We're already swaying, see?" And I *do* see. We're moving side to side, definitely not steadily, but we're doing it. We lock

eyes for a couple seconds – three, to be exact –
before she breaks off the contact. She looks away, at
the band, the red and green lights above or at the
others who have joined the slow dancing. And after
a couple seconds, she looks back at my eyes. I feel
her warm hands on my shoulders and realize that
only one of mine rests on her shoulder, while the
other hangs awkwardly at the side of my body. I
think back to how the guys do it in the movies, so I
raise the awkward hand to her hips.

"Ah, now-" She removes it with hers and places it
on her free shoulder, so we're mirroring each other.
"Sorry."

"Don't worry 'bout it." She smiles.

I listen to Springsteen without hating the song,
because I'm doing what kids do. I'm drunk with my
friend, dancing to live music in a bar and looking
towards the blue. And it feels like some higher being
went ahead and tore out a couple chapters in our
book, because how is it that yesterday I was just
Alex's student, and today we're so close to each
other – physically and emotionally – that I want to
kiss her. But I don't. Because we're drunk. Because
she's drunk. And she's been acting like there's a lot

on her mind and I don't want to add to that. Besides, this is already the best thing I've ever done. We don't need to go higher.

I've got this weird feeling in my stomach that for the first time, I'm honestly and truly, perfectly happy. And I see that joy reflected in Alex's eyes, which gives me the highest validation I've ever gotten. We continue on like this. Dan nowhere near my mind, not the junkyard, not the gang, not Mom. Just the music, the motion, the lights, the warm hands and the blue. Alex sings her heart out and I admire her. She smiles, which makes me smile. And like on cue, everyone on the dance floor, except me, joins in with the "Oooh" at the end of the song.

"You too, Brennan." She tells me and I push away the shame and join the rest of the bar. People start closing up to us, vocalizing and swaying, and Alex ends up stumbling into one of the other dancing guests. He's solo dancing and singing more off-key than anyone else, but wholeheartedly. As Alex bumps into him, he turns around.

"EY! Watch it ya fuck-" And we both stop dancing as he looks us up and down. "Well, I'll be damned."

When I realize she stumbled into Jeff, I stare at him with wide eyes and mouth agape.

"So sorry, Jeff." I hastily apologize. "She's a bit-"

"Jeffrey!" Yeah, she needs a couple seconds to register what's going on. But now that she has, she gives him a big hug around the neck. He gasps at the impact, but slightly hugs her back. He leans over her shoulder and whispers to me.

"Little one's drunk?"

"Not just her." I try my best not to keep on swaying, but even without Alex moving me from side to side, I can't seem to stop.

"Well, you're taking it better than her."

"Practice." I tell him.

She finally lets go of him and he moves past her to turn me and him away from her. He pats me on the shoulder with a wide grin, the grin he has when he's drunk and something is really amusing.

"You two have fun." Next, he leans in for a whisper. "And stay *safe*."

I push him off, but can't suppress a smile, and he disappears in the crowd. Alex is still swaying even though the song has ended and I grab her by the arm.

"Come on. Let's get."

"What!? Why? I wanna stay."

"What you want is a glass of water and a good night's sleep. Also, song's over."

"I'll ask for another one. "I've always been crazy," come on!"

"Is that a song or a statement?" I tease while dragging her along with me through the crowd – while there still is one to shield us from the counter – and after a few more stumbles and a lot of Alex's complaints, we emerge from the masses. I avoid looking towards the counter and focus on reaching the front door.

"Abel!" *Of course.* I turn around to Mom facing me from across the room. Knowing there's no use in escaping now, I pull Alex and me towards the counter.

"Eve! Hiyaaa!" As we come closer, Alex waves at her, almost slapping me in the face.

"Hiya, Love." Mom waves back irritated. Guess *she* didn't know about Alex being in the back. I can see how she finds drunk Alex funny. Still, she's worried.

"Hey Mom, can you not tell-"

"Alex!" *Too late. Elaine saw us.* "Where the hell were you?" She shouts at her daughter.

"Takin' the edge off." Alex raises one hand, making the Sign of Horns. I slap her hand so she lets it fall.

"I'm so sorry, Elaine." I try my best to apologize. Now, Taylor joins the conversation.

"So those six rounds I tapped were for you and *her?*" She points the cloth in her hand at Alex, but addresses me. Guess T didn't know either. Alex really wanted to be alone. *And then I stepped in.*

"Yeah." I admit. Alex ended up insisting I get us more beer and handed me the money for it. I couldn't decline her look and the idea of continuing my plan and getting drunk seemed reasonable.

"Six!?" Mom exclaims.

"You did this?" Elaine shoots Taylor a look.

"I did my job." Taylor throws her hands up in defense.

I try my best to form a proper, sober-sounding sentence. "Elaine, it really wasn't T's fault." *How do I tell her it was Alex's idea to get drunk and not mine? Then again, I don't want to snitch on her.*

"Whatever. I don't care. I've got enough to do here." Elaine's mad at me. She doesn't need to swear to let me know. "Take her home." She demands and I need a second to realize the order was directed at me.

"What, me?"

"Yes, you. You got her drunk, you deal with it. I can't handle this right now and you seem fine to walk her." *She's right. Besides a few stumbles and almost babbling, I feel pretty good.* And I know even without Elaine telling me to, I wouldn't have let Alex walk home alone like that.

"Uh…okay." Before I can turn both of us around to leave through the door, I feel Mom's hand on my shoulder. I face her and she leans into me.

"You be careful. Got it? Don't get in trouble."

"Got it, Mom. Don't worry." I calmly try to reassure her.

I lock eyes with her and then search the bar for Jeff to do the same with him. He winks at me and waves goodbye. I wave back with a smile.

"Alright. Let's go, Pony." I tell her and at the sound of the bell, Alex turns away from me and to the bar.

"Bye guys!" She shouts. They all turn and wave at us. The regulars with smiles on their faces – which makes me regret getting Alex drunk at the one place where almost everyone knows her *and* me – and the other guests in confusion. Everyone waves except Mom and Elaine. We leave with a chime and everyone knowing the towns princess and the town's fuck up's son are leaving together. Or the Protector of The Jukebox and the Devil's right-hand man. *I like that one better.*

Chapter Thirty-Four

It takes us a while to get to her place, but a full hour later, we're back at the junction formed by Main Road and the dirt trail. The moon's still full and lighting the way. I haven't let go of Alex's arm, even though some of the alcohol must've worn off by now. After all, it's chilly out, we've walked two miles and an hour has passed.

"You good?" I ask her as she burps almost directly into my face.

"Oh my." She covers her mouth with her hand. "I'm so sorry." But she laughs.

"Don't worry 'bout it." I let out a heartfelt chuckle at the fact I finally get to be the one to say it.

We make our way over the dirt trail and as we reach the meadow, Alex shouts "Hiya, Trixie!"

No one answers, so she shouts again. The only response is a distant barking coming from the barn.

"I think Trixie's turned into a dog." Alex tells me.

I try to reassure her with a "No. That's Jewel."

"Right, Jewel." She remembers. "Where's Trixie?"

"After what you told me last night, I suppose she's in the barn."

"Oh, I wanna see her! Come on!" She fiddles her way out of my arm and grabs my hand before pacing towards the barn. I laugh at her as I'm letting her pull me with her. *A glimpse of freedom.*

After reaching the barn, she lets go of my hand to open the gate. She juddles at it, but it won't come loose. The barking inside continues and I hear some occasional moos.

"Is it locked?" I ask her.

"Damn straight it's locked." She gives the wooden gate a kick with her boot. "Will you go get the key?" She faces me with big eyes. I take a deep breath.

"Where?"

"Dad's jacket."

"Yeah, no. I'm not gonna rummage through your dad's jacket." *No matter how drunk I am, I don't mess with dads.*

"Pussy." I know it's a joke, but it still sets my heart into a reflexive acceleration.

"Okay. I'll get it. Just…stay here." I grab her by the shoulders and pull her down so she can sit down on the ground. After making herself somewhat comfortable, she searches for her key in her jacket and after what feels like eternity, hands it to me.

"In the hall. Left side. Denim jacket." Is all she can say.

"Got it." I answer. After looking at her for a few seconds to make sure she's fine right there and now, I make my way to the front door of the Goodfellow's house. I carefully fumble with the key and twist it in the door's lock until it quietly opens. Inside, I flick on the light like Alex did last night and turn left. Above from where we placed our shoes last night, a denim jacket rests hanging next to a leather one. The leather one must be Elaine's, since she didn't come in wearing a jacket today and John definitely isn't the guy to wear a leather jacket. Same goes for Alex – though she'd look real good in one. *I have to lend her mine sometime.* With guilt, I put my hand into the pockets of John's and search for the keys. When the cold metal meets my fingers, I grab it and pull it out. Then, I turn around and leave into the room on the right. Inside the kitchen, I take a glass from the cupboard that Alex took two from yesterday. The hallway casts enough light, so I can orient myself through the kitchen. I move over to the sink and fill the glass with tap water. When I'm done, I leave the kitchen, turn left, flick off the light and quietly close the door behind me. I twist Alex's key in the opposite direction and pull it out.

Back at the barn, I see Alex hasn't moved a muscle. I throw her key and John's keys at her so they carefully land in her lap. She claps in response and then stretches one hand out to me. I take it in mine and pull her up from the ground. When she's up, I stretch my other hand out to her and she takes the glass of water from it. Immediately, she chugs the whole contents down and hands it back to me. I place it on the ground.

"Thank you."

"Of course." I smile at her.

She turns towards the barn gate and somehow manages to push the key into its lock, twisting it. The gate opens and immediately, a beige-furred creature comes rushing out of it. Alex opens her arms to embrace it.

"Hiya, Jewel." She greets her as Jewel licks her face. The dog then jumps back down and circles me while barking.

"Shh, girl! Zip it!" Alex tells her off. I stretch my hand out towards Jewel so she can sniff me and just like that, the barking stops.

"Huh. She likes you."

"I like her too." I give her a scratch behind the ear. Then, Alex takes my hand again and leads us into the barn. She searches for something on her left and after a few seconds, the barn lights up. Loud moos shoot through the air, accompanied by a whinny in the distance.

"Calm down, ladies." Alex orders and the noise decreases a bit. The barn is filled with cows on the left and right. The middle creates a pathway, so one can freely walk from one side of the barn to the other. Piles of hay rest on the top floor.

"Should we even be in here?" It feels like we've broken into a random barn in the middle of the night, rather than simply checking out her father's barn.

"Oh, absolutely not. Dad will freak out."

"What!?"

"No one's allowed in the barn without asking Dad first."

"But-" *Don't mess with dads.*

"It's fiiine. Don't worry 'bout it. He sleeps like a rock. Also, Jewel will alarm us." *And then what?* She waves me off and leads me through the barn. I look over my shoulder to see Jewel sitting at the open gate, facing the outside, watching it like she's on guard. I follow Alex without hesitation. Still, this doesn't feel right.

"Pony, maybe we shouldn't." But she doesn't answer. We cross the barn with furred creatures to our left and right. Some moo as we pass them, while the others mind their own business or continue sleeping.

"Pony." Still no answer, so I give up with a smile and a shake of my head.

At the end of the barn, we come to a halt. Alex lets go of my hand and closes up to a stable.

"Trixie, girl!" A large mass of brown with white dots gets up from the ground, shakes its head, neighs and then faces us. Alex places both her hands on the horse's head and gives it a stroke.

"So, she's the fence kicker?" I ask Alex.

"We both are. She started it, though." I stare at the both of them and for a second, they weirdly look like sisters. "You can pet her, you know." Alex turns to face me and I can finally see the blue again.

"Uh…"

"Never pet a horse before?"

"Never even been close to one before." I answer.

"Man lives in Colorado and ain't even pet a horse." She mumbles to the animal and takes my hand in hers. She places it on the horse's snout. "Here." She lets go of my hand and I'm left with the warm touch of fur under my palm. I move my hand up and down and Trixie pushes her head into my hand. I smile at her.

"She's cool." I tell Alex.

"Yeah, she is. That's why she's my muse." *Hoofed creature.*

Chapter Thirty-Five

"What's up there?" I ask, pointing at the top floor. Alex and I are lying on a thin blanket each, inside Trixie's stable, leaning into her warm body. Alex grabbed the blankets for us, so we don't have to lie in the dirty hay. Trixie's slow breathing as she's sleeping underneath us and Alex's head leaning into mine introduce unknown peace to my heart. I couldn't say for how long we've been lying here. It could be an eternity, it could be just a small fleeting minute.

"The hayloft." She answers calmly, sounding almost sober again. "I'm not allowed up there."

"Why?"

"Dad says it's too dangerous."

"It's hay. What's dangerous about hay?" I question.

"Not the hay. The height. He says *I could fall.*" She mocks her dad.

"You're eighteen."

"That's what I keep telling him."

"Hm." I nod and for a brief moment, we fall silent again, studying the science of connection. Alex breaks it first and I certainly don't mind.

"Hey, Brennan."

"Yeah, Pony?"

"Let's go up."

I lift my head to look down at her face. She lifts hers to give me her eyes, combined with a smile. *Damn.*

"You said you're not allowed."

"I know what I said. But I don't care." *Since when's she a rulebreaker?*

"But your dad."

"Don't care." She repeats and gets up. Trixie blows air through her nose at the motion, but quickly falls back asleep. I try not to disturb her and carefully get up too to stand next to Alex.

I don't like this. But when Alex turns to face me, eyes filled with curiosity, I can't help but follow her lead. So, we leave Trixie's stable, the blankets still with her, and make our way over to a wooden ladder leading up to the hayloft.

Before putting her foot on the first step, she turns towards me. Uncertainty written in her face. I shrug my shoulders, indicating she should decide for herself. *And that I'll follow her, no matter what.*

I hold the ladder steadily with both hands as Alex climbs up. I watch her feet, making sure she's got a steady grip. *At least she's not stumbling anymore.* Once she's up, I let go of the ladder and wait. Alex sticks her head over the edge to face me standing on the ground.

"You coming up?" *Again, no need to tell me twice.* I place my foot on the first step of the ladder and slowly make my way up. At the top, Alex stretches her hand out to me and I take it. She pulls me up onto the hayloft with her. Once I've got a proper stand on the wooden planks, I lean over the edge to look at the distance between us and the ground. *Feels like twenty-five feet, could be just fifteen.*

"Getting down is gonna be fun." I tell her.

"Oh, come on. We've made it up, we'll make it down. Plus, we're practically sober." I turn around to face her.

"Are we?" The question is genuine.

"Eh." She shrugs and we both chuckle.

As expected, the hayloft is filled to the brim with hay, leaving little space for the two of us to move around. The walls are just tall enough for us to walk around upright. We move forward along the edge of the wooden platform, looking down at the cows and Trixie. Everyone's gone back to sleep and I'm starting to realize how far into the night we must be. When we left, Hell's Saddle was still busy, so it couldn't be too late. Still, the only noise around is the breathing of the heavy animals underneath us and the occasional cricket in the meadow. Jewel still seems to be sitting at the barn's gate, watching the night pass by.

"So…how's it feel?"

"What?" She's walking ahead.

"Rule breaking."

"Hmm…not as thrilling as I thought." She doesn't turn around. Instead, she focuses on keeping a steady step and watching the inside of the barn below us. I focus on following her and occasionally glance over at the open gate. I don't want John to wake up in the middle of the night to see his barn open and lit. *What if he sees me in here with his drunk daughter? What if Hell's Saddle closed now and Elaine is on her way here?*

"I don't get it." She pulls me from my thoughts.

"What?" I ask her.

"T."

"What? Why are you thinking 'bout T?"

"Just..." She sits down, letting her legs dangle from the hayloft and I follow. I sit down next to her and let my leg touch hers.

"Why'd she come back?"

"Alex, you're not making sense." *Honestly, where is this coming from?*

"Think about it. She left 'cause she was hated here. The town didn't want her...people like her. So, why'd she even come back?" *Good point, actually.*

"I don't know. Maybe inside, she felt Folkspine was still her home? But you'll have to ask her yourself."

"Yeah." Her eyes are fixed at Trixie down in her stable.

"You okay?" She doesn't answer. She doesn't look at me. "Pony?"

After a moment, she simply shakes her head from side to side. *Okay.* Again, I place my hand on her thigh. This time, it doesn't happen out of instinct, but because I intentionally make it happen, looking – *longing* for the contact.

"Pony." I look at her, waiting for her eyes to meet mine. They don't. "Please just tell me already. What

[287]

is up with you?" I know my curiosity isn't the result of alcohol, but the genuine deep urge to know Alex's secret she's keeping in her soul. *Because I want to know that soul.*

"No." She stings my heart once more. *I don't have the right to be so pushy and then feel hurt at the fact she won't tell me. But man, I just want to help.*

"Will you wait for me?" She whispers.

"Of course, I'll wait." *Do I wait for you to* tell me *or do I wait for* you?

She finally looks me in the face. In the eyes. They're not teary, but about to be.

"Thank you."

And then, after five full seconds, her eyes break contact. Alex's gaze lowers, but I keep my eyes on hers. Because I want to keep the contact. But I don't force her eyes to meet mine. Then, her hand touches mine, still resting on her thigh. And my heart beats a little faster and I breathe deep and quick and I feel like I have to run away or fight back, but I know I don't need to because I'm with Alex. And I realize her eyes have lowered onto my mouth. And I part my lips a little, taking in a deep breath. A thousand thoughts rushing through my mind, but only one of them remains. *I will wait for Alex. No matter how long. I want her and I want her now, but I will wait.* And she looks back up into my eyes and the blue has never ever looked so vibrant. And the blue comes closer and then, Alex hides it behind her lids. And now my gaze lowers onto her mouth. Her lips part in the same way. And she's the one to make hers touch mine. And the fight-or-flight mode intensifies. *I don't have to wait.* So, I push my lips closer to hers and the fight-or-flight mode turns into something completely different. I'm not having goosebumps because I feel like I need to fight back, but because this is something truly good.

Something Alex thinks I'm worthy of.

Book Three

The Fence

"The only thing stopping us is ourselves."

The Female of the Species, Mindy McGinnis

Chapter Thirty-Six

Abel's hand feels so familiar. Just like when I held it in the back after Leland disturbed the bar. In those six years, I haven't forgotten the touch and his hand hasn't changed. Well, it's bigger now, but still cold, rough on the back, soft on the palm, old blood and dead ripped skin around his thumbs. What's new is the feeling of his lips entangled with mine. And, though this is the best thing I have ever done, I regret not telling him first. He deserves to know before I cross this line. But it's too late now. I can't go back and maybe I don't want to. *What if, if I told him, he wouldn't have pressed his lips into mine?* I shake off the thought and focus on his body, his taste. Beer, deep rooted pain, doubt and a glimpse of freedom. Maybe even love.

We don't stop. I keep on kissing him, because he should decide when it's too much. He should be the one to decide when to pull back. *I* can't get enough of this. And I feel like, if we stop, I can't hold back anymore and end up telling him the truth.

He doesn't stop, though. Instead, his other hand moves up my back towards my neck. There, he holds me gently. I try to push our lips even closer together, to the point where we break the laws of physics and end up intertwining our souls. *Tell him.* I work my tongue around the opening of our lips, waiting for a reaction. And thank the Lord, Abel opens his lips and takes me in. *Tell him.* We create art, we write a poem with our tongues and lips. A poem I couldn't write down on paper. A poem I want to read over and over. *Tell him.* My tongue tastes his. And suddenly it tastes salt. And I feel a sting in my heart and realize it isn't him that tastes like salt. I'm crying.

He seems to realize and pulls back quickly. His hand leaves my neck and his mouth leaves mine. He stares at me, deep into my eyes.

"Alex?" And the crying doesn't stop. The salt keeps coming and coming and it turns from a puddle to an ocean. "Hey, woah." He cups my face in his soft palms, just like Eve sometimes does with his face. "What's wrong, Pony? Did I do something wrong? I'm so sorry." I shake my head loose from his touch and it hurts.

"Don't pretend you don't know." I can't look him in the eyes.

"Don't know what?" He backs off.

I take a deep, shaky breath. *Tell him, tell him, tell him. Tell him now or never let anyone see your soul.*

"The hair, Dad's clothes...the poem?" He looks at me, raised eyebrows, waiting for me to go on.

"Ugh!" I groan.

"What? What did I do?" *Looked into my soul and didn't recognize what you saw.*

"It's..."

"Pony, please?" His eyes are wide open, pupils big. He takes his hands back to my face, wiping away my tears with both thumbs, the salt probably burning the wounds around his nails. And it feels like this is my only chance. My only chance to save myself because I feel like if I don't do it now, I will never be able to collect the strength again.

"Taylor. I'm like her."

Chapter Thirty-Seven

"Taylor. I'm like her."

"What do you mean?" I know what it means. I just need to hear the words out loud. My thumbs are wet with tears. Salty water flowing into the cracks of my open skin. I never want my hands having to touch Alex's tears ever again, but if the blue will ever start to leak again, *I* want to be the one to collect it.

"I think I'm a boy." I've never seen Alex scared. I didn't even know it was possible for Alex to feel fear. I've been swimming in it ever since I was born to be the son of Dan. But Alex? Never. That was up until now.

"You *think*?"

"I know."

"Then say it." I push.

"I'm a boy." He nods, eyes still not on mine. "I'm not me. I've been living in this…darkness. And it's like, when Taylor spoke to us that day, she lit a fire. Like she gave me a torch that's lighting up everything." The blue dances in a zigzag in Alex's eyes, looking around the barn, the air, but never at me. "And ever since then, I can see and I look at me and I'm wrong and I feel into me and I'm wrong and God thinks I'm wrong and my family… I just- I can't live in the shadow of my father's daughter anymore."

And without thinking, I pull Alex in. My hands still framing the face I've analyzed for so many years. And we produce one long verse with our lips. When I pull back, tears still roll down his face, but no new ones are forming.

"You're not wrong. You're perfect."

And I smile and I look at him and his blue and let it consume me. And, though his eyes scream anguish and doubt, for a second, his mouth forms into a smile. When it drops, my heart does the same.

"I'm tired of the dark, Abel. I want to explore the forest outside the fence. No more watching the grass grow."

"Okay, Pony. We'll work it out, yeah? You're not alone."

"You're not gonna leave me?"

I press my forehead to his. "Nah. You've seen me cry too many times. I can't just let you wander along and tell everybody what a pussy I am."

And to my luck, he chuckles. So, I know the joke worked and he knows there's no need to feel embarrassed about tears.

Chapter Thirty-Eight

"Does Taylor know?" Abel whispers close to my face, hay sticking to his long hair.

"No. Now shut it." I shush him. When tires hauled up the gravel and dirt of our trail and Jewel's barking shot through the air, waking up the whole barn, we ducked deeper into the hay. Abel and I lay flat on our stomachs on the hard wooden floor of the hayloft. The engine turns off, we hear a door open and slamming shut and footsteps that come closer with each second. Jewel keeps barking into the night, Trixie neighs and some of the girls moo. I press my eyes together, waiting for the moment to be over. Then I hear a familiar voice coming from the entrance to the barn.

"Quiet girl, it's Mom. Shh." And the barking stops. Mom's back from work, so I can only guess it must be around half past one, maybe two. All the other animals follow Jewel's lead and quiet down.

"Did you see Alex come by?" Mom talks to Jewel in her baby voice, so the dog knows she's being talked to. I take in a sharp breath and feel Abel's hand touch my shoulder. The dog doesn't make a single sound. *Good girl, Jewel.*

"Hm." She says and it sounds like she turns back around to leave the barn. With a *click*, the whole barn is covered in darkness. "Goodnight, girls."

I hear the gate rolling shut and feel for the keys in my pocket. *At least she can't lock us in.*

Abel and I both wait for a few moments before allowing ourselves to sigh. After getting accustomed to the moonlight creeping through the wooden cracks, we get up from the floor and Abel giggles at me in relief. I don't feel like giggling and I don't feel relieved.

"Dang."

"Yeah. Pretty close." He says.

"This is bad."

"We didn't get caught, though." Again, he touches my shoulder.

"And? Dad will know I stole his keys and got into the barn. What if Mom checks my room now and I'm not there and she comes back and finds us up here? What if she'll tell Dad? He's so picky with people being in here. I'm so fucked."

"Okay, chill out a moment. First of all, *you* didn't steal any key. *I* did."

"That's worse." I interrupt, but he doesn't react.

"Second of all, just blame it on the alcohol."

"You can't blame mistakes on drugs. You of all people should know that." He looks taken aback, but I can see he knows I'm right.

"Ugh! What do we do?!"

"We can stay here. You can say you wanted to see Trixie, which is true, and that we both fell asleep with her. She didn't walk to the back. She didn't check if we were with Trixie just now. Let's just go back down to her and spend the night." His mouth says one thing, but his eyes say "I want to stay with you."

"We can't stay here. It's fucking cold." And it is. It's autumn after all and deep into the night. I raise my hand to the zipper on my jacket, only to realize it's already all the way up.

"Trixie is warm. We've got blankets. We've got...us. It's a good plan."

"Dad will know we snuck in."

"And what will he do? I don't think John is the type of father to throw a punch."

My heart skips a beat because Abel is right. Neither of us need to seriously fear my dad. But he definitely needs to fear his.

"You're annoyingly smart, you know that?"

"I know. So much wasted potential." He jokes. Because he *is* smart. Maybe smarter than me. Only he never got to use it academically.

He gestures towards the ladder, indicating I should go ahead. "Gentlemen first, or whatever."

I snort, simply because it's such a bad joke and maybe because the alcohol is still working a bit. But I don't make my way over to the ladder. I don't feel any impulse to climb down this ladder. I don't want to leave the hayloft. I mean, yeah, we'll be hurled up with Trixie if we get down now. But I feel like, up here, we're different. We're finally without any filters in our actions and words. So instead of climbing down, I fling myself at him. I hug him tight and for a second, he doesn't move. I hear him taking in a sharp breath. And then, his arms close around me and we sink deep into the hay.

Chapter Thirty-Nine

Alex collides with me and I collide with the hay behind us. A metallic thump muffles underneath the dried grass and a sharp and hard material digs into my back.

"Ah-"

Alex pulls back and looks at me, baffled. "What?"

I slightly push him off me. The action hurts.

"Landed on something." I turn towards the hay and search through it with my hands. Alex joins in until we've pushed the hay to the side to uncover a worn-down metal toolbox.

"What is it?" I ask Alex, who's now sitting back down across from me.

"Don't know. Never seen it before." He lifts it up and after inspecting it from all sides, he rests it in his lap to toggle at it. After some struggling, the latch opens with a creak.

"What is it?" I repeat my questions.

"Notes." There's a flicker in his blue. *Figured.*

"Letters." The flicker slowly goes out.

"Let me see." I crawl over the wooden planks to kneel next to Alex's left.

He doesn't turn the toolbox towards me, so I have to lean in closer to inspect its content. Alex doesn't move and doesn't speak and I don't think he's even breathing. The box rests motionless in his lap, opened, revealing handwritten papers.

I place my right hand on his left shoulder and stretch the other out towards the box. I take one of the top letters in my hand and hold it towards the moonlight to read it. But before I can make out the words, Alex speaks in a quiet, almost shocked voice. "They're from Dad."

"Hold on." I squint my eyes at the paper.

"They're from Dad." He repeats and takes the letter from my hand.

"Uh, question." I raise a finger. "Who on earth keeps their own letters and why?" I judge, not considering I write letters all the time and never send them out.

"He always copies whatever he writes. Grocery lists, notes, letters." He stares down at the paper.

"Where's the sense in that?"

"Who do you think gave me my urge to organize? Also, see what it resulted in." He gestures at the toolbox. "He can read over all those, simply 'cause he wrote his letters twice. Whenever he writes to

[304]

someone, he keeps one copy of the letter to himself, so he later knows exactly what he wrote in it." He holds the letter up and reads something from it.

"*Watching the moon and thinking of you. In love, John.*"

"Did living in darkness give you night vision?" I joke, but he doesn't laugh. *Shit.* "Keep reading." I suggest, but instead of doing so, Alex neatly places the letter back in the toolbox and closes it.

"We shouldn't."

"Don't you want to know?" I think back to yesterday, when Alex pushed me to go over to James to find out about *my* father.

And after a second of mindful breathing, Alex reopens the toolbox and dumps its contents on the hayloft floor. Folded pieces of paper, postcards, notes and letters fall out. We both take one of them in our hands. I reach for a postcard and Alex grabs another letter. The lettering on the front of the postcard is big enough for me to read in the darkness. *Greetings from Montana, the Treasure State* is spread across it. I turn it around to read the written message in the moonlight. After a few seconds of squinting at it, my eyes finally manage to produce a somewhat clear picture.

The Big Sky Country and I yearn for you. Love, P.J.

Chapter Forty

Dear John,

*The creek feels unusually cold ever since you left. Please try
and come visit again soon. I found an old cabin a little
further that no one seems to use anymore. Figured we could
go for another ride next time you're back home and stay
there for a couple nights? I miss your warmth dearly.
Think of me next time you're sitting under the stars.
Love, P.J.*

"Who's P.J.?"

Reading over the letter, I *almost* forgot Abel was
right there.

"Maybe his girlfriend at the time?" I answer him and
check the date on the letter. "This one's from July
1954."

"The postcard's from May, same year." He hands it
over to me and I read over it. After finishing, I place
it on the side and pick up another letter.

*I never knew my heart had its own identity before
yesterday. If you meet me at The Big Oak tonight, we can*

talk it over. I will watch the moon and stars and wait for
you.
P.J.
And at the top: *05/23/'53*

"What do you have?" I turn towards Abel.

"Another postcard. January 1954." He answers and then proceeds to read the message out loud. "*Miss riding through Montana's mountains with you. Tara misses you too. Colorado is gorgeous. Love, John. P.S.: June sounds far away, but I'm in.* He even bought two postcards." Abel scoffs, but I don't react.

"Oh, Tara." I whisper to myself.

"Who's that?"

"Dad's old horse. Trixie's Mom. She died years ago."

"Must've been a good horse then." He tries to comfort me and it works better than I expected.

"Wait." I hold my hand out towards Abel, even though he already stopped talking. My eyes focus on a folded piece of paper on the wooden floor. I pick it up and unfold it. My suspicion turns out to be true as the piece of paper reveals itself as a photograph. Black and white and hard to see in the dim light of the moon. The edges are worn off and it feels like the paper will crumble in my hands if I grip it too tightly. So, I gently hold it between my fingers and inspect it. Then, two faces come into focus. One of them, I almost don't recognize as my dad. It takes me a short moment to see the young John Goodfellow printed on the paper in front of me. But then I remember, I've seen this version of my dad before. In an old picture with Tara. He looks exactly the same. Young and happy.

"What is it?" Abel asks, but I can't react. I look at the other face just to see another young man. Both are leaning against an old tree trunk, shoulders touching, heads covered by cowboy hats. I recognize the one my dad is wearing. Again, it's the same he still wears today. The same one that rests in his lap when he's enjoying the sun on our porch. Both men smile widely into the camera, close to each other. I stare at the photograph. I stare at my dad, smiling like I've never seen him before. And I stare at P.J.

"Pony?"

He wakes me and I slowly hand the photograph over to him.

"Oh." He says after a while. Then, he turns it around to look at the back. "Summer fifty-three." He says.

"Pony, are you alright?" The question calms me, but again, I don't react. So, Abel puts his hand on my thigh and at the touch, I feel even calmer. I'm glad to feel something familiar that keeps me grounded.

"Alex." The name finally feels like it's actually mine and not that of the role I'm supposed to play. I take a deep breath in and let it out slowly.

"What happened to them?" I ask into the air. I ask the moon, Abel, myself, God and the two young men I just met.

Chapter Forty-One

My head and eyes hurt looking at all the pieces of paper spread out in a line in front of us.

"If I have to read another word in this light, I'm going to scratch out my eyes." I complain with a yawn.

"Focus, Brennan. I think we got it." Alex slaps my upper arm with the back of his hand. Hard enough to wake me up a bit, but gently enough to not trigger something in me – which is a form of art in itself. He's leaning over the written words, over the photograph and the postcards. One hand rests on his temple as his eyes switch from paper to paper and for a second, they stop at the last paper on the far right.

"Enlighten me. Watson is gonna lie down." I lean back on the hard wood that has slowly worked its way through my jeans and flesh and into the bones of my ass. I sigh as my back hits the floor and the pain in my ass-bones decreases.

"The first one we have is from the twenty-third of May, fifty-three." I close my eyes and focus on Alex's voice. I get so lost in it, I almost miss the date. *May fifty-three.*

"Then, the twenty-sixth. So, three days later."

"Which one was that?" I ask, not remembering which paper from which date contains which words. *"I thought about what you said and I understand that you need time. I'll wait for you at the oak again. Tonight. If you come, I have my answer. P.J."* Alex reminds me.

"Right." I pretend I knew it.

"So, P.J. asked to meet at *The Big Oak* one night to talk stuff over. Three days later, he writes Dad another letter, asking to meet up again. The next letter is from Dad, a week later." He takes in a deep breath to read it out loud even without me asking. *"Thank you again for understanding. When I confuse myself, I get all scared and paralyzed. But I still mean what I said last week. I want this and I want you."* He pauses for a short second before saying his father's name out loud. *"Yours, John…*Then, it's just a bunch of notes on when to meet next, the picture and more letters. We've got *The night sky was covered in grey clouds last night and I longed for you a little harder,* by my dad. Oh, and *Thank you for trusting me last night. I'm glad about it. About it all,* by P.J." He takes another pause. "And then, there's November eighth, still fifty-three."

A cold shower washes over me, because this date is one of the only ones that stuck with me. I sit back up, right as Alex picks up the next letter in line and starts reading.

Dearest P.J.

I came home last night to my father waiting in the kitchen. I tried to sneak past him again, but this time he got a hold of me. Said he's seen us around. Didn't say when or where exactly. But he knows. He's tried to beat it out of me, but the pain just locked you even deeper into my soul. Do you think the Lord will forgive me? My father said I'll burn in Hell. Do you think so too? Do you think we'll burn? I don't want to burn.

Now, there's something I don't want to mention in here. I'll meet you tomorrow and tell you in person.

Love, John.

P.S.: The moon shone through the clouds last night. Did you see? It was like it spoke to me, louder than my father did, louder than God did.

He lays the letter back down on the ground in front of us and focuses on the next one.

"And after that, December twenty-eighth, fifty-three." Another date I realize.

"Read it, please." I tell Alex. And he barely even looks at the paper to read it out loud. Like he's already memorized P.J.'s words to John.

John my love,

When you told me you had to leave, I didn't think it to be true. But now that you're really gone, I feel like I will never see full moon again. You left and took all the light in the sky with you. Knowing you're not even just a state away, but having Wyoming part us, kills me. You know how I've always loved Wyoming from my camping trips there. Now, the whole state seems to mock me. Mock us. Sitting there, right between us, like a cold ocean, almost unable to be crossed. I'm hurting and I know you are too, but wait just a little more and I know we will be together again. I will swim through this ocean to you, even if the current drowns me in the process. How about June next year? I know it's a long time to go until then, but it works out perfectly. You can take Tara on the truck and tell your folks you're going on a camping trip for a while. I've got two whole weeks off work and could tell my folks I'm going camping too. No one'll know a thing, do not fear. I've found a beautiful creek about a two-day ride from The Big Oak. What do you think? I miss watching the night with you.

With love, P.J.

"Time passes, they meet up, the creek is colder now, they meet up again and again…" Alex fiddles through the remaining letters and postcards. "They switch from meeting in their hometown in Montana to meeting halfway in Wyoming. And then they planned on meeting in Colorado. I'm guessing…Folkspine. P.J. hit the road and…" When his hand touches the last piece of paper in line, he stops. Motionless, he takes deep breaths and I wait for him to read it out once more. But he doesn't.

"Here, let me." I take the paper from his hand and lean against him, with one hand resting on his lap. I squint at the newspaper article and ignore the sting in my eyes and head.

Young Oaksville, Montana, resident found dead in an alley last Saturday, 11/16/1954.

According to witnesses, Peter Junior Aarons, was last seen drinking at "Sky's Beer", Wyoming. "He'd been writing something in his booth and chugging down beer after beer." The barman informs us. "Said he was on his way to Colorado." Aarons was then seen leaving the bar at around one a.m. Not long after, he was found with a broken nose, in an alley not far from "Sky's Beer" and according to the local police department, he had suffered from air loss while choking and drowning on his own blood.

A service will be held on the 20th of October.

Chapter Forty-Two

Mom's eggs and the smell of coffee surround me like a hug, though I don't feel comfortable in their embrace.

"How come you're awake?" She asks as she bites down on her fork, taking in some of the egg. The metal clinks at the contact with her teeth and I feel my neck hair standing up. I look up at the clock, reading eight a.m. Mom's been up for an hour, so she's already dressed for church later. Her red waves are down and she's wearing a long light-blue skirt, with a simple white shirt tucked into it.

"Didn't sleep so good." I remove my eyes from her body and face.

"Something up, Squirrel?" Dad is full of love as ever, slurping his coffee.

Mom searches for my eyes and when I can't stand the pressure of looking away anymore, I meet her gaze. There are unspoken words between us, but neither one of us needs to talk. *The barn was open and alit, young lady. You were drunk, young lady. You didn't come to work, young lady.*

I know Mom. I know she didn't tell Dad. Internally, I thank her for it, but not knowing if she will lecture me later or not is killing me. *I know, Mom. I'm sorry for messing up.* I turn away from her to address her husband.

"All good, Dad." He raises both eyebrows with a satisfied smile and throws back the last sip of his coffee. The mug gently lands on the wooden table in front of us and Dad pushes him and his chair back. "I'll check on the girls once more. Don't take too long, ladies." He grabs his cowboy hat from the counter and starts to leave the kitchen while putting it on. He stops in the doorway and turns towards us. Towards me. And for a fleeting moment of a second, I see the young John Goodfellow from the photograph, but neither P.J. nor Tara are to be seen. "Sunday Service ain't waiting for us." But I know for a fact Pastor Raphael would delay it for a few minutes if he wouldn't be able to spot us in the crowd. Especially Dad. Sometimes I feel like Pastor Raphael is Dad's closest friend, which is both beautifully comforting and sad at the same time.

After hearing the front door quietly fall into its lock, Mom clears her throat. *Shit.*

"Jewel was barking pretty loud last night. She's real good at protecting the barn, you know?"

I press my lips together, knowing she won't even wait for an answer. "Hm." She takes her mug in hand and takes a sip from her coffee. Then, the mug meets the table with a bang. "I didn't say a word to your father. And I won't."

I look down at my eggs, ketchup spread in lines over them. Untouched fork next to the plate. I nod.

"I knew you were drunk, but we both know *very well* that's no excuse."

"I didn't make an excuse."

"Right. But you're trying to make up for it in your mind." *She's right.* I try to find reasons for why I did the things I did last night, and the only one that comes to mind, is the fact that I was with Abel and didn't really give a shit about anything else. *He anchored me.*

"The thing that matters is that when your father woke up this morning, the barn was locked and looked untouched. Except for a glass standing next to the gate, but I cleared that away." *Shit. I knew we'd forget something. But thanks, Mom.* "So, I won't say a thing, but this is the first and only time."

"Understood." The question *Are we understood?* was inaudible, but still very much asked.

"Good. Now eat your eggs." Without a word, I take my fork in my right hand and slowly pierce through the eggs.

"Do you know?" I ask before biting into the soft egg. Unspoken words fill my mouth, so there's no place left for food. Still, I manage to chew and swallow.

"Do I know what?" She asks drinking from her coffee. I part my lips.

What's in the hayloft. But I stop myself from saying it in the last second. She knows I was in there, she doesn't need to know I was *up* there.

"Yes. I know about him." She sighs. The words are almost silent, but clear. So clear, I see them written out in front of me in the air.

"And we will not talk about it."

I nod again.

After eating as much as I could fit past the words in my mouth and the frog in my throat, I get up to get ready for church. Mom's already left the kitchen to join Dad outside.

Sundays are the worst for me. I still love God and the church, but being forced into a dress makes me reconsider. And I wonder why and how Dad is still so loyal to God, even, though his father beat him for disobeying the Lord. *Then again, why do I still love God?*

Despite everything, I pull the dress over my body. I neither look down on myself, nor do I meet the mirror. I know it's white and I know it's got ruffles at the end. That's all the information I can handle. I leave my room, go downstairs, fetch my going-out boots and put them on. To this day, I still own just two pairs of boots. When my old ones became too small, I simply got two new pairs, each serving the same purpose as before. Then, I take my zip-up from last night from its hanger. There's still hay sticking to its back – along with Abel's smell. I fight the urge to raise the fabric towards my face and instead just smile at it. I leave through the front door, tap off the hay outside and put the jacket on. Dad is already parking the truck from the back of our house onto the dirt trail. He rarely ever drives, but loves taking us and his Ford F-100 to church. He loves that car so stupidly much and seeing it parked behind our house for most time of the year, nearly breaks my heart. I know those wheels yearn for a road trip. I might just grant it the wish. Dad taught me how to drive it after all. The Flying Fishbowl stays parked in front of our porch and I walk up to the truck and, when it stops, hop onto the loading space. Dad turns around to check on me and I smile at him with a Thumbs Up. He nods, shifts gears and the truck moves across the dirt trail, turning left onto Main Road at the end of it. The autumn wind whips through my hair and I pretend I'm riding on Trixie's back. Galloping out of Folkspine and through Colorado. I smile.

Chapter Forty-Three

My mouth tastes like old booze, the cig I had when I got home last night, sleep and Alex. Mum's standing in what we call our kitchen, looking out the window over the trailer park while drinking her morning coffee.

"Hey." I greet her with a slight rasp in my throat. I move over to our fridge to chug down some juice. The one Mom buys is nothing compared to Alex's Sunny Delight, but it does the job of refreshing my mouth pretty good.

"Morning, Love." She looks over her shoulder towards me.

The sour liquid washes down the booze, cig and sleep. And it almost washes down Alex, though he stays on the tip of my tongue and the lining of my lips. I look around in search of my father, the bottle still attached to my mouth.

"Already out. Don't ask me where." *Good. Couldn't bear the child molester's face anyway.* I've known for two real days, but in my mind, it feels like James broke the "news" to me ages ago. "How'd it go last night?"

I almost choke on the juice.

"Uh…" I wipe my mouth and stare at Mom while she stares at me, waiting for an answer.

"Getting Alex home?"

"Right. Good. Everything good." I clear my throat.

"That's nice." She turns back around towards the window and takes another sip from her coffee. I put the bottle of juice back into the fridge with a sudden urge for coffee.

"Is there any left?" I ask her while opening the cupboard.

"Already made your cup."

I look around and find a cup of black coffee filled to the brim on the table in the middle of the room.

"Thanks, Mom." I smile and take the cup in my hand, blowing on it once and then lifting it towards my mouth. I feel the hot, bitter coffee mixing with the cold, sour juice in my stomach. It makes my insides turn for a second.

I watch Mom, she watches the outside, we both drink our coffee. And my mind wanders to a different universe, where Mom left with her seed to a different place, far, far away from the rotten apple. *It could've been like this. Always. But with a proper kitchen.*

With a proper coffee maker and not instant coffee. With a counter. With Sunny Delight.

"What are you watching?" I finally ask her.

"The neighborhood." She doesn't turn to face me.

"Why?"

"Because it's ugly. Looks like a junkyard, don't you think?" My heart stops for a second. And then I realize, she's right. The trailer park *is* littered with old junk. Broken plastic chairs, bottles, trash cans that have fallen over. It seems like Jeff is the only one, besides Mom and me, who's trying to keep their property clean. At least from the outside.

"Yeah. Kind of." I answer and for a moment, we are both silent and I try to determine if I can enjoy this silence or not. *I can't.*

"I'm so sorry, baby." Her back is still towards me. I move up to her, lead her head into my shoulder and then place my hand flat on her back.

"Don't be."

"Can you promise me something?" I feel her shivering.

"Anything." But I'm not sure I really mean that.

"Be better. Do better. With better people. Find someone good, will you?" *I think I have.*

"Yes, Mom."

"Promise me."

"I promise."

I place my mug down, she follows after me and I open my arms for her to fall into. We both know how this goes. We hug tightly. I don't smile.

Chapter Forty-Four

"Genesis twenty-eight, fifteen." Pastor Raphael
announces. I look back down at the pamphlet resting
in my hands and read out loud.

*"I am with you, and I will protect you wherever you may
go."* My voice, the voice of Dad, Mom, the pastor
and all the other people fill the church. "Amen." I
clutch the wooden cross around my neck. It's
hanging lower now than it used to when Dad gave it
to me.

I look to my right, to him standing straight, cowboy
hat in hand, head down, eyes closed, smile on his
face. He follows by making the Sign of the Cross and
opens his eyes again. He sees me looking and gifts
me a smile. I return it.

The crowd scatters after the service comes to an end.
Some of Folkspine's residents gather in groups to
chat. Dad goes up to the pastor for a quick catch-up.
They're shaking hands and smiling at each other like
old friends, because they kind of are.

"Tell your father I'll be waiting in the car, will you?" Mom tells me, our conversation from this morning seemingly forgotten, but still hanging between us.

"Aye aye." I try to joke. We both slightly smile. *At least.*

When I turn to walk up to the altar to join Dad and Pastor Raphael, I feel two hands grabbing me by the shoulders and giving me a shake. I turn around to see Taylor standing right in front of me.

"Jesus fuck you scared me." My hand immediately lands over my mouth.

"Woah there."

I suck some air through my teeth and apologize. To her, the church and God.

"You look...pretty." She looks me up and down and I feel the need to open up a hole in the ground and fall through until I've reached the end of the world.

"Save it."

"Alright. Just didn't know you even owned a dress."

"I'd prefer to throw it out, but..." I gesture towards the room.

"Yeah." She answers nodding with her hands resting on both hips.

"Uh...*why* are you here?" For a second, I fear the question might offend her, but I know T doesn't mind. And I'm actually wondering. I know she grew up Christian, but I thought she left that part of her behind long ago? Like she's just read my thought, she answers.

"Still a Christian at heart." She raises her right hand to her heart and I think back to when she laughed about Abel saying *"If God fucked you up, you fuck Him up."*

"But I thought you said-"

"Yeah, I know. That was six years ago. Yadda yadda. Guess I found my way back." I can't help but question my way with God. If I have to part ways with him to be me, like Taylor did. But if she found her way back, then maybe I don't have to part ways in the first place.

"How?"

"It's not about your folks or other Christians or the Pastor or whoever. It's about love. Yours and God's. And it's no one's business to interfere with that." And again, I hear Him speaking through her. I feel Him. "If you really love Him, then He loves you. Don't let anyone take that away from you, just 'cause they think they're a better Christian than you."

"You should become a preacher."

"You're cute." She bumps me in the shoulder and we chuckle.

"Well, I'm glad you've found back."

"Me too, Sweetie. Me too." She takes a step towards me and leans into my ear. "I just hope Pastor Raphael doesn't recognize me. Last time I was here, I was stuffed into my best Sunday shirt, stubble growing on my chin and all." She giggles at me and I know exactly what she means, so I giggle back. Once again, she's beautiful. Her hair is open and styled into a perfectly round orb around her head. Again, there's gold spread across her eyelids and red on her lips. She's wearing a long black skirt and a white tube top tucked into it. Her shoulders are covered by a knitted red scarf.

"What is it?" She looks at me baffled and I quickly stop staring.

"You did good. No way he'll recognize. You're pretty." She lifts one corner of her lips and her pupils dilate, making her eyes look even darker.

"Thanks, little one." At the nickname, I push her arm with my hand. She throws both her hands up.

"Alright. Pastor's staring at me. I gotta bail." She nods her head at the open door. "See ya, Love." And she's gone with a wave.

[329]

"See ya!" I shout after her.

Then, I turn back to the altar. Pastor Raphael and Dad are looking in my direction, at Taylor leaving. I walk up to them and greet the Pastor with a firm handshake.

"Ah, glad you're here too, Alex." He tells me and I smile. We let go of each other and I step closer to Dad, so we're both facing the same direction.

"What were you talking about?" I ask Dad, but Pastor Raphael answers.

"Your father just told me about the lady you were just talking to." My heart accelerates a bit, but I compensate for it by taking deep, calm breaths.

"Oh. She's a friend. A good one at that." I tell him.

"Well, she seems lovely. Tell her to come say Hello the next time she's here. I'd love to get to know every new member of our church." *New. That's good. I don't think he recognizes her. I hope Dad didn't say anything.*

"Will do." I nod at him. Then, I turn to Dad. "Uh, Mom told me to tell you she's waiting in the truck."

"Right." He answers and turns to the pastor. "Well then. Wife's calling."

"Of course."

The men say their Goodbyes, Pastor Raphael shakes my hand once more and Dad and I step down the altar towards the door.

"I didn't tell him." He says while walking, not looking at me. His eyes fixed at the open door. I look up at him and nod. "Thank you."

"I'm surprised he doesn't know. Ya know how fast news spread around here." It's only a matter of time before one of the other church-goers snitches on T and tells the pastor about her. But at least it hasn't happened yet and most importantly – even if, it wasn't my dad.

"Yeah. I guess she was lucky." I answer and before I can stop my mouth, it keeps on talking. "Uh, Dad?"

"Yeah, Squirrel."

"Were you always a Christian?"

"Well, I grew up like this. You might not have known ya grandparents, but they were far more strict than I am with you." *You expect me to thank you?*

"And you never once doubted it?"

His feet stop moving and we stand still for a second. His eyes quint at me, trying to look past my words and into my brain. *Do you doubt God, Squirrel?* But he doesn't ask it.

"I did." He takes a deep breath. "When I was young, about your age, I had a fight with my old man. He told me about sins and the consequences." *Told me* as in *beat me up about it.* I swallow hard.

"And did it help?"

"Not at first. God punished…" He looks to the ceiling for help. "He punished someone else for my sins. I was spared. And I haven't sinned since."

Chapter Forty-Five

I walk past James', listening to the muffled metal
and rock coming from the basement as I pass the
basement window. For a second, I consider
crouching down to knock, but my knees won't bend.
So instead, I simply walk by. But my mind stays
right in front of my uncle's house. I take a step
backward, grab it by the throat and drag it along
with me.

I keep on walking, past closed Hell's Saddle, past the
hair salon, past the alley that one gay guy got beaten
up in – that could've easily been Glen or me if I lost
my control – past all those houses built with solid
walls on a solid foundation with a solid roof on top.
I keep my feet on the curb, eyes towards them,
shielding my face from the sun standing high. I start
to switch sides and just as my foot lands on the tar, I
hear a high squeaking brake and jump back onto the
curb.

"Jesus, Brennan. Want us to run you over?"

"Pony!" He's sitting on the loading space of John's
Ford, leaning over the edge with his arms resting on
top. I catch a glimpse of his collarbones peeking out

from white cotton and lace and the same grey zipper from last night. *Last night.*

"He-llo?" Alex waves his hand mid-air. I look up at his eyes. My mind goes blank for a second. Then again, it screams at me to reach out for Alex's soul.

"Hey." *It's a hot autumn day, right? The sun? My face is hot 'cause of the sun.*

"Hold on. I'm coming down." He lifts himself up and jumps down the loading space. It is now that I realize he's wearing a dress. He pats the metal of the truck twice and throws a Thumbs Up at the side mirror. John starts off the truck with a double-honk.

"So, suicidal much?"

"What?" It sounds more suspicious than I wished for. More caught.

"Crossing the road without looking?" He crossed his arms in front of his…chest. One mystery I can check off.

"Oh- that. Sorry."

I register the fact he's got two bulges resting right there, wooden cross hanging over them. I register them, but I don't care, so I look away from them. In fact, I look him fully up and down before I can even realize. Legs covered in subtle light hairs, cowboy boots – the going-out type – white cotton reaching

[334]

just below the knees. Alex seems to realize I'm inspecting him.

"Ah shit." He zips up the jacket with disgust written across his face. "I forgot. We just came from church, so…"

"No no. I'm sorry. I didn't mean to stare." I'd offer him my jeans, but I don't exactly want to walk around Folkspine in my boxers. I tap my body up and down, looking for something that would help. I can't find a thing and just feel bad.

"It's fine." Alex says and I stop the hectic motion.

"Okay." I stand back up straight and stare at Alex. His face, for that matter. "You look nice, though." Because he does.

"Eh. Save it. T already gave me the newsflash. You guys don't have to climb up my ass." I want to suppress the smile, the laughter, but when I see Alex's mouth curling up, I let out a snort. Without another word, he starts walking and I simply follow like a guide dog. Though I'm not leading. *Ah, who am I kidding. I'm a lap dog.*

"Where'd you meet T, though?" I ask with my arm brushing against Alex's. Walking side by side across the curb towards out of town.

[335]

"Church. Can you believe it?" There's joy and excitement in his voice.

"T? At church?"

"I'm tellin' you. It was great!" He's a few steps ahead now, walking backwards and gesturing with his hands in the air like a kid.

"Isn't Pastor Raphael…" I can't find a proper word for "strict prudish Christian with no intend of integrating anyone that doesn't follow his ideas of a mannered life without sins." I'm out of breath just after coming up with that description.

"Yeah." Alex doesn't put up with my long thinking pause. "Didn't know you guys knew each other." He adds.

"We don't *know* each other. He's the pastor in a small Christian town. Who *hasn't* heard of him?"

"Touché." He turns back around and slows down so we can walk side by side again.

"She said she's still a Christian by heart." He says after a short while. I never really got the whole religion thing, but seeing Alex's face beam at the connection between God, Taylor and himself, makes it seem beautiful. For a second, I consider asking if he'd take me to church with him once, just to see yet another part of his world. *Because I want to know every part of it.*

When we exit town and I realize we're walking in direction of the farm, I utter a "No." My feet stop moving forward and I stand there like a kid refusing to go to the dentist.

"Yes." He says, grabs my left arm just above the wrist and drags me along. The touch stings like dirt under skin. I suck warm air through my teeth and squeeze my eyes shut. One second later, the pressure around my jacket, bandage and open skin loosens.

"Shit." Is all he says as we're standing there, on Main Road. He locks eyes with me, double blue looking right through my body, into my soul. I know he sees the anxiety written in my brown. He can probably hear my fast-beating heart, see the frog in my throat, smell the sweat dripping down my temple.

"He doesn't deserve you." Alex tells me, but I don't get a single word.

"Who?"

"Dan." And I realize I can easily get out of this. Blame it on Dan. *Or show Alex a part of my world?*

"Oh. He didn't-" Is all I can say before choosing the first option. "Yeah. Thanks."

And at that, he gifts a tiny smile, almost big enough to make me forget about last night. The *bad* part of the night. The part where I was lying in bed, tossing and turning, getting up to the bathroom…like so many nights before. Almost big enough, but not quite.

And being back with Alex, I wonder why I even got up to the bathroom in the first place. Because just right now, even with us being physically further apart than yesterday, there's not a cell in me feeling the urge to do it. I'll just blame last night on…*what? Yesterday was fucking great. Why'd I do it?*

Chapter Forty-Six

I lead him across the dirt trail towards the meadow, with our fingers intertwined instead of mine gripping around his wrist. We reach the wooden fence, marked by years of repair, and a wave of melancholy washes over me. I shake it off as I hear Jewel's barking coming closer, her furry beige body shooting across the meadow, climbing underneath the fence and circling me and Abel. We both crouch down to pet her and each receive a lick on our hands. She pauses at Abel's arm, the one I accidentally hurt earlier, and sniffs over it. He quickly pulls back and looks up at me with an unconvincing smile. I get up from the ground and tell Abel to wait there.

"You keep an eye on him." I point a finger at Jewel, who barks in response. "Atta."

Abel smirks at the joke and I quickly turn away from the dirt trail to live out the blush crawling up my face.

Inside the house, I take off my boots, run upstairs, grab the pair of jeans that have been resting on my chair after I snuck up to my room last night, and put them on. I switch out the dress with a shirt and throw the jacket back on, leaving it open now. Downstairs, I switch to my muddy boots and leave the house to join Abel at the meadow.

He smiles when he sees me walking up to him, leaning against the fence with his back, arms propped on top of it, his black sweater lifting to reveal two inches of dark-haired skin peeking out from- *Jesus.* I smile back. *No, I blush back.*

"Where are your parents?" He asks looking around.

"Drove straight to one of my dad's friends. Farmer stuff." I explain and he nods more satisfied than necessary, but just right.

"So," he backs off from the fence to come closer to me. One of his hands rests on my cheek, the other holds my hand. "Can I?" He locks eyes with me.

"Do you remember what I told you last night?" Slight fear rises up my stomach towards my chest. *What if we only kissed because of the alcohol? Out of the spontaneity of the action?* I keep my eyes on his.

"Did I forget to tell you, I'm half gay?" He keeps his eyes on mine. And I keep mine on his. I smile.

"I'll ask again. Can I, Pony?"

"Please." And we add another verse to our poem. I feel my body drawn towards his, like magnets operating under our skin. We close up, chest on chest, and I don't give a fuck.

A whinny breaks the magnetism working between us and we both turn towards Trixie, suddenly peaking over the fence, lifting her upper lip at us. We both laugh at her and let go of each other. It doesn't hurt, because I know this isn't just one fleeting moment that could never repeat itself. There's relief in knowing Abel Brennan still wants to kiss me. And something else is telling me I want more than just a kiss. I don't want a verse or a poem. I want the full book with all its pages, prologue, story and afterword.

I turn towards the gate, tell Trixie to back off and lead Abel and me onto the meadow.

"If you expect me to get on a horse, *this,*" he gestures at the air between us "is over." I know he's joking. Not because I can hear it, but because the smirk on his face is undeniable.

"And what is *this?*" I mimic his hands, teasing.

"Don't know, but I can't wait to figure out." And he winks at me. It's cheesy and should make my skin crawl with cringe, but it doesn't. It makes my knees weak.

"Okay. No riding for you then." I keep the joke that would follow to myself, because that's not a joke a good Christian should make. And I don't want to share James' sense of humor.

We walk across the meadow, following Trixie who's already settling herself into her stable, passing some of the girls grazing, resting or pissing. I watch them, wondering how ethical a saddled cow is. He seems to think the same, because I hear a suppressed snort coming from him.

"Same goes for the critters BTW." He says as one of the girls sticks out her tongue at him.

"Are you fine with walking beside me and Trixie?"

"That I can do." He responds.

We've been keeping Trixie's gear at her stable for quite a while now, which kind of annoys me because I've just gotten strong enough to carry her saddle, saddle pad and bridle from the furthest end of the barn towards Trixie's stable without my arms burning or me running out of breath. Abel watches me getting her ready, not questioning how he even ended up in this situation in the first place. I glance up from the brush moving over Trixie's coat.

"Uh…where were you walking?"

"Huh?" He's leaning against one of the pillars holding Trixie's roof.

"I just went and took you with me. I never even asked if you wanted to come along." Suddenly, I feel incredibly stupid. Naive even. *Why would I think Abel would automatically follow me around, stopping whatever he was doing, just to stay in my company like a dog?*

"You don't have to ask me to follow you, Pony." His expression is warm. Like I could wrap my body around his face and heat up after a snowy walk through Colorado's mountains.

"And I was walking nowhere. I always take walks without any destination."

I simply nod at his response and get back to work.

Chapter Forty-Seven

We take a familiar route. The one across Main Road, onto the other dirt trail and through the woods. Only this time, it's light out and I don't need to feel stiff, because I'm fine. And I'm *actually* fine because I have the acknowledgement that Alex still wants my company. That yesterday wasn't a mistake for him. It makes me feel higher than after any joint James ever gave me.

Trixie's hooves collide with the ground in a rhythmic pattern, almost like a song. I walk beside her, keeping my hand on her body, but longing for the one sitting on top. Alex moves in sync with Trixie, hips adjusting to her pace. I try to look away, but my eyes won't react to my brain. And something else *is* about to react to it.

"You alright?"

"Uh-" I look up at Alex's face, not sure if the sight will make my brain quieter. "Uh huh." I nod.

"Pervert." I back off a little, shocked at the...*well, truth.* But then I see a smile spread across his face. Not the "Haha, that was funny smile," but the *other* smile. The "I know what you're thinking and I'm thinking it too" smile. So, I bury my face in the hand that isn't touching Trixie's body and pray for my body to obey me. *There. Alex made me pray. He's a real good Christian.* And gladly, my body does obey. For now.

Back up in the treehouse, I feel like I'm not in the same place I was two days ago. This time, I'm with a boy – that I have kissed multiple times by now – and this time, I know about my father, and I know about Alex's dad and I know what Alex's collarbones and legs look like. And I think I *know* Alex. And I want him to *know* me.

The sour taste of apples rests on my tongue and the seeds and stem are scattered on the wooden ground of the treehouse. We're leaning into each other on the mattress, looking down at the notebook in his hands. It's one of the poem-notebooks and I patiently listen to him flipping through the pages.

"Okay, you ready?" He asks stopping at the page he was looking for.

"Shoot." And I close my eyes, feeling Alex's body pressed to mine and listen to the poem.

I used to find comfort in the darkness of the night.
'Cause the stars and moon lit my way.
My way to you.

Now, the stars have fallen.
The moon watches me like a judge.
Shouting its disapproval.

Now, I have fallen.
The past watches me like a judge.
Shouting its disappointment.

I used to know love like a song.
'Cause you were the melody and the lyrics.
I sang along.

Now, love is an unfinished symphony.
I write another song, similar to ours.
Sounding right, but still off-key.

Now, my heart's unfinished.
I listen to its beat, still the same.
Sounding right, but in a different tone.

"Yeah," I reopen my eyes, "you *have* to do something with your passion, dude."

"*Dude.*" He mimics me and I laugh.

"No, I mean it. You should publish some."

"I don't know."

"You gotta stop hiding. You should bring yourself and your art out there."

"Look who's talking big." He smiles down at me resting on his shoulder and I smile back.

"Why doesn't it have a title?" I get back to the poem.

"Nothing felt right." He pulls up his upper lip with a shrug.

"How 'bout *God's Eye*?" I suggest and instantly Alex shoots up, looking me straight in the face.

"What?"

"God's Eye." I repeat a little confused.

"Why? How?" He asks like I stole the title from someone else.

"Someone always watching above, judging you and disapproving of a certain love? Sounds like God to me."

His eyes stay on mine for a few more seconds, shouting disbelief and amazement at the same time. He grabs a pen lying around and adds the title. I smile, proud of myself for naming one of my favorite artist's poems.

"I'm guessing you didn't show him."

"I did not." He nods.

"Yet?"

"Nah. I don't think I will. Remember: only Mom and you." *Jeez, I'm privileged.*

"Maybe break your rule again? You wanted to break out, this is a tiny step towards it. Besides, I think he'd appreciate it."

"Yeah, I'm sure he'll be thrilled to know I broke into the barn, went through his probably most prized possession and analyzed it."

Fair enough. I raise one hand and nod at losing the argument. But I see Alex reconsidering. A tiny part of his heart telling him to give his father a piece of literature made only for him and the ghost in the moon.

We settle back onto the mattress, my head in his lap.
Lap dog. Woof woof.

"What's so funny?" He asks studying my expression.

"I'm a dog."

"I was *just* thinking that." We laugh.

And we laugh a little more. And somewhere between laughs, we somehow ended up entangled, his hands gripping my hair, my knee between his legs, his lips on my neck and mine slightly agape.

"No." To my surprise and shame, it almost comes out as a moan.

"What?" He pulls back, licking his lips. *Shit Brennan. Don't mess with Alex. Don't mess this up.*

"Do you really want to?"

"Do *you*?" He looks almost pissed off.

"Yes. I'm asking you." He simply nods, pupils dilating. And that should be enough of an answer, but somehow, it isn't.

"I need to hear it."

"Brennan." It's his teacher voice coming through as he grabs my face with both hands, eyes switching from one of mine to the other and back. "I want this. Okay?" I nod unable to speak. "I want you." He adds and before one of us can say anything else, my lips press against his. It's the taste that makes my body succumb to my brain. The taste of desire coming from both tongues. And if that isn't enough, Alex lifts himself off the ground, lowers himself onto my lap and keeps working with my neck.

"Alex."

He bites down onto my skin.

"Alex?"

He pulls back staring wide-eyed at me. And we realize at the same time that his name didn't come out of my mouth. The only thing my mouth is producing right now is saliva. Lots of it.

"Yeah?!" He shouts back.

"Can I come up?" John asks.

Our mouths fall open in sync, our heartbeats probably accelerating at the same pace. *As if my heart wasn't working fast enough already.*

"No! I'll uh- I'll come down." Our bodies lose contact and I feel my hand reaching out towards Alex. He combs his fingers through his hair and tugs at his shirt, looking at me with a big question mark written across his face. I nod with a Thumbs Up.

Chapter Forty-Eight

"Why are you here?" I ask Dad like this isn't *our* spot. And I feel bad for temporarily making it Abel's and mine.

"Trixie and the gear were gone, so I figured you'd be here." At the sound of her name, Trixie looks away from the low-hanging apple she's drying to bite.

"That doesn't answer the question, Dad."

"Aight. I wanted to come talk to you." *Fuck. Did Mom snitch? And since when isn't silence the ground principle of Dad's and my relationship?*

"About what?" I place myself in front of the ladder like a doorman, positioned just like Jeffrey sometimes is in front of Hell's Saddle, indicating we will not go up to eat chocolates and apples on the mattress. Because Abel covers the mattress and something else was about to do the same just shortly after Dad interrupted us.

"Mister Beckham." With my mind entirely focused on Abel and last night's mysteries, T completely slipped my mind.

"Miss Beckham." I shoot back and he almost rolls his eyes at me. But instead of doing so, he takes a deep breath in and releases it with a quiet sigh.

When he doesn't speak up, I do it like always. I take the word. I lead the conversation on. Every time Dad comes up to me to talk about something - which isn't often – he ends up going non-verbal and I have to pull the words through his mouth.

"What about her?" I cross my arms.

"I don't want to see him at church anymore."

"You got no say in that." I try to keep a respectful tone, but feel the anger slowly slipping to the front of my tongue.

"No. But Raphael will take my side if I end up telling him." *Raphael. No Pastor in front.*

"Is that really what you came here for?" The anger has made its way off my tongue and into my words.

"I thought we covered that earlier."

"Yes, Squirrel." He ignores the second part of my speech.

"Don't Squirrel me right now!" He backs off, giving me a face I've never seen before. Disappointment mixed with annoyance.

"What?" He asks me. *What a stupid question.*

"Stop talking about Taylor like she's the Devil's offspring crawling right out of Hell and into Folkspine." *Wouldn't be a long way to crawl.*

"You know nothing. The Lord-"

"Oh, shut the fuck up. *You* know nothing! The Lord can kiss my ass." I'm out of breath, internally apologizing to God and preparing myself for the analysis of Dad's next words. Only, they never come out of his mouth. He stares at me. Too long. Too deep. And I regret what I just said because maybe Dad *knows* very well. Dad knows and if P.J. in the moon does too.

He turns towards Trixie, plucks the apple and offers it to her. Then, he takes her reins, unknots them and climbs up her back.

"What!?" I shout at him, begging for him to speak to me. To tell me he's angry, disappointed, shocked, sad or whatever. But there's nothing but the clicking of his tongue coming from his direction. Trixie doesn't obey him, though. Instead, she turns to me, staring deep into my eyes. *I know, girl.* She seems to hear my thoughts as she snorts and turns to walk towards our farm, carrying Dad on her back.

I watch them going smaller and smaller in my vision until they've vanished and just as the disappear behind the trees, my eyes go blurry from tears. They form in my eyes at the realization that there's no future for me here. No future in this family, this church, this town. I can put up an act to please those around me. I could, but I won't. I've done that for too long. I've been Mom and Dad's daughter too long. I have to let her go.

I break down right here and now – onto the ground. I hear Abel jumping down the ladder and running up to me. He takes me in his embrace and rocks us back and forth. The continuous routine of the motion calms me. Abel calms me. His smell and warmth.

"I'm so sorry." He whispers into my ear. I beg my body to stop crying, but instead, I let out another loud sob.

"I have to leave." I somehow manage to press words holding information past tears and snot.

"Like break out?" He asks with calmness in his voice. I nod hidden behind my hands. And at that, he lifts me up from the ground, sits me down leaning against the tree trunk and climbs back up the ladder. When he comes back, the sobbing has turned into a subtle tear rolling down here and there. He's carrying as many notebooks as he possibly can.

"You're staying at my place tonight."

"Abel, I'm really not in the mood right now."

"Jesus, no! I mean, you need to not sleep at home right now. Trust me. We'll go back, grab your other stuff and if you still feel the same in the morning, we won't waste another second."

"We?" Is the word that I seem to take most from out of his speech.

"Yes. We." My body answers with another sob.

"Okay, okay. Come on. Get up." He lightly kicks at me, given his hands are still full with my works. I sniff, wipe my face with the sleeve of my zipper and push myself off the ground.

"There you go."

Back at home, I pass Mom and Dad sipping coffee. Neither Dad nor I say a word, leaving Mom in confusion. I go upstairs, grab some clothes, my diary, the going-out-notebook, my cap and other essentials one might need when running away from home. *I'm running away from home? With Abel Brennan?* And then something completely different pops into my head. *I just almost had sex with Abel Brennan.*

"Honey? Where are you off to?" Mom asks as I leave the same way I came from, full backpack on my back, bags over my shoulders. Her tone indicating Dad didn't tell her about our crash-out.

Now Dad knows something Mom doesn't, and Mom knows something Dad doesn't.

"Having a sleepover." It's a bad lie. Mom knows I don't have any friends. Well, except for Abel now.

"With whom?"

"Some people from school." Not *exactly* a lie, since I'm his teacher.

I look between her and my dad. She's confused and in disbelief, worried. He's angry and questioning, silent.

"Speaking of." Mom raises an eyebrow. "You've got school tomorrow." *Shit. I actually forgot.* I try to come up with an answer, but there's not a single one. And then, to my surprise, Mom adds.

"It's fine. Your grades are good. I'll call you in sick." Like she forgot our little dispute this morning. Like she's trying to make up for it. And I feel the need to thank her for that, so I tell her the truth.

"I'm staying with Abel." I correct myself, also knowing Eve will tell her anyway, and I'd rather she'd hear it from me. As expected, her eyebrows rise again – this time both – and her mouth is slightly agape. Dad gives me the poker face, but I see his chest rising and falling heavily.

"Okay." She tries to sound genuine, but there's more worry and even more confusion in her voice. She switches her voice to a mix of boss mode and mom mode. "Don't get drunk or your father and I will have a *talk*." I look at my dad, who looks at his wife all confused.

"Yes, Mom. Thank you." *For letting me do this.* I nod and then add "See ya," knowing this isn't the final goodbye. I'll come back tomorrow morning, because there's still some stuff I need to do before abandoning the meadow and going off into the forest. And then, just as I'm about to leave, I think further, planning out how Abel and I are going to bash against this fence with full force and there seems to be only one option.

"Uh...Dad?" I break the silence – bad silence – between us.

"Yeah?"

"Can I borrow the truck? We might wanna drive around town." Never ever have I tried so hard to sound like I'm not lying. Never ever have I even just thought about lying to my dad like this and it's pretty obvious.

"Sure." There's something else he wants to say. Something about the first fight we ever had. I'm guessing it's an apology. Or maybe him giving me the truck right now *is* his apology. There are a thousand things I could say myself, but only two I'd *want* to tell him. *I'm sorry you lost your love. I'm sorry, but your daughter is dead.* But I don't say them.

Dad fiddles in his pockets and throws me the key to his truck. I catch it and the sudden feeling of holding freedom in my hand makes me want to not waste a second.

"I'll be back in the morning." Is all I say.

"Be careful." Normally, she would've added a heartfelt Sweetie. "Remember what I told you about interco-"

"Jeez, Mom! Alright, I'm leaving."

"I'm just saying!" She shouts after me as I leave through the front door and I can only imagine the look that Dad's shooting at Mom right now. *Oh no, sex. Eve, why'd you pick the apple? You doomed us all.* I scoff as I walk out of the house.

Abel is resting against the meadow fence again, smiling as he sees the bags stacked on my body.

"You really mean it."

"I think I do." But I can't break a smile. My bags

land on the ground in front of him and I turn away from him and walk back to the house.

"Where you going?!" He shouts after me like I just betrayed him.

I raise my hand to the sky, letting the car key jingle and reflecting in the sunlight for him to see.

I park the truck from the back of our house on the dirt trail right next to Abel. I roll down the window and tell him to load the back. Without a word, he throws my bags and notebooks into the loading space. Then, he walks around the truck and opens the passenger door.

"I'm not supposed to get into strangers' cars."

"I've got candy in the back." I finally crack a smile and mean it. He gets in with a chuckle and we drive off onto Main Road, into downtown. He's leading me to the trailer park and I realize I've never even been here. I've lived in Folkspine all my life and never went to the trailer park. Because I never had a good reason to. Now I do. Two, actually. Getting away from home and being with Abel.

I park the truck in the unofficial parking lot – a flat gravel space right in front of the area.

"Is your dad home?" I ask turning towards Abel.

"Don't know. Hope not. Don't care."

"Hm." I want to get out of the truck, but I feel my body stiffening up, gripping the wheel, remembering all the stories about Dan.

"Hey. Don't worry, yeah? I've got it." Again, his hand rests on my thigh and I place mine on top.

"Yeah." I whisper and like on command, Abel opens his door and gets out of the truck. I do the same, grab my backpack from the back and tell Abel to lead the way.

Chapter Forty-Nine

We pass my neighbors' homes and the closer we get to mine, the more ashamed I suddenly feel. Alex seems to notice as he squeezes my hand, fingers locked like puzzle pieces.

Mastiff barks through Jeff's trailer when we close up to it and I shout a "Stop barkin' critter!" copying Jeff's tone.

"That's a loud ass dog." Alex comments.

"Nothing compared to Jewel, huh?" I answer.

And just shortly before reaching our trailer, the door to Jeff's opens.

"Son. Wanna come in for-" He's in a white shirt and boxers, sleep and last night resulting in a hangover painted across his face and hair. "Little one?" He spots Alex, who waves at him.

"Hiya Jeffrey."

"Ah." He's lost his cover. He's full-on confused and doesn't hide it. "Whatcha doin' over here?"

In response, Alex raises the hand holding mine, so Jeff can see our bodies connected. For a short second, mine protests, not wanting Jeff to see. But I quickly surrender and let Alex lift our hands.

"Oooh." He points a finger at us and Alex lets our hands drop. "Ah, you kids. I remember when I was your age..." If we don't leave right now, Jeff will, for a fact, talk to us about his past for at least a full hour. And though I'd love to hear the story, which I've probably already heard multiple times by now, I wave him off.

"Alright, Dad. We're gonna go now, yeah?"

All three of us realize at the same time. Alex's mouth drops open, revealing his tongue. I force myself to look away from it and back at Jeff, whose eyebrows are raised high into his forehead, mouth agape and slightly turned up.

"You have fun." His mouth closes and forms a proper smile and I see his eyes relaxing into something that might be the love of a father. I bury my face my hand and drag Alex with me towards our trailer.

"Bye, Jeffrey!" He waves at him before we disappear behind the metal door.

Inside, my body relaxes at the slight feeling of home, and at the same time, tenses up for the same reason.

"Uh…" *Come in* doesn't make sense, since we're already inside. *Home sweet home* is definitely not an option. So, I settle for the best possible option. "This is me." I'm still holding Alex's hand. I see him looking around, but not saying a word. He doesn't look like he judges what he sees, he simply takes it in. All the beer cans, the old food, Dan's clothes everywhere. Mom is nowhere to be found, and luckily, the same goes for my father.

"Are we alone?"

"I sure hope so." I answer. We move across the living space into my room. I see Alex stiffening up with the familiar cringe one gets when entering someone else's room for the first time.

"Here, give me that." I let go of his hand and take the backpack from his shoulder to place it next to the doorway. I look back up at Alex inspecting my room, standing still like I did on James' stairs. And suddenly, I feel extremely aware of what my room looks like. There's a single mattress on the floor, the bedding thin and marked by old blood stains. My closet is filled mostly with long-sleeves. Plain black or black with band logos printed in the front. There's a white shirt hidden in between. Even without unfolding it, I know exactly what the front looks like. *Devil's right-hand man* is written in big black letters on the front. Jeff has got a matching one, saying *Devil of Hell's Saddle.* It's nice thinking about Jeffrey organizing matching shirts for me and him. He could've gotten a *Protector of The Jukebox* one for Alex or a *Hell's Boss* for Elaine or a *Gossip-Queen* one for Mom. But he didn't. It's just him and me and when we're both in security mode, we do feel like a unit. I love that grumpy old man.

I've got a small wooden table which currently holds the notebook I'm working on, an ashtray and a copy of King's "The Body." Of course, that's the first thing that catches Alex's eyes. He finally moves from his spot and walks up to it.

"Hm." He nods satisfied, holding the book in one hand. Then, he looks back up around the room to inspect the Metallica poster above my bed and the graffiti of a dick with a face having a puff next to it on the wall. He stares at it like a painting in a museum.

"Ah- Sorry. Alan did that." I take a step forward as if I'd be able to block the view somehow.

"So many artists in Folkspine." He jokes and I feel a little less embarrassed.

"I wanted to cover it up, but…"

"Yeah, no. It's like a memorial, right?" He turns over his shoulder to smile at me and I sigh in relief.

"Exactly." I never really let the grief of losing Alan get to me. Still, I never had the guts to remove him from my past. And I guess James feels the same.

I stand in my doorway, watching Alex as he turns around in my room.

"Sorry, it's not much." Another wave of shame washes over me.

"No, it's not…You are, though." He adds and I move from my place in the doorway towards him. I take his wrist in my hand and walk us out of the trailer.

"Where are we going?"

"Can I show you something?" I stop once we've exited the trailer.

"What?"

"My soul."

Four years. It's been four long years since I last went here. I never came back out of the fear of running into what remained of the gang. But then again, I also never wanted to go back to James' either and ended up there two days ago and almost today, too.

Right now, it's like I'm on vacation with Alex and we're going to all the sightseeing attractions. But without the tourists, children's laughter and the general understanding of what happened here, at least that counts for Alex. But I'm back. And I was scared to go back to this place where I almost saved myself. I'm standing in the exact same spot, looking straight ahead. I see the truck that James propped the beer bottles up on. His pale face sometimes flickers into my imagination, like I'm going back in time to relive the moment.

"The junkyard?" Alex's voice shakes me from my nightmare.

"Yeah."

"Okay. Why?" He takes a step closer to me, so he can look right where I'm looking. At the truck, only he doesn't see the bottles. Or James or Alan and Glen or the moon or the campfire.

"Can you promise me something?" I beg and he nods. "Don't think I'm a freak." I don't wait for an answer and fumble in my back pocket. My fingers touch the familiar piece of metal and I pull the bullet out, holding it up into the sunlight for Alex to see.

"A bullet?"

"My way-out ticket." I offer as an explanation.

Alex pulls his eyebrows down and together in confusion, so I turn around and place the bullet on the ground. Right where I picked it up four years earlier. When the metal was still warm.

I turn back to Alex, make a gun with my fingers and point it at my temple. My heart accelerates in response. Like my body can't determine the difference between cold metal and semi-cold skin. Like I've actually gone back in time. I wonder what might've happened if I just did what James told me. One shot, knocking down a bottle. That's all he wanted. And instead, I tried to take his cousin away from him. To be honest, I'm not sure if I ever would have left the gang otherwise. Maybe, I would've ended up like James. Rotting away in my room, drugs, music and porn all around me. Maybe, I would've ended up like Alan – dead. *How come it's more deadly to stay in the gang than holding a barrel to your skull?* So – weirdly – having metal and hair touch was kind of a good thing. Because if I wouldn't have, I might've become a dick and Alex and I would never have become…whatever we are. My mind switches from the past lying on the floor, to my future standing right next to me.

"No." The future says and I take my hand back down.

"I didn't do it. Glen stopped me. It landed on the ground and fired at the impact." I explain.

I wait for disappointment, shock, anger. But it doesn't come.

"So, the guy that held you at gunpoint was…"

"Me. Yeah." I confirm. And again, there seems to be no emotion coming from Alex. Instead, he walks past me towards the bullet on the ground. He picks it up, looks at it resting in his hand and then up at me.

"You always carry it around?"

"Always. I can't let go of it." I answer and hold my hand open for him to drop the bullet into. His gaze wanders from my eyes, to my hand, to the bullet in his and back to mine. His fingers close around the metal and he turns towards the trees surrounding the junkyard. And before I can stop him, the bullet shoots through the air for the second time in its existence and lands in the thick of leaves and twigs. I want to shout at him. I want to be angry. But to my own surprise, I'm not. It's like he ripped an old band-aid off my heart, that was no longer necessary because the wound underneath might have already healed without my knowing.

I'm standing right there, right where I was four years ago. When I was determined to end it all. Only now, I see my future and it's standing right in front of me with its blue eyes fixed on mine.

We spend the next hours resting in the sun while lying with our backs on the hood of an old truck – not the throne – and listening to the creaks and tumbles of the junkyard.

"You always annoyed me, you know?" Alex says staring straight up at a crow flying over the trees.

"I know." Even I hear the smirk in my voice.

"And I always thought you were just another Brennan." This time, I don't answer. Hearing Alex compare me to my father, James and my grandfather hurts, because if he thinks I'm just a Brennan, then it might actually be true. Then, I have nothing ahead of me. Just dark paths leading into my family's footsteps. Mom once told me Dan is the way he is because his father was even worse and it made me wonder what will happen to me. What if I become a father someday and mess up just like my father did, because his father did? William Brennan was the worst alcoholic Folkspine has probably ever seen. It got to a point where he came to work drunk, got even drunker and attacked customers like a hyena with rabies or something. His work partner, Elaine's father, kicked him out. He whored around town, got a girl pregnant and only went to visit the kid, Dan, whenever he wanted to let off some steam. I have no pity for Dan whatsoever, but I know that no child deserves a father like that. I'm almost grateful Dan isn't as bad as that. Almost, but not quite.

"But," he continues, "I know you're not and I'm really glad about that."

"Me too." I look away from the sky above, away from my family and to Alex on my right. I inspect the slight bump on his nose, the thick brows, the brown hair framing his face and all demons fall off my mind. I breathe deep.

"How do you feel?" I ask.

"'Bout what?" He keeps his eyes on the sky.

"Everything." Meaning probably breaking out tomorrow, the fight with John, being confused with God, having been at my place, us suddenly being together all the time, having told me his secret and and and.

"Now *who's* being a therapist?" He mocks.

"We've been spending a lot of time together. I'm starting to get the hang of it." He turns towards me, but doesn't answer.

"So?" I push.

"Fucking confused and…scared." Given the expression in his eyes, that's exactly the answer I expected.

"What about you?" He asks me. And I take a moment to keep my eyes on Alex's, considering the options I have for an answer.

I choose "High."

Chapter Fifty

We're lying on our bellies on Abel's mattress with a notebook each in front of us. His cheap-looking record player fills the air with "Rebel Yell" and we focus on the paper below us. Our arms occasionally stretch out to the pizza that Eve warmed up for us and we lick the grease off our fingers so we don't damage the paper. I suppose Taylor and Mom work the bar tonight and Eve's got the day off. She reacted as expected when she came home to her son and me sitting in his room, laughing on his mattress.

"Alex? What- Is everything okay?" She said after walking into Abel's room and pausing. We reassured her that everything was fine, though we both know we aren't *actually* fine, and didn't give her any more details. But we were laughing our asses off over the story Abel just shared about Jeffrey.

He used to sneak out at night when he was younger and got so wasted one time that he climbed back into the window of his neighbor's house. He only realized he wasn't sleeping on *his* bedroom floor when he woke up a couple hours later to his senior neighbors having loud sex in the dark, in the same room. So, we seemed fine for the moment, which is what we told Eve. When she turned around and left to probably call my mom, I addressed the elephant in the room and asked Abel about her.

"What about your mom? I mean, when we leave. *If* we leave."

"This isn't the first time I'm making the decision to leave." He answered like he was already prepared for the question and I thought back to the bullet. "But this time, I know how to write a goodbye letter."

"Wait. That was four years ago, right?"

"Yeah"

"I remember that night. The bang." I shook my head. "We started school two years earlier. You could've written a letter then. I mean- not that you should've, you know, pulled the...uh."

"Pony." His eyes landed on mine. "I know how you mean it." I took a deep breath in and let it out slowly to nod. "I didn't write one because I didn't know what to say. I mean, I kinda knew, but I couldn't, if that makes sense."

"It does." I reassured him because everything he says makes sense.

"I started writing another letter when I was younger, though. Like an apology to her. You remember I tried to teach myself? Well, I lost it and never finished it." *Can it be?*

"Where'd you lose it?" I glanced over at him.

"Hell's Saddle."

"I have it."

He turned to me. "You have it?"

Mom, im ~~soray~~ sorray

~~do~~

"I have it. In my note-notebook. We never figured it out."

"Dang. There's some poetry in that, don't you think?"

"Yeah." I flipped through the notebook in front of me to add *Stolen Apology* to my list of poem ideas and felt Abel's eyes on me.

"Yes. I'll read it to you." He smiled, satisfied. "Back to work." I reminded him. So, I flipped back to the page I was working on and Abel turned back to his notebook marked with a big five on the front.

We give each other the privacy of not looking at the other one's words, but still lie side by side, shoulders touching.

[374]

Writing a goodbye letter to Mom and Dad is easier
than expected. Still, my stomach fills with angst and
doubt so I have to take breaks between sentences. I
look over at his side from time to time. His pen
doesn't seem to stop, like this is a test that he's
studied weeks for, writing everything he knows as
fast as possible so he doesn't forget a single
information. We both don't say a word, so it's kind
of like when you're at a funeral, sitting in the front
row. You wouldn't talk during that either and this
does somehow feel like a funeral.

I write down what I think is the last word and take a
look at the full page. Reading over it, Mom's red
waves pop into my mind. Then, Dad's cowboy hat,
Trixie's spots, Jewel's circling, the girls. I glance over
at Abel, looking for help. His hand pauses over the
paper and he looks up to meet my eyes.

"Done?" He asks.

"I think so." I feel my eyes dropping, mouth pressing
shut. Abel musters my face with worry, but I know
he relates to my expression.

I feel like it's my turn to ask "You?"

"Almost."

I roll onto my back and fold my hands over my
chest.

"This is insane." I tell the ceiling.

"What is?" I hear Abel's pen sliding across the paper.

"All of it. Those letters, leaving town…us."

"Yeah, we're insane." He drags the last syllable to a comedic length, so I push my elbow into his side.

"Careful! I'm writing."

Chapter Fifty-One

When I'm done with my letter, I copy Alex's position so we both stare at the ceiling. I keep my eyes on the spider web that's been sitting in the corner for a while now. In an attempt to feel less lonely at home, I named the spider. Though I haven't seen Maverick in weeks. I never felt the strength to check if his corpse is lying tucked together in the corner on the floor. Alex pulls me away from my thoughts.

"What about Taylor? We can't leave without telling her." He says it like he waited all the time for me to finish writing, so he could finally ask me this.

"You mean we should write her too?" I ask.

"Uh, I insist." He corrects.

"We don't know where she lives, do we?" If he's got a spare key to Hell's Saddle, maybe he knows where T lives too.

"No. But we can slip a note into her locker in the back." With the key. *Seems like we've had the same thought.*

"Smart." Knowing it, makes my heart warm up. But

saying it, makes it jump with pride.

"I know, thanks."

We turn back around to write our goodbye to T.

"Hey. Let's do a poem."

"A poem?"

"Yes. I realized I've written a poem about everyone I love, except Taylor."

And without being asked, I recite the list. "Mom, *Forbid The Rotten Apple*. Elaine, *Phoenix*. John, *God's Eye*…oh and *Sound Of Silence*." I glance over at Alex, waiting for approval and that I should go on.

"Trixie, *Break The Fence*-"

"That one's for me too." He interrupts. And I'm glad to know he himself is on his list of people he loves.

"Right." I answer and get back to the list.

"Uh…wait. That's it."

"No." His eyes stay down on the paper. "There's one more." And the blue goes up to my face and his lips curl up. But he doesn't go on and I don't have the guts to ask the question.

Writing to Taylor is somehow way harder than writing to Mom. Not because we don't know what to write, – the words come naturally – but because leaving her might be one of the hardest things. Then again, her words from four years ago, are what made the stone start to roll in the first place.

"I'll miss her." Alex says when we take a second to think of the next sentence.

"Me too." I reassure him.

"I'll miss them all." And I wish I could say the same, but honestly, I'm just glad I finally have a good reason to get away from my father. That reason being Alex…and suddenly myself.

"I know." Is the best I can say. And I'd love to add "You don't have to leave, though." But I fear that might actually make him stay. *Make us stay.*

I wake up to objects clattering in the living space. Alex is sleeping on his belly, one arm around my neck, hair tickling my chin. The light coming from Jeff's trailer shines through the splits in my curtains, casting stripes onto Alex's back. *Dressed* back, one might add.

"Abel's got someone over. Keep it down." Mom says, muffled by my closed door. *"Someone."* She doesn't specify and I'm thinking that's probably her try of not getting Alex involved. I appreciate it. I look over to him and his brown hair hanging over his face as he's breathing constantly and slowly, deep and steady. At the same time, my breath fastens just like my heart rate.

"Who?" My father shoots back, louder than necessary. Provoking.

"A girl." I cringe at Mom's quiet answer.

"Fine. At least I can stop worrying my only son's a fag."

I don't care about waking Alex up when I throw my blanket to get out of bed and probably smash my father's face in.

"Hmm?" He moans turning around. "Abel?"

"Go to sleep, Pony." I don't face him. My focus is on something else entirely. Without another word, I open my door to join my parents.

They're facing each other, the table that used to hold my coffee just this morning standing between them.

"Abel." Mom spots me first. I don't care that I'm just in sweats and a shirt, revealing the stained bandage on my left arm. *It's not like Mom doesn't know, but I don't have to rub in her face how fucked up her son is.* I look at Mom's eyes, following her gaze, which lands right on the red and white cotton.

"Abel." She repeats my name, this time with a different meaning and I feel embarrassed by the stupidity of doing too much and having to put on the bandage in the first place.

"See? The boy's a freak!" My father shouts pointing a hand at me. We all hear Mastiff starting to bark, but none of us care. Knowing Jeff is right over there, probably looking out the window, ready to come over here in less than three seconds if the situation escalates, makes me proud. Proud to have a dad who hates my father just as much as I do.

I walk up to him. Slow and steady, locking eyes with him. On any other nightly dispute, I would've kept my eyes on the ground to not accidentally step into whatever my father shattered across the floor. Not tonight, though. Whatever flew across the trailer just a moment earlier can cut my feet up as much as it wants. I've got a goal and will take all the obstacles lying in my way with me. When I've reached the goal, I'm right in front of him, our faces four inches apart. I stop walking. My eyes still fixed on his. It'd be an insult to Alex to call my father's eyes blue, but sadly they are.

"Wh-"

"Dan." I interrupt.

"The fuck you want." He comes a little closer, eyes squinting, nose high. In fact, he comes *too* close, but I don't give a shit.

"You out of here." I pronounce every word so clearly, like when Alex read out sentences for me to copy. Which feels like centuries ago.

"What did you just say to me?" A drop of his spit lands right on the mole on the right side of my jaw. I wipe it away with the back of my hand.

"Get. Out." I see Mom in my periphery, but her head isn't turned to me and her husband. Instead, she's looking behind me. I don't turn to check.

"Listen to that mouth of his!" It's directed at Mom, but he too doesn't face her. "Know what?" He continues. "I never gave a crap about you. And I didn't give a crap when you tried to kill yourself." For a split second, my guard drops. I feel my eyes switching left and right between his. I want to look at my mom, I want to see her reaction. *Did she know? Did she suspect? Or is she shocked?*

"Yeah. James told Ramy, who told me." *Keep James' name out of your poisoned mouth.* "And wanna know somethin' else?" He doesn't stop. "It's a shame Glen interrupted you. 'Cause holding that barrel to ya face was probably the smartest thing you've ever done."

[382]

Since overthinking the whole thing today, I actually agree with him. Only he talks of the possible outcome in which I'm dead now. And then it hits me. *Dan wants me dead. And I won't do him the favor. I will live.* More spit lands on my face and I keep it there. We keep our eyes where they are, interlocked with each other. I take a step back, increasing the distance between us. He scoffs at me, a smirk breaking on his face. Victory written across his eyes. And I think back to how good it felt to fight hate with hate. So, I place my thumb over my knuckles. "Abel, don't!" Mom screams at me. But I pull back and send my skin and bones crashing into my father's jaw. The jaw I inherited. Mom squeals like a pig seeing the one before it getting slaughtered. Like she doesn't get I'm doing this for her too.

He falls to the ground, spits out blood to the side and looks through his eyebrows up at me. And in that moment, I think back to my rule. The rule that said, I'd only use my fists to protect the ones I love. The rule I just broke, *right?* And looking for an explanation, Alex's face pops into my head. The face whose words and actions suddenly made me not hate myself. I realize, my father's hate towards me is bigger than my own.

Chapter Fifty-Two

The trailer door opens to Jeffrey standing in the moonlight. Abel still hasn't realized I'm standing right behind him and Eve glances back and forth between Jeffrey, her son, her husband and me. Dan gets up from the ground with a grunt and everyone is silent. Abel is catching his breath, shoulders rising and falling, head towards Dan struggling to get up.

"Abel." It's Jeffrey, determined and confident. *Why is his name basically the only thing that's been said in the last few minutes?* "Ya okay?" Jeffrey's voice has switched to a soft, worried tone.

"Yeah, Jeff. I'm fine." Abel answers shaking his hand, just like he did after punching Leland.

"I know yer fine." Jeff answers and sticks his head further into the trailer to look at me. "I was asking the little one."

Abel turns around in an instant, his eyes still filled with anger and adrenaline. He wipes his face with the back of his hand. "Shit."

And suddenly, I realize I'm not just someone watching the situation unfold, but someone who's somehow involved. I shake my head, mouth agape, trying to reassure Abel and Jeffrey that I'm fine, but I don't know if I am. Seeing Abel punch Dan was something entirely different from seeing him punch Leland. It's way more intimate and serious and fucked up and far from my concept of reality.

With every step he takes towards me, Abel's eyes slowly settle back into the calm brown orbs I know them as. His trembling right hand touches my upper arm, rubbing up and down.

"Sorry." He whispers, but I shake my head with a rushed "Don't be." Dan has managed to get up from the floor and stands upright in the middle of the room, hand raised to his jaw. He turns to the door, right at Jeffrey.

"What?" He asks, sounding like a lamb surrounded by wolves, with all of us staring at him. Even Eve's got the predator's look in her eyes.

"I think you heard him." Jeffrey answers. "Get. Out." *Apparently, trailer walls are thin.*

Abel is still by my side, hand still trembling across my arm. I take his hand in mine and give it a squeeze, trying to steady him.

"The fuck?" Dan answers and Abel steps forward again.

"Get out. Take your crap and piss off."

Jeffrey cracks a proud smile, knowing Abel can handle himself, but glad to lend a hand if needed.

"Who do you think you are?" Dan's voice is slowly giving in.

"A faggot." Abel leans his head to the side, mocking. "Who do you think *you* are?" His voice is steady.

"I'm your dad." Dan pleads pathetically, almost sad.

"No." Abel shakes his head. "You're a pussy. And a pedophile at that. A fucking addict and a rapist."

I turn to Eve, who's now got her hand over her mouth, tears in her eyes. *Did she know?* She hasn't said another word since the impact of bones on bones. Dan turns towards her, begging with his eyes and voice.

"Eve. Do something, my love." His voice shakes. He doesn't even believe himself.

Now, it's her turn to take some steps forward. Her face closer to his than it has probably been in a long, long time. I don't know what I expect from her. Another "Get out" or a spit in the face or a slap or a kick in the nuts? But what she ends up doing seems far more loaded with power. She stares him down. Just like Abel did, but with even more hate. A hate so deeply rooted, I've never seen anything like it. More tears form in the corner of her eyes, rolling down while growing in number and size, but she presents them with pride. They're not a sign of weakness, but of the amount of strength she's had to gather to stand living with this man for so long. But she stands her ground. She stares the creature down. The rotten apple. And he crumbles down under her eyes. Molding away until there's only the seeds and stem left. Eve picks the remnants of the ground, opens a hole in the earth and drops what's left of her husband into the most stinging corners of Hell.

Dan does what he's probably never done in his life. He obeys. He turns to the door that Jeffrey is holding open. Without another word, without his stuff, without bumping Jeffrey's shoulder, he leaves. Jeffrey's dog barks louder than it did before, just as Dan passes their trailer. The door falls shut after Jeffrey steps inside Eve's and Abel's trailer. At the same time, the energy changes and I feel like I shouldn't be here. Like I invaded a ceremony that wasn't meant for me, because I haven't been there to read the ancient texts and runes.

"Son." Jeffrey finally says out loud.

They walk towards each other, steps in sync, and Abel falls into Jeffrey's embrace. They pull each other closer and closer until Abel decides it's time to let go. His back is towards me, but I hear him sniffling and see him wiping away a tear. He then turns towards his mom, who's still standing stiff and tall. When her son's touch shakes her awake, she smiles. Brighter than when greeting customers at Hell's Saddle or when waving at me or laughing with Mom. They too hug. I'm left standing between what suddenly looks like a loving family. And there's doubt creeping up on that joy. I think of my family. God at the top, Mom and Dad one step under and the girls, Jewel, Trixie and me at the bottom. *It's the love that keeps me in.* I remind myself. But, *never love your master.*

Chapter Fifty-Three

Mom and me clean away the trash and clothes from our couch. She and Jeff sit down on it, leaving little space for anything else. I grab two chairs from our "kitchen" and place them by the couch. One for Alex, one for me. He accepts and sits down without a word. I turn mine the wrong way and sit down with my head resting on top. Alex glances towards me, eyes stuck on the mole on my jaw. I look back and squint my eyes in confusion. I don't get an answer, just a quick smile and then he looks away.

"Everyone fine?" Jeff's the first one to speak.

Mom and I nod, Alex lets out a small "Hm."

"Jeff, you don't have to stay, you know." I tell him and Mom nods.

"Nah. Except you guys need some space to chat." He nods at Mom and then at me.

"I guess I should go then, too." Alex is already in motion to get up, but I grab his shoulder and pull him back down.

"No, don't go." His body's still stiff, ready to leave.

"Please?" I cringe at the tone in my voice, but when

I hear Alex sigh and feel him resting back in his chair, that cringe vanishes.

"Jeffrey, I really think there's not much to-" Mom speaks up.

"Mom." I interrupt.

"Yeah, Love?"

"Could Jeff, Alex and I have a chat?" I try to sound as loving as possible, because that's exactly how I mean it.

"Son, I think ya mom should know if you have something to say." *He really is in Dad mode.*

"She'll know soon enough." I reassure him, without looking at Mom. Then, I turn to her.

"We'll only be a couple minutes." And without Jeffrey's or Alex's agreement, I get up. Alex follows without a word, but shoots an apologetic look at Mom.

We leave the trailer and step into the night and just before Jeff joins us, we hear him saying "I'm sure they're fine."

Alex and I both shiver under the dark, cold sky, since we're both just in shirts. Jeff closes the door behind him and like we asked him to, hands each of us a jacket.

"Thank you." We both say and put them on. I

happen to grab my father's jacket and put it on with hesitation. That leaves Alex with my leather jacket. It probably smells like cigs, but he puts it on anyway. I glance over at him standing in the light coming from our trailer, wearing shorts, his T-shirt and my leather jacket. And I was right. He *does* look good in it. *Damn.*

We smile at each other, trying to strengthen ourselves and each other.

"So, what's up?" Normally, Jeff would've put on his "I'm one of the cool kids" voice, but this time he really means "What is up?"

I take Alex's hand in mine and look at him, waiting for permission. He squeezes my hand and nods. Then, I focus on Jeff.

"We're planning on breaking out." I say it quietly. *Thin walls.*

He stares back and forth between us, arms crossed, confused.

"*Getting* out. Like, running away." Alex explains. But Jeff doesn't break an expression. Instead, he just nods. And looking at him, I realize I didn't write a goodbye to him. Because I couldn't. *How do you say goodbye to your dad?*

"When?" He asks.

"First thing in the morning. Given, we don't change our minds overnight." Internally, I thank Alex for leading the conversation even though it was my idea. Jeff looks up at the moon. John's and P.J.'s moon, mine and Alex's. Everyone's moon.

"You've got about three hours." He informs us.

"Knew it." Alex muffles to the side.

"What?" I ask.

"Nothin'."

Jeff steps back in. "So, is this why you're here?"

"No. Kind of." Alex looks at me. "I had a…fight with my dad. Which is stupid 'cause…" He gestures towards our trailer.

"It's not stupid." I reassure.

"Kids. Why'd you come to me with this?"

And right when I open my mouth to answer, I realize I don't have an answer. Other than, maybe he's the only one who wouldn't judge. He always lets me do my stuff, holding his hands out for me if I ever feel like I might need them. That's how we roll.

"Will you take care of her? Mom, I mean." I look to the ground, feeling the saltwater form again.

"Please, Dad. It's the only thing I'm asking."

Alex takes his other hand to ours, cupping mine in both, thumb rubbing over my skin.

"Ah, stop that." Jeff's voice breaks a little, but he smiles at me. "I've been takin' care of ya two for years. 'Course I will." There's not a speck of shock or pity in his voice. It sounds more like I just insulted him with the question. Like I doubted the obvious. I look up at him, at his white moustache, the big nose, the wrinkled eyes. And I see what I think God might be. I see God, who I never knew existed, in the face of this man.

And I realize I don't have to go back into my room and write a letter to Jeff, because I can write one right here and now.

"Thank you." Is all there is to write. Because he knows all the rest. God smiles at me, proud and guiding.

"Come say bye in the morning, will ya? I can't have *this* be it." He flaps his hands around.

Chapter Fifty-Four

Like Jeffrey predicted, we wake up three hours later to the sun slowly creeping up the sky. I let my eyes adjust to the light and my mind to where I am. Or who I'm with.

I'm still in my shirt from yesterday and Abel's jacket on top. It smells like him. Cigs. But then again, that's what the whole room smells like.

I look over at him, worn-out shirt on pale skin. The fabric is so stretched out, it reveals his collarbones. My eyes trace him. His breathing is calm and steady – thank fuck. The bandaged arm rests stretched over his head, so his shirt lifts a little. Abel threw the blanket off himself in the middle of the night, so there's nothing covering his pelvis, decorated with a stripe of hair from top to bottom. I spot a mole on his hip and think back to my night sky poem. I look around, searching for more. There's one left of his belly button, another one on his right upper arm, another one on his right collarbone. Another one sticks out from under his boxers. *Jesus.*

"Like it?" His voice is still deep with sleep, and there's that smirk in it again.

"Hm," is the next best noise I can produce.

"There's more."

I don't answer. Because I can't. *Dang.*

He sits up and, with a groan, stretches his arms out over his head. His shirt lifts a little higher, but falls back down when his arms drop.

"And?" He asks.

"I wrote a poem about them." I confess.

"Oh." His eyes adjust to the sunlight and he stares at me. "I meant, do you still feel like breaking out. But also...read it to me, will you Pony?" The smile on his face looks like victory. Like he finally knows I wrote one for him.

"Oh." I feel embarrassed for misunderstanding his question, but the way he answered washes the shame away. "I've got it memorized. I'll recite it to you on the road."

The smile spreads until his face is lit up again.

"Really?" He leans forward, eyes about to pop out of his head.

"Really." I nod.

He mumbles to himself "Shit man," and then at me "I can't believe it. I've been wanting to get out for years now and all it took to do it was you."

I sit up, lean over and kiss his lips.

Chapter Fifty-Five

We act quick. Like there's a timer running and once
it goes off, we've failed because we've spent too
much time thinking about leaving that we chicken
out and end up staying. Which is what neither of us
want.

Mom is already out when we wake up and I couldn't
tell if I'm glad about that or if I want to cry my eyes
out. She's my mom. She's all that held me in
Folkspine. And saying I'm just leaving because I fell
in love with a boy would be a lie. I'm leaving
because this boy, whether out of love or friendship,
has taught me. Taught me all that's hidden within
me. There's more than my father's blood rushing
through me. There's art and literature and strength
and weakness and grief and love for myself rushing
through me. There's a past rushing through me that I
don't need to hold onto. I don't need to hold onto
the bullet. There are other ways to save myself and
Alex showed me. *"You have a life out there,"* I told
him. And I might not have realized when the words
came out of my mouth, but now I do. I have a life
out there too. A life outside the Brennan blood.

So, the both of us get ready. I grab my stuff, my clothes, notebooks and records - 'cause *why not*. I throw back a coffee and Alex poor people's orange juice. I grab the note and place it on the table, where Alex's "Forbid The Rotten Apple" already rests. I look at my letter once more, imagining what Mom would feel when she comes home later to an empty trailer. No son, no husband. And I hope she finds peace in that. I don't know where Dan went or if he'll be back. I can only hope for my mother's strength and put faith in Jeff's support. I fight the urge to read over my letter once more, to cross out words and add others and Alex pulls me away. "Come on. It's fine. We gotta go over to Jeffrey."

I tried to write this letter when I was a kid. I never was able to. Now I am.
Mom, I'm sorry.
Do you forgive me? I can't always be strong. Not for you and not for me. I'm both lion and lamb. And the lion is willing to rest so the lamb can live in quiet for once. And while the Devil haunts your Eden, I have to push aside the lamb and become the lion. But I can't do that anymore. Mom, I love you with everything I have and I beg of you, get out. Break out. Someone close once told me I should

*break out if I ever felt trapped. No matter who built my
cage. That I should never love my master. Dan put the
both of us into a cage and I gnawed at the bars for nineteen
long years so we could be free. Mom, the cage is open. You
can choose to break out or you can choose to stay inside. If
you stay, please promise to bite the hand that feeds you.
Resist. I haven't got my lion from Dan, I've got it from
you. And if you break out, then I promise you everything
will turn right. You will figure it out.*

*One more thing: Please look out for James. I know you two
were never close, but the kid needs someone he can trust.
Tell him I forgive and love him. He'll know what I mean.*

Chapter Fifty-Six

Jeffrey opens at the first knock while his dog barks
from within the trailer.

"Shut the fuck up!" He shouts over his shoulder and
lets us in. The dog lies down on the ground with a
groan and wags its tail at Abel.

"Hey buddy." He crouches down to pet him and
Jeffrey looks at the both of them with his arms
behind his back. He's already on the verge of tears
and I see him suppressing them. Successfully.

"I uh...I got somethin' for ya." He says and Abel
gets up from the ground. "I wanted to give you
Mastiff. You know, to protect ya. But you don't
need him and I sadly love that stupid dog too
much." Jeffrey chuckles. "And I thought ya might
need this better." He pulls an envelope from behind
his back and hands it over to Abel. I watch how his
hands shakily open it and how his eyes peak inside.
"No." His head shakes from side to side. "Jeff, I
won't."

"Yes. Now shut your face and just fucking take it."
*Mental note: Mom swears when she's stressed or pissed off
and Jeffrey swears more than usual when he's about to cry.*

"Where'd you even get that from?" Abel looks back up from the money.

"Rodeos pay off good. And the ladies loved watching me ride them damn bulls."

"You did not do rodeos on bulls." Abel questioned.

"Fucking yes, I did. When I retired from it, I didn't know what to do with the money, so I kept it for a special occasion. Which is now."

"You could have gotten a pretty little house on Main Road with that."

"Fuck no." *Lots of fucks this morning.* "I like it here. And I can keep an eye on your trailer." He bumps Abel's side and after a teeny tiny chuckle, both take a long look at each other, speaking their love for each other through the silence, like I used to with my dad. Jeffrey is the first to open his arms and Abel crashes into his body, holding him tight.

"Fuck." The old man breathes and Abel sniffles in response. My heart warms up at the sight of them, while the knowledge of them breaking up drags it down into my stomach. Jeffrey does it like I do – he waits for Abel to let go. And when he does, both wipe their noses with their sleeves. Now, Jeffrey turns to me with open arms and I too hug him tight.

"Thanks, little one." He whispers in my ear.

[400]

"What for?" Tears roll down onto his shirt.

"Savin' my son from this fuck ass town." I chuckle into his body and give it a squeeze before letting go. "Now git before I stop you." He tells us both and we each look him in the face once more. Analyzing his white moustache and the wrinkles all over, so we never forget the Devil who went against the other Devil.

"I said git! Go on." He turns us around and pushes us out the door. "Piss off now." And the door closes behind us with a bang, leaving Abel and me standing in the trailer park.

"You think he's crying?" I ask over Mastiff's barks.

"Like a baby."

Chapter Fifty-Seven

Again, I'm not sure Jeff knows how thankful I am for him. For the money, for being a dad when I needed it most and for throwing me and Alex out of the trailer – I never would've left otherwise.

"Stop that." Alex punches my arm lightly.

"Stop what?"

"Being all sentimental about Jeffrey. You're making me sad."

"I didn't even say anything."

"You should know by now that we don't need to talk to understand each other."

"All right, all right." I open the door to the passenger side, get out and Alex does the same. We're standing in front of Hell's Saddle, staring up at the sign above.

"In, note, out. Got it?" Alex turns to me.

"Yes, Sir." I nod and we move towards the front door. Alex pulls a key from his pocket and unlocks it. I get the strange feeling that some privileged people probably get when they're at school on weekends for a project or something. Seeing a place that's normally packed and loud, all quiet, empty.

"Weird." Is all I can say to describe the place.

"I know, right? Now come on." He takes my hand and leads me through the beaded curtain. My eyes are already focused on the back of the hall, where the women's lockers are waiting for us. We come closer and closer until I suddenly feel the wall pressed against my back, with Alex standing right in front of me. His hands hold my shoulders, just like six years ago. Only this time, his eyes don't say *What is wrong with you and your family?* But *I want you, Brennan.* I lock with the blue and count. When we've reached three seconds, the connection remains and I press my lips together in a smile.

"What about *in, note, out?*" Five.

"You should stop blindly listening to me." Now he's the one to smirk. Eight.

"But, our rules." We smile at each other, knowing for a fact, I never cared for the rules. I just cared about Alex. And now, he doesn't seem to care either. He's the one to have our lips touch – harder, longer. His hand moves from my shoulders to the back of my head, his finger entangling with my hair. I take his face in my hands, trying to pull us closer together. Our tongues dance and I hear him let out a quiet moan in my mouth. *Fucking Christ.* But my body's doing a real good job of obeying my mind and I take my hands to his shoulders and turn us around, so he's the one with his back to the wall. "What do you think you're doing?" He says between kisses and I know it isn't a question. He turns us back around, my back to the wall. *Glad we got that figured out.* I smile into his mouth.

"Ahem." The sound breaks us up and we're both panting, looking towards the beaded curtain. Taylor is standing between the beads, arms crossed and a mocking smile on her face. "Well, well, well." She shakes her head.

"T!" Alex exclaims. "We- uh…" He looks at me for help, but I can't give any. I'm focused on making my body obey. That includes pushing away the anger of us not being entangled anymore.

"Don't even try." She waves us off and comes closer. "What are you doing here?" Alex asks.

"I left my wallet in my locker." She points down the hall and Alex and I share a look.

"What?" T asks.

"We wanted to give you something. That's why we're here."

"You expect me to believe that?" She raises an eyebrow.

"Nah. But it's true." I finally say something. "We wanted to give you a letter, but we didn't know where you lived so we figured we'd stick it in your locker."

"And you couldn't have waited until I got to work?"

"No." Alex says. "We're…God, I wanted to do this in secret."

"Yeah, I can see that." T chuckles.

"Not like that. We're leaving and we wanted to keep it a secret until we were gone." I offer as an explanation.

"Leaving?" She looks back and forth between the both of us. Instead of saying something, Alex pulls the folded poem from his pocket and hands it to T. She takes it in her fingers and starts unfolding.

"No!" Alex exclaims. "Wait with that till we're gone. Please."

"Kid. You're scaring me." She takes a step back and puts the note in her pocket. Then, she places a hand on Alex's shoulder. I watch with envy – *which is stupid.* "What do you mean you're leaving?" She asks again.

"You of all people should know what it means." I offer.

"Shit man. You're finally getting out?" Her eyes widen.

"What'd you mean *finally*?"

"You're not as sneaky as you think you are. You guys are a thing, *obviously*." She chuckles and then turns to me. "He is living the most fucked up life I've ever heard about." Now she turns back to Alex.

"And you are so obviously not who you're supposed to be." He takes a step back and stares at her.

"Don't worry. I didn't tell anyone." She reassures.

"How do you know?"

"Uh, since you asked me about it six years ago? And you're not really hiding it. The way you stood in that dress at church yesterday, your face when guests think you're a boy, the hair, the clothes."

"Well, at least someone got that." He eyes me from the side and I bump his shoulder.

"Wait… shit. Does he know?" She addresses Alex, but points at me.

"Yes." I answer.

"Thank God." She looks up at the ceiling and we all fall silent for a moment, looking at each other.

"Well, I don't want to stop you." Taylor backs up to a wall to give us free way to the beaded curtain.

"Absolutely not." Alex steps forward and takes Taylor from the wall to give her a tight hug.

"You've got no idea how much you mean to me, T." Alex says into her shoulder.

"Jesus Christ, child." T hugs Alex tighter and I hear a sniff coming from her nose. *There's too much crying today.* "Get in here." She takes one arm from Alex and opens it for me to join them and I do and I feel both breathing and hear us three sniffing.

Golden sin

In an unknown past wrapped,
She came in with golds and reds.
Saying: Break out if you feel trapped.

She then read out her page.
Her past unfolded and sick.
Said: No matter who built your cage.

Do it for your own health.
Stare them down, stamp them over.
Your parents, adults or yourself.

For she once was a Sir.
She makes us both promise now,
That we shall not love our master.

Whether we are right or wrong,
Even God shall never know.
Only we know where we belong.

Chapter Fifty-Eight

I stop the truck on our dirt trail and feel my heart banging up to my throat, pushing at it. I try to work against it with deep breaths, but it only seems to grow worse and worse. Abel watches me from the side, but I keep my eyes on the farm and Dad standing in the meadow, a shovel filled with dung in his hands. He looks at his truck and me behind its wheel. I step back down on the gas, pass the meadow and move further to park the Ford in front of our porch. Now, I glance over at the Flying Fishbowl.

"What do I tell them?" I don't know who I'm asking. It could be Abel, myself or God. Or all three together. But only Abel answers.

"What feels right."

I turn off the motor, unbuckle my seatbelt and tell Abel to wait for me. My boots hit the ground and I move to our front door to step in. Mom is reading over some paperwork in the kitchen with a coffee mug right next to her.

"Mom?" I ask quietly. She looks up from the table.

"Morning, Sweetie." My heart breaks at my mother's love. At the fact, it probably won't be enough to love her son. I clear my throat, but Mom speaks first. "I called you in sick. Fever." It lets me know Eve hasn't come home yet and hasn't read Abel's letter and hasn't called Mom about it.

"Thank you." I look around and take in our kitchen. The table where I've been eating Mom's eggs all my life. The fridge that always offers Sunny Delight. The photograph of my parents and me right next to it. I look away.

"Uhm...we'll be out again." I point my head at the door, but Mom's eyes are back on her work.

"Uh huh." I look at her and her red hair and I imagine the light she used to cast. She still shines bright, she's still pretty. But she doesn't shine for me like she used to.

I've got the urge to go over to her and ask her for a hug, but I feel repelled. Because if I go over and hug my mom, I'll stay. So, I don't. I turn around and leave the kitchen.

"Oh, Alex!" Mom shouts after me and I stick my head back in. "Make sure to catch up on school from today." Her eyes are still down.

"Yes." I don't breathe.

I grab the letter from my pocket, along with "God's Eye" and "Break The Fence," and place them folded together on the dresser in the hallway. I followed Dad's strategy and copied both poems, so I can take one with me and leave one with my family – same goes for Eve's poem. I move out the front door before I can stop myself, take a deep breath in, pass the truck and Abel in it and go over to the meadow.

Dad is still working on getting rid of the dung when I join him. Jewel watches him and runs up to me when she sees me. I take her in my arms and hug her tight.

"Mornin', Squirrel." He places the shovel in the ground and wipes his forehead.

"Hey, Dad." Jewel jumps back down and circles me.

"Is it fine if we keep the truck for one more day?" *I hate the way lies make my stomach feel.* Dad's eyes switch back and forth between me and his four-wheeler.

"Sure." He shrugs his shoulders.

"Thanks." I smile at him, trying to push past yesterday's argument.

"Is Trixie in her stable?" I ask.

"Last time I checked, she was."

"Alright. Be right back." Dad goes back to work and I turn away from him to move towards Trixie. I take the privacy to let a tear roll down my cheek. When Trixie comes into view, I can't hold the others anymore and water drips from my chin without pause. Trixie stares at me and whinnies.

"Hiya, girl." I take her head in my hands and place a light kiss on her snout. Her fur is warm and the kiss feels like nothing out of the ordinary. Because I've kissed her so many times, because I love her dearly. But this kiss is out of the ordinary. I pull back and look at her eyes while she looks at mine.

"You get out too, yeah?"

She snorts and stomps her front leg.

The truck and Abel come closer as I walk up to Dad again. I feel my eyes stinging and know they're red for sure, so I keep my head down.

"Bye, Dad." I try to hurry past him, but just before I reach the fence, I hear the shovel being pushed into the ground.

"Uh, Alex?" *God. I wanted to make this quick.*

"Mhm." My eyes are on the wooden planks.

"Can you turn around for a sec?" *Shit.* There's no use in trying to get out of this situation. So, I do as I'm told and do Dad the favor of facing him. He holds his neck with one hand, the other still on the shovel, and looks to the ground.

"Squirrel, I wanted to apolo-" His eyes meet mine. And they speak. They say *What happened?* They say *Are you okay?* And they say *Is this because of me?* And I couldn't really answer a single one of those questions. His eyes speak, but his mouth doesn't. The look on his face is everything he needs to give me. And I guess he knows this, because he goes on to finish his sentence.

"I wanted to say sorry. For yesterday. I shouldn't have run off like that and I shouldn't have dragged your friend through the mud." *Yeah, you shouldn't have. But what you don't realize is that by doing that, you've dragged your only child through it too.*

"Thank you...for apologizing." I take a step towards him, my eyes swelling up again. And I thank the Lord that he lets go of the shovel and opens his arms for a hug. And while I'm in his embrace, I wonder when the last time was that we hugged.

"I'm sorry for what I said about God."

"He'll forgive." He holds me a little tighter. "And I do too."

I tried to hide like Taylor did, but I can't. I'm not that strong and she wasn't either. But I'm strong enough to break out and leave. I love you both like I love apples and warm summer nights and live performances of Parton and Springsteen. But I don't love you enough to let my light burn out. Because I know you don't love me enough for who I am. I pray the Lord will give you peace. He didn't seem to have any left for me, so now I have to go chase it on my own.

"I have found whom my soul loves." Song of Solomon 3:4 That someone is Abel and who I really am. And Dad, I know you once had found someone like that too. I know all about it and I'm so sorry. I watch the moon and think of you and P.J. and I do it with love. But I cannot hide like Taylor did and I cannot pretend like you do.

Mom, you're the fire that has been lighting my way, but I'm holding my own torch now. Don't blame any of this on Taylor. She's opened my eyes and that is the hardest thing I've ever had to do, but I'm willing to take the rest of my life with my eyes open.

Your son

Chapter Fifty-Nine

His knuckles are white from gripping the wheel too tightly. He killed the truck a bunch of times and hasn't really spoken for hours.

The wooden sign in the distance comes closer and closer until I can read the *Leaving Colorful Colorado* and we pass it. Having left the state, his body relaxes slightly and I feel like I'm able to breathe better.

"Alex?" He doesn't answer. His eyes are focused on the yellow and white lines. The cross on the rearview mirror swings from side to side. The sun burns through the window onto our skin.

"Pony?"

"I feel bad."

"For leaving?" I watch his profile. The bump on his nose, the eyes staring straight ahead. And I feel at home, finally.

"No. For feeling good about leaving." He turns his face to give me a smile and I feel mine lighting up and I let it shine as bright as it wants to.

"So, where do you say we're going?" I couldn't care less where we end up. As long as it's far away from Folkspine and as long as the blue stays close.

"Montana. I want to see the oak. Let the past haunt me for a while and then we can go wherever."

"Like?"

"Like…the Pacific Northwest. Oregon, Washington."

The truck keeps moving, taking unknown routes. And with every mile, Alex relaxes further.

"I have to say, the forest is way better than the meadow." I love that he still remembers me talking about the forest out there.

"You haven't even really seen the forest yet."

"No. But I can smell it, see it in the distance, hear it calling out to me. To us." Again, he smiles at me. And it's different than the smiles before. This one is the result of excitement and not the effort to push aside fear and doubt. "I can't wait for all the poems we'll write. There's already so much in my mind. My fingers are all itchy for a pen and paper."

"Mine itch too. Just for something else." I smirk at him.

"Don't you dare! I'm driving." *Pull over.* But I don't say it. Because I long for the connection of our souls more than for the connection of skin.

"By the way, you said you had a poem?"

"Night Sky Skin." He nods.

"Tell me." And he opens his mouth and the words start flowing like a preacher's.

[417]

Night sky skin

Bright on dark.
Dark on bright.

Opposites united.
Envious watcher, guided.
Canvas showing contrast.
Blank space under, masked.

Dark and bright.
For his life is the dark,
I wish upon him the light.

His skin touched by stars.
Dark spots, but they shine so bright.
Light, I want to fill up jars.

Keep him safe,
For his soul is scarred.
The light is what I crave.

1987

Epilogue

"You two brothers?" The old guy behind the reception counter sounds like an investigating officer.

"Uh." Alex looks at me, searching for rescue.

"Yes." I look at the blue next to me, but my voice is directed at the reception officer. He raises one of his white eyebrows at the both of us and takes a moment to analyze each of us before nodding. He takes more time on Alex's face than mine and I feel him holding his breath next to me.

"Good." The guy finally turns around, grabs a key from the wall and places it on the counter between us. "'Cause this is the only room I got left for tonight and there ain't no two beds. I don't want no fucking fags in my motel."

"Of course. Can't be careful enough nowadays." I nod past the heartbeat closing up to my throat and take the key. Alex is still stiff and not really breathing, but standing tall and broad. _He's good and this isn't the first time we're in a situation like this._

"Come on." I take his bag in my hand and tell the receptionist Goodbye and Thanks.

[421]

"He don't talk much, eh?" He nods at Alex. *If only he knew the mouth on this boy.* I almost slip out a laugh.

"No, Sir. He doesn't." I answer instead and we turn around and start walking towards – I look down at the key – room thirty-two.

"Hey!" The man shouts at us and Alex draws in a quick breath.

"Yes?" I turn around and ask.

"Top floor, all the way back." He explains while fishing something out of his teeth with his fingernail. I swallow past the disgust and thank him with a smile.

The door to room thirty-two closes. I lock it behind us and throw off our bags while Alex falls down onto the double bed.

"Oh my God." He sighs.

"I'm sorry." *For you having to interact with such a prick and for having to lie all the time.*

"No- No, I mean. He believed it. Like, he really believed I was your *brother*." He sits back up, a smile beaming across his face. The smile of freedom, of victory, love.

"Yeah. He did." I light up, walk up to the bed and lean down to kiss his face. He melts into me and smiles into my mouth.

My body gave up trying to obey long ago, and I don't want it to anymore. Neither Alex nor me suppress anymore. Instead, we finally let go. We've been on the road for almost a year now. In that time, we've done it in his truck, in motels, under the stars, in creeks and woods. In Wyoming, Montana, Idaho. He pulls me in and I get down on the bed with him. He crawls up to my lap and sits down, hands wrapped in my hair.

"I think we might have some fags on the property." He smiles while his face comes closer.

"Yeah? Better call them out then." I smile back and we entangle our lips, our tongues, our legs and arms. I thank whoever is out or up there for having this be my life. For Alex being here with me, for giving me the push to break out.

After leaving, we've quickly established a routine. Live on the road, sleep on the loading space of his truck if it's warm enough, sleep in motels if not, kiss, write poems, see the states, connect our bodies and souls – but it never feels like a routine. *'Cause how can something this good be a routine?* We become one, like

[423]

so many nights before, and I love being the one Alex trusts to do this.

"If the Lord knew what we were doing." He says between heavy, short breaths.

"I don't care. I've been in and out of Hell before. I'll gladly do it again, if it's the price I have to pay for this." I kiss him deep.

"Mhm. I'm pretty sure this is heaven." He answers as the wooden cross dangles over me.

"Your parents would be stupid not to love their son." It should feel off limits to talk about Folkspine, but it isn't. We often talk about our families, T, Hell's Saddle, the gang. And I think he might want to go back one day.

"How do you know?"

"'Cause I love him. I love you, Pony."

"Do you love yourself?"

"Yes." I say without hesitation.

"I love you too."

The End

"I'm getting rid of everything from the past so I can be reborn in the future."

Norwegian Wood, Haruki Murakami

Playlist

"Maps" – The Front Bottoms

"Poet" – Bastille

"The Devil Is Human" – AURORA

"Homewrecker" – Willow Avalon

"Way Out There" – Lord Huron

"Feathered Indians" – Tyler Childers

"You're Gonna Go Far" – Noah Kahan

"Time To Run" – Lord Huron

"Bullet With Butterfly Wings" – The Smashing Pumpkins

"The Drugs" – Mother Mother

"Soldier, Poet, King" – The Oh Hellos

"Who Laughs Last (feat. Kristen Stewart)" – Lord Huron

"Save Me From Myself" – Noah Baker

"Drunken Poet's Dream" – Hayes Carll

"Take Me To Church" – Hozier

"Pale Beneath the Tan (Squeeze)" – The Front Bottoms

"I'm On Fire" – Bruce Springsteen

Author's note

There's a bit of me painted across Alex and Abel. I eat my eggs with ketchup, I struggle with being Christian and queer, I carry a tiny notebook in the cigarette pocket of my jacket, I prefer animals over people (love goes out to my cats) and I think being trans is a pain in the ass. I also love Metallica, I take walks without knowing where I might end up, I scrape the ever-living shit out of my cuticles and I love myself only because those around me tell me I'm worth it – Thank you for this, Amy and Leni. I love you dearly.

This book has been with me for half a year now. It started with a simple diary entry. I wanted to write down what I thought my life would be in an alternative universe. Before I knew it, Alex and Abel were born. Alex was the first character to appear, simply because he's based on me and my imagination of who I could be. That's also why we have the same name. Alex was called Alex before I knew he was a character and not me, and when the story evolved, it became impossible to name him differently.

The Norwegian musician AURORA calls her albums her children and now, after half a year of working on this, I know exactly what she means. Break The Fence is my child. Those characters are my kins and my blood flows through every chapter, every page, every sentence and especially every poem. So, if you sat down to spend your time with me and this story and these characters, I want to thank you. From the bottom of my heart, thank you for allowing me to share my art with the world.

There are some more people I want to thank. Daniele, thank you for being there to give me professional opinions and tips on how to make this book happen (check out his own works: Daniele Rizzo, Carciofo Comics). Thank you for telling me how proud you are of me. Mrs. Peltner, thank you so so much for always encouraging me to keep on writing. Thank you for motivating me. While writing, I´ve been thinking of the small notes you added to my exams, and those words kept me going on days where I though I might not be able to finish writing this. Now to those that saved me; Thank you so incredibly much, Amy and Leni, for loving me. Thank you for being proud of me and thank you for supporting me. Abel was saved by Alex. Alex was the one to throw away Abel´s bullet. You guys threw away mine. There´s a chance, I wouldn´t be here right now, if it wasn´t for you and what you give me.

And what you´re giving me is not just your love towards me, but my own love. And I hope every day, that I give back the same to you. Lastly, I want to thank God. It's cheesy, I know, but thank you for being a light in my life. Thank you for showing yourself to me to give me strength in the journey I´m starting right now. Thank you for loving me regardless.

I want to share this story and mine hidden within it. I want to share it to help myself and hopefully be able to help others too. I want to show a little piece of my soul through these words.

Exodus 14:14

The Lord shall fight for you.

And if you don't want to hear that, then…what doesn't kill you makes you stronger. Or something like that.

And now, please enjoy some more poems of mine.

Call Upon Me

Visit outside, where I walk and yearn.
Visit at night, when I toss and turn.

Fill the hole the devil dug.
Fill it up with luck.

Call Micheal upon me.
Have him make the demons flee.

Know your mother birthed a wonder.
Know she gifted faith like thunder.

Listen to my plead.
Answer me and lead.

Cain I Be Abel?

Being able to gift God.

Lord, can I?

Let us live in brotherhood.

Lord, let me love you.

Let me gift you.

Take the golden weeds.

He's a shepherd.

Able to gift you the living.

Lord, take mine too.

Can I make him young forever?

Can I take him upon my land?

Upon the gold.

Make it drink on the red.

Gifted red on my land.

Lord, will you take it now?

Brotherhood never able to be again.

Death can never be for me.

Death was for him.

Immortal's Death

To Willi, with love

I've seen you in the dark.

You're a sight that makes me frown.

Still, you light my path all the way back home

Baby, you are all around,

When you should be underground.

Aren't you cold?

You're everywhere,

When you should be nowhere.

Aren't you alone?

You're in the grass and in the wind,

In the clouds and in your kins.

Next to me, right here next to me.

Your presence warm as ember,

While your skeleton's colder than ever.

(Darling, are you dead?)

(Darling, are you gone?)

J. Doe

Let me ask you once,

If this is what you seek.

Do you want to be my creep?

Or just to feel unique?

I'm asking for a favor,

Begging for a savior.

Now, be my J. Doe.

Become unknown.

For I need to let you go.

For I have to be alone.

Leave my cranium.

Don't even be a memory.

Swear you'll leave my atrium.

Swear it'll be my remedy.

Oh, J. Doe…

Savior in disguise

In The Night of The Moon,
The Devil knocked on my door.
He broke my windows,
Let the flowers in my garden wither.

Once I invited him in,
The torment stopped.
He became an angel within my walls.
Once he left my door,
His head was horned again.

Sometimes, I still hear the knocking
And open the door.
He either showed me the way,
Or disturbed my silence.
Now, in his eyes I have a name.

Jesus' transformation

Hoofs and wool,
Pierced by nails.
Whips and thorns,
Staining the white red.

Mane and claws,
Rising on day three.
Protecting the herd
With His light.

New God

"Run," roared the orb of light,
Outshining the moon.
Cold wind gushed out of its void,
So sharp it pained like needles.

"Shout," ordered the God,
Never seen before.
Growing louder every second,
Drumming in one's ears.

"Fear," pleaded the monster,
Hissing through teeth.
Rising higher in the sky,
About to leave the mind.

"Hug me," said the human.

.